now

you

KNOW

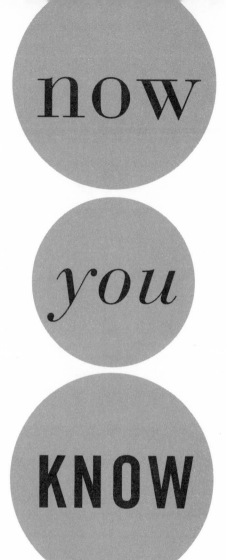

now

you

KNOW

Susan Kelly

PEGASUS BOOKS

NEW YORK

NOW YOU KNOW

Pegasus Books LLC

45 Wall Street, Suite 1021

New York, NY 10005

First Pegasus Books edition 2007

Library of Congress Cataloging-in-Publication Data is available.

ISBN: 978-1-933648-61-3

10 9 8 7 8 6 5 4 3 2 1

Printed in the United States of America

Distributed by Consortium

For Sterling, Stafford, and Preston, who adapt.

And in memory of Suzanne Tanner

At heart, of course, a story itself is consolation's instrument.

— RICHARD FORD

September 4, 1947

The designated dorm room was more glorified corridor than bedroom. Like mirror images, the right and left walls were lined with a single iron bedstead, a bureau at its footboard, and a closet door. Between the two beds stood a radiator and a window overlooking the Emerson Seminary entrance three stories below.

The speckled black linoleum floor was obliterated by belongings—an open trunk spewing sweaters, two laundry bags stuffed with blankets and sheets, a jumble of shoes and sports equipment and books, none of whose titles Frances Simpson recognized as required texts for freshman English. She picked one up: *Brideshead Revisited*.

The custodian had deposited her trunk in the only available space left: the narrow aisle between the twin beds. Frances stepped around the mess left by her assigned but absent roommate, scraped her shin against the wing nut of a tennis racket press, sat on the stained mattress ticking, and opened the trunk. Full bottles and jars and a plastic soap container were fitted in one quadrant of the upper tray. Stiff coiled belts kept folded underwear and slips from encroaching on the area allotted to sock balls and the satin lingerie bag for her stockings, an afterthought graduation present from her father, who'd purchased the first item he saw in the Montaldo's display case, Frances was certain, just as he did at Christmas for her mother. Frances stood and opened the window to relieve the musty stuffiness of the dorm room.

The door slammed open so suddenly that the brass hook attached to its back rammed noisily into the closet door, leaving a mark on the wood. "Oops," the girl said and peered at Frances. "Whoa. Thought for a minute you were dead."

"Wh—pardon?"

"The way the sun's coming through that window, lighting up the back of your head. Looks like you have a halo."

Frances reflexively touched her light hair. Whoever she was, the girl with wiry black hair and eyes silver as the tiny diploma charm dangling from the bracelet on Frances's wrist was the loveliest person she'd ever seen.

"Welcome to our grim and squalid abode." The girl stuck out her hand. "Libba Charles."

Frances thought only men shook hands, but she took it. "Frances Simpson."

Libba gestured to the room, its minuscule dimensions. "Didn't you have any pull?"

"'Pull'?"

"I requested a Southern roommate. Doesn't everyone know everyone else down here from four generations back? I thought a Southerner would naturally pull some strings, shake the genealogical family tree to get us a decent room." She rolled up a sleeve of the man's shirt untidily tucked into wrinkled Bermudas. "Instead of a shoebox."

Frances didn't know how to respond. It *did* resemble a shoebox. But she hadn't requested anyone as roommate. Her mother had suggested she not begin college by singling herself out as someone who asked for special favors.

"Well," Libba said, "one out of two's not bad."

Frances couldn't resist. "What was the other one?"

"I already told you. A Southerner." Libba lifted a sneakered foot and nudged the trunk tray with its neat configuration of personal possessions. "You look pretty Southern."

"Alabama."

Libba positioned herself between the two beds and stretched out her arms to either side. "If my fingers were six inches longer I'd be able to touch both walls at the same time. Where's your mother, casing the joint?"

Frances opened her mouth. That's precisely what her mother was doing. An alligator belt unspooled in her fingers.

"I'm dying for a Coke." The door slammed again, and Libba was gone.

Pamela Simpson came in, her arms filled with student store supplies. She frowned at the disorder and picked her way gingerly across it. "There's a hotplate in the Commons area so you can heat soup if you're studying late at night. And an iron." She stacked new notebooks, diagonally blazoned EMERSON SEMINARY across the front, on the scarred bureau top, then removed them again. "Do you see that dresser scarf? I packed it under your summer robe, next to your kid gloves."

Frances extracted the white linen rectangle. She hadn't known what a "dresser scarf" was when she'd seen it on Emerson Seminary's ARTICLES TO BRING, listed just below "white gloves" required for trips out of school. But her mother had known. Her mother, in fact, already owned a dresser scarf; several. "I bought a pennant for the wall, too," Mrs. Simpson said, taking an elongated triangle of navy felt from the student store sack. "Now, what do you need help with?" she asked, raising her voice to be heard over a sequence of grinding thunks in the stairwell just outside the room. "I'll make your bed for you."

Again Libba Charles appeared in the doorway. This time she was pushing a two-wheeled dolly, with a chest of drawers leaning upright against its metal bars. She tipped the carrier and the chest rocked forward and free, solid and enormous in the cramped room. Again she stuck out her hand, this time toward Pamela Simpson. "Libba Charles."

"What's that?" Mrs. Simpson asked.

"A dolly from the library. They won't miss it. I hated to ask one of those poor porters to bring my things in. It's hot, they're sweating."

"I didn't mean the dolly, I meant the . . . ," Pamela Simpson said. Frances watched. So far, this scene was the most interesting aspect of going off to college. "I'm looking forward to meeting your mother, Libba. Where is she?"

"Which mother would that be? At any rate, none of them are here."

Mrs. Simpson blinked, plainly flustered by the plethora of information Libba had provided in her unrelated utterances, and returned to a topic she was sure of. "An extra chest of drawers wasn't on the ARTICLES TO BRING list. There's barely room for the two that came with the room."

"We'll make it work."

"I would imagine it's against the rules. Suppose everyone brought extra furniture, what then? Frances has a slipper chair she'd loved to have brought—"

But Libba was out in the hall, stashing the dolly in a linen closet. In the room again, she leaned over, pulled a handful of bundled wool from her trunk, regarded it, then rewadded the sweaters. "Won't be needing these." She pushed the trunk under the bed. "Does it ever get cold?"

"November," Frances said, happy to oblige.

Mrs. Simpson reached to tuck her daughter's straying bra strap beneath the sleeveless blouse, where it belonged. "I'll make up your bed while you unpack, Frances," she said, and stepped dramatically over a cardboard carton of papers, books, record albums.

"Careful with those," Libba said. "They're my most treasured possessions."

As Frances's mother leaned into the trunk for folded sheets— graduation presents as well, bearing her daughter's monogram stitched in pale pink—a pushpin protruding from a bulletin board slanted against a battered leather suitcase snagged the hem of her skirt, ripping the seam. She sighed loudly.

"You know," Libba said thoughtfully, "it's too crowded in here for all three."

"Three chests," Mrs. Simpson agreed.

"Three *people*." Libba drummed her fingers against the offending wooden bureau. "I bet Frances can make her own bed. And lie in it, too."

Pamela Simpson straightened. "Come out in the hall and give me a kiss good-bye, Frances."

Frances obediently followed her mother out of the room. She had no trouble maneuvering around the room's disarray. "Sweetie," Mrs. Simpson said, raising her voice slightly to be heard over the noise of other arriving girls. "Take my advice. Study hard. Be good. Never borrow clothes or money or anything else from a roommate. It only leads to trouble. I'll call you. The phone's—"

"— just down the hall," Libba called from inside the room.

Mrs. Simpson tensed, lowered her tone as she turned for the stairs. "If I were you, I'd look out for her."

When Frances came in again, Libba was examining the length of ironed linen that lay across the top of Frances's bureau. "What's this, a napkin?"

"A dresser scarf. It's required."

Libba rolled her eyes.

Frances picked up the pristine Emerson Seminary pennant. "Here," she said, "use this." And laughed, the first time Libba Charles was to hear that laugh, neither trill nor tinkle nor peal, but loud and unforced and unique.

As she grew up, the oldest sister Alice had difficulty deciding who to admire more in the Em Sem opening day scenario: the roommate who knowingly broke the rules, the roommate who wouldn't complain, or the parent who fought for her child's rights. Alice admired her mother's obedience to a parent yet scorned it. She admired Libba's presumption yet resented it. She admired her grandmother's adherence to principles, yet was embarrassed by her interference.

"I should have known then," Frances laughed years later. "Hand me the cruet."

"Known what?" Libba said. "Don't use too much vinegar."

"To steer clear of anyone with so much nerve."

"You should have known then that your redeemer had cometh to teach you the meaning of chutzpah. You should thanketh me on your kneeseth for giving you balls."

"Libba," Alice's father complained from behind the newspaper, but he laughed.

"What's 'chutzpah?'" Alice herself asked. "When's supper going to be ready?" The story became a metaphor for Alice, a life-theme of torn-betweens.

"Has she done anything about that chest?" Frances's mother asked over the telephone several days later.

"Yes," Frances lied, a first.

By October, Frances was wearing Libba's pilled and raveled sweaters. By October, Libba was picking up the care packages Pamela Simpson mailed weekly from Alabama to her daughter in Virginia, and reading aloud the letters enclosing a ceaseless litany of social and academic advice. By October, the radiator was scorching their faces at night and waking them with its predawn clanking, and warping the covers of the books Libba carelessly left atop it. By October there were eleven gashes on the closet door, which Frances drew a line through as a running tally of Libba's slammings. By December they knew they would room together again, knew they'd request the same shoebox of a room, knew what the other was thinking, knew what childhood refrains they'd been raised with.

"Here's what I was told from the moment I could talk until the moment I got on the train to come to Em Sem: 'Lower your voice.'"

Frances laughed, that blurt of hilarity, juicy and joyous. "And here's what I was told: 'Laugh like a lady.'"

By December, Frances Simpson and Libba Charles, the modest, obedient, Southern girl with the startling laugh and the brassy, ballsy Yankee gal with the startling good looks were inseparable. Classmates couldn't conveniently pigeonhole this perfect pairing of opposites in temperament, behavior, appearances, upbringing. The relationship between light-haired, fair-skinned, hazel-eyed Frances Wilson and dark-complected, gray-eyed Libba Charles was so unlikely as to seem both inexplicable and ludicrous: calm, reticent, unassuming, and accepting Frances indivisible from restless, reckless, critical, and aggressive Libba. As cliques subtly, invariably formed, the wilder girls—the smokers, the rule-breakers, the burgeoning beatniks, the literati—sought out Libba as an obvious recruit to their nonconformist ranks. The traditionalists—the daters, the shoppers, the studious, the carefully groomed and attired—let Frances know she was welcome in their studious, social midst. Both groups were ignored. Other girls speculated, whispered and conjectured behind their hands, unable to comprehend this bond, even less able to penetrate their cocoon of inseparability.

"How can you stand it?" a classmate asked Frances. "Libba's such a slob."

"Bite back, Frances," Libba said, "defend me."

"How can you stand it?" another asked, "waking up every morning next to someone so beautiful?"

"Bite back," Libba said, "that's a cut to *you*. Defend yourself!"

"Double O's" they dubbed themselves. For they discovered they were both only children of only children. Or in Libba's case, the only original child in a choppy sea of step siblings and broken marriages. At holiday tables set for three, Frances sat lonely and bored. When someone managed to pull a meal together in whichever family Libba found herself during the holidays, she sat surrounded by relations she couldn't quite place and adults who threatened to break into bickering over something as insignificant as the consistency of the gravy.

"How old were you when they divorced?" Frances asked Libba of this inconceivable world: crowded, boisterous, argumentative.

"Eight, ten, fifteen," Libba shrugged. "Depends on how you count them. The original one? Or my mother's next divorce or my father's or—never mind, doesn't matter. I'm not getting married."

"I am," Frances said, and pressed the sleeve of a shirt with the iron her mother had been so pleased to discover in the dorm's Commons. "I want to feel secure and loved. You will too."

"Oh, I won't. *Au contraire*. I want to feel free and irresponsible. Besides, you can be loved without being married. Hurry up with that." The only things Libba ever ironed were cheese sandwiches she'd wrapped in tinfoil.

"But what about children?"

"You can have a child without being married, too."

"Oh, Libba, be serious."

"I *am* serious."

"Maybe you can, but I want lots and lots. No one's ever going to be as lonely as I was."

"I wasn't a 'child.' I wasn't even an offspring. I was a 'product.' Says so right on the divorce papers, plural. You're the one majoring in husbandry, you have the children."

"What are you majoring in, English?"

"I'm majoring in experience so I can describe something with authority when I begin writing novels."

Frances lifted her chin with small triumph. "But who's going to describe the experience of having children for you, of being a family?"

Libba switched off the iron. "You."

As a child, the middle daughter Allegra took piano lessons just as her older sister Alice did. But unlike Alice, Allegra refused play the assigned pieces. She wasn't interested in *Für Elise* or the theme from Hansel and Gretel or the Toreador's song from *Carmen*. Allegra took piano lessons only long enough to be able to pick out the song her mother and Libba sang snatches of, a song from Em Sem nickelodeon days. *If you'll be M-I-N-E mine I'll be T-H-I-N-E thine and I'll L-O-V-E love you all the T-I-M-E time. You are the B-E-S-T best of all the R-E-S-T rest and I'll L-O-V-E love you all the T- I-M- E time, rack 'em up, stack 'em up any ol' time.*

Libba and Frances were never sure whether the piano teacher gave up on Allegra or Allegra gave up on the piano.

"'What do I intend to be?'" Libba had echoed the guidance counselor's question. "Tough with a capital T." Libba had shrugged when the story traveled the dorm and reached her. "She shouldn't have asked me what I wanted to *be*. She should have asked me what I wanted to *do*."

"Poor Libba," classmates said, and Frances knew what they meant in the low-flying radar of denigration. Libba was quick, decisive, clever and self-sufficient, traits that in a midtwentieth-century Southern milieu translated as abrupt, shrewd, manipulating, caustic. Not to Frances, who watched Libba pitch the oranges provided nightly to the dorms out the open window at teachers who—innocently, unfortunately—chose to leave the college after dark. Not to Frances, who watched Libba sit in that same window, legs drawn to her chin, and smoke illegally, languorously, inches away from a tumble down a slate rooftop and three stories to the sidewalk. Not to Frances, for whom Libba Charles revealed a previously unglimpsed world of insisting upon what she wanted, of challenging what she didn't, and of questioning what she did.

Edie—the youngest daughter, the last—spent hours closeted with the pebble-grained Em Sem yearbooks, locating her mother and Libba among the slick pages of black-and-white photographs: Glee Club, Altar Guild, Debating Team, athletic and academic and social clubs. And in the formal Senior pictures, too: ovals that encapsulated page-boy hairstyles and curving shoulders bare but for a modest yet provocative drape of black fabric below which Edie could only guess at bosoms. The Em Sem yearbook pictures were nearly all she had with which to glimpse or imagine her mother's life before she became a mother, and nothing was more fascinating than a mother before she became A Mother. Unlike Alice and Allegra, Edie hadn't been around to hear her mother and Libba's laughed conversations and reminiscences and jukebox tune duets. Because Edie wasn't so much as a twinkle in her father's eye then, as they say. Edie wasn't supposed to have been born at all.

After two weeks the chest was still there, stolidly blocking passage. Mrs. Simpson decided it was time to get tough with her daughter, who seemed, after two weeks away from home, to be just the slightest bit tougher herself, in an unattractive way. "If you don't turn that girl in to the Resident Adviser I'll do it myself."

Frances had returned glumly to the room. Flat on her back on the bed, Libba was walking her bare feet up the walls, leaving a staggered, shadowy path of footprints toward her bulletin board covered with lists and quotes and cartoons and celebrity—not family—photographs.

"That was my mother on the phone."

"Ah." Libba got up, began inching the chest toward the deep

closet. "Let's make a deal," she said, grunting. She succeeded in wedging the chest inside the closet, scraped the coathangers to one side, then scrambled up to perch atop it. Her eyes gleamed in the semidarkness. "A perfect place for writing."

"What's the deal?" Frances reminded her.

The proctor called from the hall. "Lights out in ten minutes."

Frances reached for the brass hook, and her nightgown.

"The deal is," Libba said, "that if you promise not to tell anyone I have this chest in *my* closet, I promise not to tell anyone that you're so modest you dress and undress in *your* closet."

The immoveable object opened her mouth to protest. The irresistible force lifted her eyebrows.

"Okay," Frances said. "The chest stays."

I would look out for that girl if I were you, Mrs. Simpson had told her only daughter, Frances.

"It's not exactly what she meant," that only daughter would tell her three daughters, Alice and Allegra and Edie, "but as it happened that's exactly what we did. We looked out for each other."

CHAPTER 1

The periods of sleeping—they won't let themselves think it's unconsciousness—have grown longer.

The inert figure in the hospital bed looks far older than her sixty-three years, supported and suspended by a network of plastic tubing entwining her body like tangled yarn, connected to a clicking, flashing, humming monitor with an inhuman life of its own.

They stand by the bed and stroke limp fingers or pass their strong, young fingers over their mother's forehead where, unlike the slack flesh everywhere else, the skin over the skull is taut, plasticlike. Her mouth works occasionally, the tongue moving against dry lips Alice and Allegra and Edie take turns coating with petroleum jelly they squeeze from a crumpled tube. No respirator, they'd agreed. No accordionned tube looking like a vacuum cleaner hose. Just morphine for the pain. If she should swim through the fog of drugs to speak, they want to hear their mother.

It's a warm Sunday in September of 1993. Edie, standing at the foot of the bed, wears a loose pink jumper made of a fabric so thin that her nipples, raised by the constant chill of the hospital, are clearly visible. Occasionally, she unconsciously rubs her breasts, trying to soften the hardness grown uncomfortable. At the window, Alice is wearing a khaki skirt the way her mother taught her, a seasonally-appropriate "transitional cotton." Allegra's ratty, bookstore-logod T-shirt isn't tucked into her jeans, and she leans against the wall and shifts from one leg to the other. The other foot she presses to the cream-colored wall, leaving shadowy mismatched footprints much like those Libba Charles left on the Emerson Seminary wall fifty years earlier.

By now, the nurses waive the visitor regulations. They know the Wilson family drifting in and out of the ICU waiting room where John Wilson sits now with strangers keeping similar vigils, existing on prayer and fast food. A room where the smells of disinfectant and flowers and medicines blend in a singular odor endemic to hospitals. The sterile language of terminal illness has long since become a second language to them. Cancer has been killing Frances Wilson by degrees for more than two years.

She'd been restless since lunch, when Edie brought milkshakes for them all. Caramel, chocolate, strawberry, peach. Allegra attempted a joke about the flavor of glucose. John Wilson didn't touch his, and Alice flushed the thick melted liquid down the toilet. Now, at six, they're hungry again. They've gone on living.

"Take your father home and get something to eat," Libba says, coming into the room. She tugs the pale gray cardigan sweater she'd borrowed from Frances's drawer around her body. "They said nothing would happen tonight."

No one asks for the definition of *nothing*. The daughters hesitate.

"Ginny Murphy brought lasagne," Alice says. Allegra makes a retching cough and Edie instantly looks up, thinking the noise has come from their mother.

"Fine, then," Libba says, "stay," and leaves them.

As though the curt tone of voice has reached and woken her, Frances Wilson's eyes open.

"Mother?" Edie says.

Allegra and Alice take two steps to the bedside, unconsciously lining up in order of birth. Alice at the pillow, Allegra at her mother's hips, Edie at the sticklike thighs. The cluster of bones that is Frances Wilson's hand, criss-crossed with white adhesive, rises from the sheet.

"Mother?" Edie says again.

Three heads lean toward the wasted figure beneath them. "We're here," Allegra says.

"What is it? Do you want Daddy?" Alice says. "A nurse?"

"Do you need anything?" Edie asks, fitting her hand to her mother's neck.

"Hush," Allegra says. "She's trying to talk."

The piteous eyes take in the three heads leaning toward her and flash with absolute recognition. The daughters wait. "We're here," Allegra says again, gently, and bites her lip.

Their mother's voice is soft too, almost a whisper. But her words are unmistakable. "Look after Libba," she says. "Promise," then closes her eyes.

CHAPTER 2

They can't remember a time they haven't known her.

Libba was always there. On Labor Days and July Fourths, an anniversary celebration in August. At their christenings and confirmations and birthdays and graduations and weddings. Stealing their mother, stealing the show. Or she was there for no reason at all. Mostly, in fact, she was there for no reason at all, unless you counted Frances.

She was there before they themselves were. Weekends, when Libba visited Frances and John in White Plains, she slept on the nursery's single bed while an infant Alice slumbered beside her in the crib. Pasted to an early page in Alice's baby album is a card that reads *To Alice from her first roommate, your pal Libba Charles.* The scribbled, saved memento seems both touching and quaint, except that if you ask Alice, there's never been anything remotely touching or quaint about Libba Charles.

"A piece of work," Alice remembers her father calling Libba.

The note had accompanied Libba's baby gift to Alice, a silver teaspoon. Not a pablum spoon, but a full-sized teaspoon in the Shell and Thread pattern that became Alice's flatware pattern. A choice in which, Alice has remarked more than once, she herself had no choice. "Why did Libba get to decide?" she asked her mother as a child, fingering the shiny spoon, trying even then to unravel her mother's relationship with Libba Charles.

"It wasn't deliberate forever-and-ever," Frances said. "Libba's not that territorial."

Alice grew to doubt this. Libba was territorial about Frances.

And even when she wasn't there, she was there in their mother's references: Libba's books, Libba's ideas, Libba's travels, Libba's pranks.

"LKF," Libba said. "Your mother was so modest she dressed in the closet when we were in college. I never saw her—"

"That'll do, Libba," Frances said.

Ten-year-old Alice looked down at Libba, doing leg lifts on the carpet. "What's LKF?"

"Little known fact," Frances answered from inside the closet. "Is this a valid complaint from someone who jumped naked into a country club swimming pool at a debutante party? Pay attention. You promised me a closet consult."

"Why?" Alice had asked breathlessly, thrilled with the vision, the lawlessness of Libba's outrageousness.

"Somebody dared me to," Libba said without pausing in her exercise. "*Je jette* the bouclé suit. Too Jackie Kennedy. Next? And that two-piece brown horror. That's an HWC outfit."

"Which you gave me."

"What's 'HWC'?" Alice asked.

"Heavy with child," Frances said, and a look passed between them.

They always talked like this. Around her. Above her. Hopping from subject to subject with their verbal shorthand and abbreviations. Alice had known the two to make written lists of topics they intended to cover because their conversations would veer into so many tangents when they were together after an absence.

In Alice's memory, Libba and Frances talk, endlessly and everywhere: on the terrace, heads thrown back with hilarity; stirring coffee as they talked in the low voices of confidences at the kitchen table; in the den on winter weekends, with four socked soles to the fire and their hair fanned out behind them on the rug, or falling to the side, exposing a pale stripe of neck. Grown women curled and girlish, lazy and laughing.

Frances changed in Libba's company, transformed from *my mother* to *Libba's friend*. Her posture and demeanor and features relaxed. She laughed more and minded less. She was prettier, younger. Happier. Alice loved her mother's loosening and, lacking even the vocabulary at seven and eight to describe it, was envious of Libba's transforming power. Alice sensed she herself couldn't effect the same hocus-pocus on her mother no matter how many A's she brought home on her report card.

Allegra's childhood memories of Libba differ from her sister Alice's. With Allegra's birth her parents returned to the South, to North Carolina, and though Libba's weekend visits became less frequent, they became more vivid. Wilder. Louder. The talking and laughing and lounging continued, but in party form.

"Libba's the best kind of houseguest, Alley-oop," Frances said to Allegra. "An old shoe, doesn't require a thing."

But despite the playful nickname, Frances didn't pause in her housework to gently tug Allegra's hair as she said this; didn't smile and wink at her. Because as far as Allegra could tell, Frances was too busy preparing for Libba, who supposedly needed no preparations. Buying unusual foods like avocados and mushroom caps and oyster crackers and toothpicks with colored cellophane hats. Putting flowers in Allegra's room, which she was required to move out of for Libba. Allegra silently disagreed with her mother's assessment of Libba. The Wilson household changed indeed, not only to accommodate Libba, but to revolve around her.

A current crackled through the house when Libba arrived Friday afternoon, and through Frances as well, a current of mischief and merriment that preceded the evening parties. Bedtimes were ignored, chores were left undone, meals were hurried.

"Mommy, ugh," Allegra once complained after cutting into a hastily browned hamburger patty. "I can't eat this. It's still red and squishy."

Libba had leaned over to inspect it. "Looks like a hemorrhoid."

"Libba!"

"What's a hemorrhoid?" Allegra had asked, but Libba only shrugged. Not to Allegra's question, but to Frances's laughed objection.

Friday and Saturday nights the house filled with people. Music blared, glasses ringed tables, shoes were abandoned in corners, cigarette butts were stubbed into every conceivable container. Allegra was intoxicated by the swaying creatures in the living room, her mother shuffling off to Buffalo in a long slubbed-silk hostess skirt, Libba doing the Twist. Alice was gone in Allegra's memory, old enough to spend the night with friends while Allegra watched television as late as she wanted in her parents' bedroom. She was shooed from the kitchen table crowded with bottles, marbles of olives and onions, napkins disintegrating with wet, where they mixed concoctions with beautiful names: John's Gee and Tees, fizzy yet clear as water; Frances's amber-tinted Manhattans; Libba's lemony-pale Tom Collins. The rosy slush of blender drinks in the summertime, peach and strawberry daiquiris. Allegra had mixed her own drink, tonic and ice with a pretty green accent of lime wedge. Bitter to the tongue, but so entirely grown-up. Now Allegra realizes that those parties were the beginning of her drinking, imitation gin and tonics that with time became pilfered drinks, fully alcoholic.

At one and two in the morning Libba and Frances could be found in the den cluttered with party debris, dopey with fatigue but jawing about one of the dates Libba occasionally brought, wry men full of innuendo and uninterested in Allegra or Alice, and especially not in baby Edie. Or the extra man Frances had invited. "Imports," Libba referred to them.

Woken by laughter, Allegra wandered in from her bedroom. "Aren't you going to bed?"

"I'm too tired to go to bed," Frances said. She wasn't answering Allegra, though; she was telling Libba. Allegra felt foolish standing there in her nightgown while Libba and her mother, garbed in hot pinks and fluorescent geometric prints, were draped across furniture.

If party evenings were late, mornings were even later. Libba slept with a machine on the mattress beside her pillow that whirred a hushed drone meant to blot out the shrieks and punches of Saturday cartoons, or Edie's toddling whining. "Shush, girls," Frances would whisper loudly, "Libba works. She comes to rest."

Allegra knows now the hijinks that transpired those nights. The hat parties, when pots and lampshades and ice buckets became bonnets and berets and sombreros. Dirty-themed charades with outrageous cheating; a neighbor's tractor mower hijacked for a midnight joy ride.

For forty-eight hours that current fizzed and burned, until Sunday night when, hoarse and exhausted—hungover, Allegra knows now—Frances was in bed by eight, leaving Allegra bereft and mystified and slightly anxious at losing an adult to sleep before her own bedtime. It was worrisome. Weren't parents supposed to stay up? "Where's Mommy?" she asked her father.

"Already asleep," John Wilson said. "The weekend wore her out."

But Allegra didn't think the weekend had worn out her mother. Allegra believed Libba Charles had worn her out.

Edie doesn't remember the parties; she doesn't remember swapped laughter and secrets on the bed or terrace or sofa. What Edie remembers of Libba is that Frances went *away* with her, on weekends to the beach or the mountains or weekdays to a conference or to New York or some college in some state Edie had hardly heard of. Libba breezed in and swept up Frances and her luggage, waved from the car, departing and taking Edie's mother with her. Leaving Edie to love her father best, though she was lucky even to have been conceived, much less born after a long and difficult pregnancy.

"My mother's famous friend" was how Edie described Libba Charles to her classmates, using Libba as social currency for playground popularity. If the parties when Libba visited contributed to Allegra's drinking habit, Edie believes she's grown up unanchored and uncommitted because Frances was gone, away with Libba.

Because their mother loved Libba, the three sisters understood they were meant to love Libba, too. But Libba was difficult to love, dryly witty or aloof or puzzlingly adult. Most of all, it was difficult loving someone who siphoned, by her presence, even by her phone calls, love from a person who was supposed to belong to you. Hard to stand on the outside looking in to a relationship in which you seemed superfluous. Easy to resent the person responsible for compromised affection. A person who predated you; who knew more about your mother than you ever would.

But Alice and Allegra and Edie couldn't erase Libba, forget her if they tried. She was singular. A character. A personality. Quick, brash, mercurial, effusive, and impossible to categorize. "A living outrage," John Wilson also called Libba Charles, "wide open."

"What's she like?" people pressed them as adults, having read her books, and the sisters themselves would be hard-pressed to describe this bundle of contradictions.

"Intriguing," Alice once offered, though she has a few more adjectives she'd currently use to describe Libba: thoughtless, caustic. When Alice was a child, Libba thought nothing of correcting her English: "Don't say this girl *she* hates my guts." "Don't say can't hardly."

"Why isn't Libba married?" Alice once asked her father.

Behind a shield of newspaper, he'd said, "Because she beat the boys at everything. Tennis, studies. Let that be a lesson to you."

From the kitchen Frances amended her husband's answer. "Because she doesn't want to be married." Though she had eventually married, twice; to Sam, a poet and Russell, a book reviewer.

"Mysterious," Allegra said. "Where do you live?" she'd asked Libba, who seemed to come from nowhere. Allegra had never seen a picture of a house, an apartment.

"Web City," Libba answered.

"Where's that?"

"I'll tell you when you're older." And when Allegra turned sixteen, she had: "Halfway up a spider's ass."

"Complicated," Edie, as usual, hedged. Once a popular, entertaining fixture on the speaking circuit, twenty-five years earlier Libba Charles had abruptly ceased giving any sort of speech or interview or lecture about her life and her writing. But she'd had no qualms about mining personal morsels of her close friend's— and her daughters'—lives for material. "Coarse," Alice would add. "She cussed." Not *cursed*, the prissy term Frances used, but *cussed*. "Try this, it'll knock your dick off," Alice had heard Libba say to John as she handed him a martini.

"Lucky," Edie would shake her head. Wherever Libba went, she always managed to see somebody famous: Jackie Kennedy shopping in Saks, Walter Cronkite on an airplane, Paul Newman in a bar.

"Dowdy," Alice said, because Libba dressed in the same ratty clothes every visit. Jeans and men's shirts, madras Bermudas, the same piqué cocktail shift summer after summer.

"Libba's not dowdy," Frances said. "She's so beautiful she doesn't have to bother with what she wears."

"Funny," Allegra would say. She remembers the imaginary aerosol can Libba pointed at Edie when she toddled toward her with zwieback-gummed hands or a snot-candled nose. "Look what I've invented," Libba said, index finger pressed to an imaginary button. "It's called 'Babe-Away.'"

"Generous?" Allegra tried, remembering the presents Libba brought to them. Soundtracks from Broadway musicals she loved, singing loudly along with *My Fair Lady, West Side Story, South Pacific,* unembarrassed that she mangled the tunes, mispronounced the lyrics. Sometimes the gift was nothing more than a swizzle stick from a swanky bar, but once, for her godchild Allegra, she brought a thigh-high battery-operated green plastic robot that staggered across the floor when the switch was clicked on.

Yet the gifts were given carelessly. Libba didn't stoop to their level, inquire condescendingly about school. When she talked to Alice and Allegra and Edie it was as an adult; a forthright manner of address that delighted and terrified and angered them. Because Libba had come to see their mother.

Discipline was lax and meals slapdash because their mother was hurrying to be with Libba again, to turn her attention back to Libba. When Libba was there Frances was present but unavailable, and the sisters were excluded and invisible. They felt abandoned on Libba Charles's behalf. Because no matter who else was there, in the end it was always Libba and Frances.

If you were to ask each daughter to explain what it was between their mother and Libba Charles, they'd tell you the stories they knew. Dressing in closets, swimming naked on a dare. Libba with the Em Sem night watchman, Frances with the fratty from State. Libba with the multiple mothers, Frances with the omnipresent one. Stories that were told to them, or stories they overheard. The daughters would tell you that even their names were a story, that they'd been named for the sisters in a poem Frances came across in the anthology text of an Em Sem poetry class, Longfellow's "The Children's Hour."

"Listen," Frances said.

> Between the dark and the daylight,
>> When the night is beginning to lower,
> Comes a pause in the day's occupations
>> That is known as The Children's Hour.

> From my study I see in the lamplight,
>> Descending the broad hall stair,
> Grave Alice and laughing Allegra,
>> And Edith with golden hair.

From their mother's bedtime recitations the sisters knew the occasional verse by heart, the way other children knew Goldilocks and the Three Bears. "I don't want to be grave," Alice complained.

> A sudden rush from the stairway,
>> A sudden raid from the hall!
> By three doors left unguarded
>> They enter my castle wall!

I have you fast in my fortress,
And will not let you depart,
But put you down into the dungeon
In the round-tower of my heart.

"I notice there's no mention," Libba had said, "of who fed them and who bathed them and who got them ready for bed between the dark and the daylight, while the master of the house read his newspaper." But she was teasing, knowing Frances adored not only the rhyming cadence but its conjured images: the snug fire-lit study, the rambunctious girl-children who would never grow up and old and away, the forever-and-ever no-matter-what love of a parent. The sisters had adored it, too, until the story behind their names embarrassed them, like being forced to wear matching dresses to Sunday school. Or middy blouses.

"We know all the stories," grave Alice and laughing Allegra and Edith with golden hair would say, would sigh, now that they've grown up and old and away, just as their mother feared. "The stories are all in Libba's novels."

But they'd be wrong. Because as Libba herself could tell them, novels have unreliable narrators. And every character has a different point of view.

● ● ●

April 1, 1951

"I rue the day I ever introduced the two of you," Libba said. She gave the diamond on Frances's finger a cursory glance. "Water it, maybe it'll grow."

John and Frances laughed. "She's just jealous," John said, and tightened his clasp on Frances's neck.

Frances put her hand in the pocket of his new suit. "Isn't he handsome, Libba? I love the way men look in seersucker suits. Poochy and puckery and rumpled, like they've just gotten out of bed."

"Want to pursue that train of thought?" John said.

Frances laughed, pulled her hand free. "No, I want Libba to help me pick out my wedding dress."

"*Libba* as fashion consultant, marriage mentor? You've lost your mind."

Libba eyed him, poked Frances. "Do you really want to marry a man whose mother delightedly told her friends, 'And his fiancée is already an Episcopalian!' Think about this, Frances. Consider the implications."

"Did I tell you that story?" Frances laughed. "And did I tell you that

I love him?" She smoothed the wavy brunette hair at his temples.

"Nix on the nuzzling," Libba said. "If you come to Maine with me for the summer, I'll help you pick out your wedding dress. You can do your student teaching there and I'll pen my first masterpiece in a windswept shack near a rocky beach."

"That hardly sounds like an even swap," Frances said. "Besides, I have a wedding to plan."

"*Au contraire.* Your mother has a wedding to plan. *You* are extraneous."

"Not to me," John said. "But why not? I'll be in New York anyway. It's closer to Maine than Alabama. Go on, hon. After four years, it's yin and yang's final days as roommates. Your next roommate is me." He pinched her bottom, ducked into the front seat of the car, and pulled out, playfully fishtailing down the driveway so that the car's fins seemed to wave good-bye.

Libba stuck out her lip in mock petulance. "How can you do this to me? I want to be first in the hearts of my countrymen. Countrymen meaning you."

"It's a wedding, not a funeral. I'll be there for every important occasion in your life, I promise. And promise me you'll be there for all of mine. Beginning with my wedding."

August 1, 1951

Frances opened another mirrored door in the windowless room hushed with pale beige carpeting. She slowly moved heavy white dresses across the rack; this one with seed pearls, this one with tulle, this one with organdy, or lace, or netting. So many choices. She wanted white that wasn't white; the color of magnolia, kid gloves, whipping cream. Libba could describe it. Frances looked over her shoulder as a stout woman with a severe bun showed her into the dressing room. Libba had gone to the next block to pick up pictures she was having developed. "Is something wrong?" the woman asked.

"I'm looking for my friend. She's helping me decide."

"What does she look like?"

"Black hair. Beautiful."

"I'll let you know when she comes. But it should be *your* choice. Try the high collar first. I'll bring you a crinoline."

In the elevator, Libba studied the photographs. There was only one of both of them, from the afternoon they'd hiked in Acadia Park and asked another walker to take the picture. They stood on a hillside above the ocean, their long coats whipped by a stiff wind. In July, dead summer, as bleak a backdrop as you could imagine, and nowhere near the romantic picture Libba had verbally painted for Frances.

Libba knocked on the dressing room door. "You found me," Frances said. "I'm on frock number seven."

"Miss Havisham out there directed me." Frances stood on a raised block upholstered in the same pale carpet as the floor. "On a pedestal," Libba said. "How nice. Think you'll stay there? I got the pictures."

"Any good ones?"

Libba showed her the two of them side by side, huddled as one figure against the wind. "Take a last look at your independence. Is that a smile or a grimace? *Why* did I ever get that Carson McCullers haircut?"

"Can I have it?" Frances said from beneath a billowing umbrella of shapeless cloth she pulled over her head and shoulders. "Help me with the buttons."

Libba worked two dozen buttons carefully through the silken loops of the closely fitting low-waisted bodice. "Feel secure yet? The major benefit of being engaged is that now you can do anything to your hair and he still has to love you. That's what *I* call security."

The saleswoman's head appeared around the door. "I knew the ecru would be best with your fair skin!" She beamed. "Come take a look."

Frances moved carefully down the short hall of dressing rooms, her fingers on the shifting, swishing fabric. She stood before a demihexagon of mirrors and looked at herself: the creamy gleam of satin falling in long vertical waves from her hips, the tightly shirred bodice outlining her waist, the organdy cap sleeves clinging to her shoulders. For a long silent moment she regarded the wide-eyed person who faced her, fingers spread against her pale chest as though asking *Me?* Suddenly she pressed her palms to her eyes and broke into tears, overcome.

Libba tapped her cheek, said wryly. "I guess this means you're really going to do it."

Frances choked a sob of disbelief, gratitude, joy. "It's what I've always wanted. It's *all* I ever wanted."

"I'll just, um, fetch a tissue," the clerk said.

Libba stepped outside the bay and opened the flanking mirrored doors on either side, behind which more wedding dresses hung. She drew the doors together, enclosing the two of them in a compact silvery pentagon of mirrored walls. Wherever their eyes fell, the vanilla dress and Libba's yellow shift, Frances's cap of fair hair and Libba's ebony frizz, repeated themselves, unavoidable. They were surrounded by eerie, mesmerizing multiples, reflection upon reflection upon reflection of identical images tunneling smaller and smaller until their bodies were nothing but distant tinted blurs against silvery walls.

"Oh," Frances breathed, whispered. "We're inside a kaleidoscope. Like repeating a word. Foot," she said, "foot, foot, foot, foot, foot, foot, foot. Until it doesn't have any meaning."

A knock sounded outside. "Are you ladies alright in there?"

"We're—" Frances began.

"We're just pondering infinity," Libba answered, and lifting her hand, pointed. Countless replicas of her finger pointed on, beyond and beyond. "Look at that, Frances. That's forever and ever. That's 'I do.'"

September 24, 1951

"It's been a month. Has your mother forgiven me yet?"

"She'll never forgive you. The maid of honor making a rehearsal dinner toast with the letters of the alphabet? By the letter F it was clearly an off-color disaster and you had twenty letters left."

"Oh, that. I meant forgive me for asking how many people she'd invited to the wedding. I had no idea that asking specifics was the height of tacky. Speaking of specifics, how is it?"

"How is what?"

"Post marital sex."

"Libba!"

"Well, why not? It's always struck me that men talk constantly about sex until they're married and then clam up. But with women, sex talk is taboo before the wedding. Afterward, carnal conversation is fully boo."

"Maybe I haven't been married long enough. Ask me later."

"You can count on it. Meanwhile, are you using birth control? Or is John being a good boy and doing the honors?"

"You know very well I'm not interested in controlling birth. The babies can't come fast enough to suit either of us. How's the daytime journalism and the nighttime novelizing?"

"Both are missing something crucial."

"Plot?"

There was a pause. "Egad, I think it's you."

Frances smiled. "I miss you, too. Start spending the weekends in White Plains. You can write in peace."

February 9, 1952

Side by side on the postage-stamp concrete terrace, they hiked up Bermudas and rolled up camp shirt sleeves and peeled off loafers and socks. Libba squinted into the miraculous seventy-degree February day. "The glare from my white legs is worse than the sun's," she said. "We look like we've been playing the organ in the Luray Caverns."

Frances laughed. "You'd have never known about the Luray Caverns without me."

"I won't go into all the things you wouldn't know without me. Such as John."

Frances tapped the wide arm of the Adirondack chair. "Weren't we lucky? These came with the house." Behind them, John mowed neat stripes in the fledgling, minuscule yard, ducking at each corner to avoid braining himself on the metal support poles of the clothes line.

"Like the chests that came with the room at Em Sem?" Libba fell silent for a moment. "Still glad you swapped independence for security?"

"Does a different date every night of the week make you feel secure?"

"Sure."

"Not secure enough to bring any of them out to White Plains, I notice."

Libba gave her a coy look. "There's only one twin bed in the spare bedroom." She stretched, turned her head from the ratcheting noise of the lawn mower. "Does John have to play Farmer in the Dell on the one day I'm not laboring in the *Fortune* salt mines?"

"The lawn mower came with the house, too. It was in the base-ment with the chairs."

"Mmm," Libba drowsed. "I hear a refrain."

"Can you hear this, Libba?" Frances whispered, leaning. "I'm pregnant."

"Omigod." Libba's eyes were closed, but she grinned broadly. "I can't bear it. You'll produce before I publish."

Before Alice was born in September, and Libba became her first roommate, the lawn mower expired. Soon after, the fold-down attic steps Frances had been so pleased to discover in the house, collapsed, and the toilet in the single bath cracked and leaked. Not long after Alice's birth, "It came with the house" became not just a refrain, but the title of Libba's first novel.

And there they were on page nine, suburbanites sunning their legs on a sunny, gift-from-God winter afternoon, though Libba had made it a Sunday in March instead of February. There was John, recast as an Edward, shearing liriope instead of grass. The Adirondack chairs were absent, though, as was the lawnmower. And in Libba's portrayal of a newlywed couple, *it came with the house* became less a statement of delight in accidental treasure than an ironic comment on the aspects of marriage—material and otherwise—that began as bonuses but mutated into liabilities. It was the first time Libba Charles wove Frances Wilson's life into her fiction, but not the last.

January 11, 1953

Frances smoothed invisible strands on Alice's four-month-old-but-still-bald head and pulled down the collar of her day gown. "Karen Little two blocks up invited us for Sunday brunch."

"Did she come with the house, too?"

"Please? She's reading it."

"Nope, nada. You know I hate that kind of social outing. Besides, I remember her. I have no interest in robots. I'll babysit for Alice while you go."

"Well. She's a friend."

"How good a friend? As good a friend as me?"

"Of course not. Stop that. But I like her. She's—"

"Let me put it this way: If Karen Little's mother died tomorrow, would you go help in the kitchen?"

"No."

"Would you make potato salad to take over to Karen Little's house?"

"No."

"Would you go to her mother's funeral if it were out of town?"

Frances chewed a fingernail, frowned, hesitated.

"I rest my case."

Frances laughed. "It's something that's always worried me, to tell you the truth. When someone dies, how do you know if you're the level of friend, a good-enough friend, to go over to the house and greet people and help in the kitchen?"

Libba leaned her elbows against the table, cradled her face in her palms, and watched Frances spooning pablum into Alice's obediently gaping mouth. Then she caught herself unconsciously opening and closing her own mouth, and straightened. "You'll know."

CHAPTER 3

"Who cares what your sisters think?" Teddy asks. "They're not your mother."

"In a way they are," Edie says. At thirteen and nine years younger than Alice and Allegra, Edie was nearly an only child. She thought her mother's death would bring her closer to her sisters, make them more like friends than older siblings. "You three must be so close," people had repeatedly said at the funeral. But they'd never been in school together and now live in cities distant enough to preclude casual visits or participation in each other's lives. They have their families, or in Edie's case, a husband who wants a family. They have their work, though not in Alice's case, who doesn't work, ("Not for a salary, anyway," Alice is always quick to add when someone asks what she *does*.); and recently not in Allegra's case either, though at one time she was earning fifty dollars an hour grading standardized writing tests. And though slight tensions persist, Alice and Allegra and Edie would scoff at the suggestion of sibling rivalry. Not only are they too old, they've had rival enough in Libba Charles.

"When's the last time you even talked to either of your sisters?" Teddy asks.

Edie counts back from today, the end of May. "Six weeks ago."

At Easter, another holiday in a year of first-after-Mother's-death events—first birthday after, first Thanksgiving and first Christmas and first New Year's after—John Wilson informed his daughters that he was moving into a condominium. "This is too much house for me alone. And too full of memories." So on an April Saturday—"Divvy Day" Allegra named it—the sisters met in Raleigh, chose numbers from a toboggan hat their mother had knitted decades earlier, and spent a morning in the sad task of dividing her things among themselves. Excepting jewelry, Frances had designated nothing.

From her horizontal position on the bed Edie squints into the sunlight streaming through the shutterless, curtainless wall of windows that form three walls of the pentagon-shaped bedroom in her house. Teddy's house. The house that Teddy bought for her. For himself. Well, that's the trouble, Edie thinks. Teddy has his own apartment, where he lives. Mostly. Though it's a very nice apartment, with a beautiful view of the Battery. It is a clear, late May morning, and she has two hundred spinach-and-filo pastries to assemble for an engagement announcement party tonight. Teddy bought the catering business for her, too. "Alice thinks our living arrangements are strange," she says.

"People in Charleston are used to strange arrangements," Teddy says.

Edie and Teddy eloped ten years earlier, but haven't lived together for six years. They've never gotten legally divorced, or even separated, and Edie tells people that they stay married because of financial reasons, though she has no idea what "financial reasons" encompass. Edie isn't quite a kept woman. She's more than a mistress and less than a wife, though she and Teddy have great, athletic sex. Edie blushes, thinking of their Thursday night together. She just can't quite be *married*. She just can't quite grow up.

Through the years, she and Teddy have half-heartedly tried to see other people, but always return to each other. Edie knows the arrangement looks odd. The fact is that though she and Teddy love each other, when they live together everything is ordinary. There's nothing romantic about it, nothing spontaneous.

"Come on," Teddy says softly, curling beside Edie, spooning her, cupping a cheek of her rump with one hand. After ten on-again off-again years with Teddy, morning sex still embarrasses her; all those limbs thrashing through, well, *day*light. It's another contradiction of Edie's that Teddy and other men find charming, but only perplexes or exasperates her sisters. Alice and Allegra regard Edie's situation as world-on-a-platter. Teddy clearly adores her, he's independently wealthy—his family owns some entire island off the South Carolina coast, for God's sake—but Edie can't commit, doesn't care, still drags her bohemian days behind her like one of her drapey crepey shawls. Unless she's giving it away to a charity that temporarily catches her interest, Edie cares nothing for money.

It isn't just morning sex Teddy wants. He wants a child. Edie doesn't know what she wants, which is nothing new.

A downtown church bell tolls nine, and Edie thinks of the tanned, long-legged coeds walking to summer school classes down

Glebe Street at the College of Charleston. Ten years ago, with two years at two different colleges behind her, she'd been one of them, pursuing design. Straight academics hadn't taken; maybe graphics would.

"Is that a biological clock I hear?" Teddy whispers on the bell's final peal and taps his forefinger against her nipple. It obligingly hardens, encouraging him.

But Edie's afraid to have a child, and not only because her marriage to (*with?* she thinks) Teddy is . . . indefinite. She's afraid she'll have to grow up if she has a baby; afraid that she won't be able to, well, have sex in the morning if she has a baby who's crying. And afraid, she thinks in a small guilty corner of her heart, that the child will love its father more than it loves her—just as Edie herself did, even though she was Frances's miracle child.

"Tick-tick, Peedie," Teddy clucks, using her childhood nickname, short for Precious Darling. His breath is warm in her ear.

Edie hitches her shoulder. Ear kisses give her goosebumps. Lying on the cabinet beside the ornate, silver-handled letter opener she chose on Divvy Day, is Libba's letter. Edie sees her mother slicing the tool's ivory blade through the envelopes of early get-well cards. She sees her mother after the first radiation treatment, her high hopes amid fatigue.

Libba doesn't have children, Edie thinks. "I'm only thirty," she says to Teddy, not angrily or accusingly, but with genuine wounding.

Teddy smiles at her. "I know." All her life Edie has had a troubled sweetness and an appealing inefficiency about her that's irresistible to a particular kind of man. As a result she has more male friends than female. Other women feel threatened by this sweetness, her questionable availability, her attraction for the kind of man who wants to take care of a woman. She has no close female friends, no relationship with another woman that compares even slightly to her mother's friendship with Libba Charles, which baffles Edie, and makes her jealous.

Edie knows she'll never be able to decide by herself whether or not to go to Vade Mecum. She's the original go-along-girl, for whom the expression *Whatever* seems to have been specifically coined.

Teddy gently parts Edie's legs with his knee. She turns to him, kisses his chest, and remembers that she hasn't taken the filo dough out of the freezer to thaw.

While Alice waits for the final load of laundry to finish tumbling in the dryer she stamps her daughters' names onto waistbands and collars and sock heels. Though Catherine and Frannie aren't leaving for summer camp for several weeks, Alice performs chores long before they need to be done. With four children, she believes that efficiency is the only means of keeping chaos from the door. Her older sons, Luke and Thomas, have summer jobs, Luke assisting in a vet's office, and Thomas working at IHOP. Minimum wage—and God, but Luke smells funky every afternoon when she picks him up—but good résumé builders.

The dryer bell buzzes. Alice checks the contents and mashes another fifteen minutes on the timer. While she's in the kitchen she writes *Check out summer reading books from library for camp* on her calendar, plucks two bananas black with ripeness by their stiff withered stems from the fruit bowl and puts them in the freezer for banana bread later, then returns to the stamping assembly line she's arranged on the den coffee table where she doesn't have to worry about spilling ink.

The low cobbler's bench is stippled and scarred by four children's worth of carelessness with crayons and markers, gouges from straightened paper clips or other items-become-tools that her children created with whatever they found in their pockets. Luke, Thomas, Frannie, and Catherine are seventeen, fourteen, eleven and nine, and Alice plans to redecorate the room when they're old enough to stop ruining whatever they come in contact with. "One of these days," she's told her husband, Rob.

Trouble is, that day is nearly upon her. But despite appearances, inertia hampers Alice, has stopped her in her decorating tracks. Inertia, or grief. She pauses midstamp and gazes into the adjoining room where she's placed some of her mother's possessions that have become her own: a cut-crystal candy dish, a porcelain compote.

Alice believes she can predict now whether a parent has died by the contents of people's homes. Her friend Margaret's house, for example, while also child-filled, is still sleek with contemporary furnishings— lamps, artwork, *objets*. But a house with a milk-glass pitcher on a table, or folding television trays in a closet, or a stern-looking ancestor portrait hanging over a fireplace announced inheritance. And loss.

Alice debates calling Margaret for advice about going to Creek Cabin. Alice meets Margaret for coffee every Saturday morning to discuss their children, compare rules and gossip and allowances so they'll be in parental sync. So their children can't raise the tired comparisons of who else gets to do what when. Margaret and Alice agree that, deep down, children like limits.

But Margaret has recently taken on contract work for banks and nonprofits, planning employee luncheons or charity benefits down to the last fork and flower, and she's full of that these days, not whether nine-year-olds should be allowed to spend the night out on two consecutive evenings. Now Margaret's Saturdays are filled with what she used to do on weekdays—errands and exercise, bill paying and telephoning, house cleaning and clothes washing—and Margaret has broken three coffee dates in a row. If her mother were alive, Alice would call her, say lightly, "I have this friend—you know Margaret—who no longer has time for me," and her mother would understand that she was saying, "I have this life, and I'm no longer sure where I fit in it. What did *you* do when you were too old to be necessary, and too young to be an empty-nester?" But she can't ask her mother; her mother is dead. And her mother, of course, had had Libba.

Alice picks up Libba's letter and rereads it. She tries to muster anger toward Libba, reasons for which she can locate in nearly every chapter of Libba's ten books. After scanning the note over his wife's shoulder, her husband Rob said, "Are you going to go? I thought you were way down on Libba."

Way down can't touch it, Alice thinks. But the trouble is that Alice can't think of Libba without thinking of her mother's final words. *Look after Libba. Promise.*

Alice straightens her shoulders. As if Libba Charles has ever needed looking after. Another buzz, and for an instant Alice mistakes the shrill ring for the dryer. But it's the telephone, and Edie.

"I haven't even thought of her in six months," Alice lies. "I'm not going."

"Why not?"

"Pick a scene, any scene. How about throwing up at the circus from *Father of Girls?* How about my having a pacifier until I was six in *Necessary Concessions?*" As the oldest, Alice has seen herself the most often in print—Libba's books.

"I thought I might go," Edie says.

"Don't be pathologically nice. Has Daddy said anything about Libba being at Vade Mecum?" If anyone had talked to John recently, it would be Edie.

"No."

"So she's cabin squatting. Up there hatching her plots."

For the hundredth time Edie wonders how Alice came to be so certain about everything, when she herself has never been sure of anything. But just as Edie prepares to say good-bye, Alice stops her. "What does Allegra say?"

"Allegra doesn't put down her book long enough to answer the phone." The recording on the answering machine at Allegra's house is less greeting than warning: "This machine is low-tech, so make your message short." Edie pauses. "She's probably getting reacclimated from the . . . clinic."

Alice is silent. Finally she says, "We're preaching to the choir with Allegra anyway. She's the only person besides Mother for whom Libba can do no wrong."

"Did Libba call or write you?" Edie asks.

"Wrote. Letters are so cowardly. She'd never have the nerve to call."

Alice is wrong on two counts, and both sisters know it. Lack of nerve has never prevented Libba Charles from doing anything, and her chief means of communication is writing.

"What did she say?" Edie asks. "Did you save it?"

Alice flashes to her mother waving one of Libba's letters, filled with gossip and details Libba invariably regretted as soon as the ink was dry. "No you can*not* have it back," Frances would laugh as Libba begged. "I'm keeping it for your biographer. *The Collected Letters of Libba Charles.*" Outside that charmed circle of two, Alice had watched and wondered if her mother kept *her* letters.

Alice reads in a rapid monotone. "'Dear Alice, If you'd like to meet me at Creek Cabin on June 20th there are some things of Frances's you'll likely want. I'm writing Edie and Allegra also. Libba.'" Paper rustles. "Two sentences after nine months of silence? And what does that mean—'likely want'? What we *wanted* all those years was—" Alice is about to say *Mother's undivided attention*, but changes her mind. She's the strong one. Everyone has always said so.

"She was Mother's best friend—" Edie tries again.

"For reasons that are unknown to me." Alice's voice cracks as she hangs up the phone. She puts down the letter, aware that it's unlike her not to answer it, deal with it, and move onto the next task. The dryer's insistent second buzzing through her empty house startles her. Empty of children, who are busy and absent with summer jobs or vacation's freedom.

Opening the dryer door, Alice thinks *I can't make any decisions now,* though she knows her sisters believe her unflappable, equate her efficiency with emotional toughness. She pulls the sheets and towels from the metal well, and holding them to her chest, walks upstairs toward her bedroom. Some days Alice finds anger easier, but not today. Some days, Alice had found, all you can do is hold the comforting if temporary warmth of laundry to your chest. She tumbles the linens onto the bed for folding.

Instead of folding, though, Alice crumples to the bed herself, gives up the pretense of doing anything worthwhile. She lies at an angle, watching the tulip poplar branches beyond the window. Since Alice began crying when her mother died, the branches have completed three seasons of foliage changes. Though she is forty-one years old, for nine months Alice has spent some portion of her scheduled day in her well-kept house lying on her neatly made bed crying with an inexhaustible grief. It's too hard to cry sitting in a chair, there's nothing to do with your hands, nowhere to rest your head, no room to pull your legs to your chest. It's easier to cry on a bed. And that's what Alice is doing: crying inconsolably for her mother who's been dead since September. Alice knows it's time to move on, she knows she needs to get on with her life, and beyond her mother's death. Trouble is, she no longer knows what her life is. Trouble is, Alice can't get beyond her mother's death until she gets beyond Libba Charles.

Allegra knows what her trouble is; she's been trouble since she was a child. Though Libba objected, Frances installed a hook and eye on Allegra's bedroom door before she turned three because it was the only way to keep her contained during afternoon nap-time. Allegra knows the story. But she never napped anyway; Frances came in after an hour's time to find the room destroyed. It's a family joke that the real reason Edie was born so long after Alice was not because of Frances's likely infertility, but because it took John and Frances nine years to recover from Allegra.

She drove her parents to distraction with teenage shenanigans: boys, broken curfews, complaints from other parents. Behavior that was beyond garden-variety adolescent mischief. Behavior that was reined in at boarding school, but not terminated; where she stretched the limits of the rules and grading system. You could read all about her suspensions in *This Go Round:* being confined to campus for squirting a senior prefect with a water gun during chapel, for keeping a poster on her dorm room wall covered with filthy graffiti about her teachers. Until, only days from graduation, Allegra herself was terminated. Expelled for drinking, caught spiking Cokes with vodka from a PhisoHex bottle. In *This Go Round* Libba made it a mouthwash bottle, with food coloring.

Allegra is lying on her bed, too, the way she had the day after her mother's death, when she left the two dozen people milling about her parents' home to go upstairs and lie down on her childhood bed. Allegra thought she'd scream, thought she'd choke the next person who said *I'm sorry*, that she *was in their prayers*.

Alice had found her. "What are you doing up here?"

"Counting the stripes," Allegra calmly replied. And she was, just as she had as a child when she was punished or grounded: counted the wallpaper's vertical blue stripes per wall. Allegra was thirty-eight. She'd forgotten how many stripes there were.

"Edie and I could use some help with the guests," Alice said. Alice herself had done some counting once. When her children were one and three and six and nine she put a notepad at the top of the stairs and made one mark for each time in a single day she'd had to climb the steps. Her top total had been thirty-two.

Libba's face appeared over Alice's shoulder in the door frame. "Allegra," she'd said.

Allegra had looked at her. "You're my godmother, not my boss," she'd retorted as a child when Libba had told her to turn off the television. Libba had passed a palm over her forehead, concealing her expression and, amazed that she could provoke a hurt reaction from Libba, Allegra had switched off the set. And that day after her mother's death, she'd obeyed Libba again; gotten off the bed and gone downstairs. She'd needed a wine refill anyway.

Now Allegra looks at the bracelet she's wearing, which her mother had left specifically to her. It pains Allegra; reminds her of jewelry she's carelessly lost through the years, beginning with a similar gold bracelet whose clasp had been repaired that Frances had mailed to DeWitt Academy in the same package as a winter coat. Allegra had pulled out the coat and thrown away the box, failing to notice the letter from her mother, or the bracelet. The rest of Allegra's special-occasion jewelry had been lost at college, fallen off her wrist or neck or ears while she stumbled around fraternity houses on decidedly unspecial occasions. She fingers the cool gold links. Special-occasion jewelry hadn't been necessary at Blair Clinic.

Though losing a pound of gold is the least of Allegra's troubles. In her day she'd stolen a neighbor's car for a weeknight joyride, spun wheelies on golf course greens, snuck liquor from the cabinets of rented vacation houses.

Allegra has spent the last four weeks exiled at Blair Clinic learning more about her trouble. "I'm Allegra and I'm an alcoholic." Just as in the movies, with more alliteration. She thought the one positive thing that would come out of her mother's death was introspection and inspiration; that she'd finally begin writing as she's always wanted, but instead it's just ninety meetings in ninety days. And guilt.

Allegra picks up the mirror of her mother's matching dresser set that she selected on Divvy Day. Not out of vanity, though Allegra has always been the prettiest of the three sisters, until the extra weight of alcohol and the limited grooming of a near-recluse took their toll. But because it was Allegra who comforted her mother when the hair began to fall out in chunks, telling Frances she was still pretty; Allegra who held the mirror to Frances's face when she was too weak to hold it herself. Those sunken eyes, Allegra remembers, hating the doctors, the nurses, the scientists, all the caregivers and geniuses who couldn't save her mother. Hating herself as well.

A knock sounds on her bedroom door, and the gentle tap breaks Allegra's heart. The child behind the tap is accustomed to closed doors, because Allegra had wanted privacy to drink. "Come in."

Brent's head pokes through the door. "Can Travis come over, Mom?" Travis lives next door, Allegra's friend Susan's child. At Susan's house, at any normal mother's house, children didn't feel they had to politely inquire whether the next-door-neighbor's child could come over to play, to watch TV, to shoot baskets.

"Sure, honey," Allegra tells her seven-year-old. Her voice is gentle. She fears she might never make up for times she's raised her voice or simply not answered at all. Brent's eyes widen with gratitude, and Allegra wonders what lies behind those eyes, stashed away in his subconscious; what troubles he'll tell an analyst one day. What he'll blame her for, hold against her forever. *My mother wasn't maternal*, he might say.

"But," she begins, and when Brent halts as if leashed, another piece of Allegra's heart crumbles off. "Has Travis asked his mother if it's okay he comes over here? Make sure Susan knows." *I want to know my children are safe around you* Susan had said. Ex-friend Susan, with whom Allegra had shared so many late afternoons sitting cross-legged on their parallel driveways, rumps on the warm concrete, hands around a glass of wine, killing time talking while their children pulled wagons and raced tricycles up and down the driveway, or drew on the cement with fat stubs of colored chalk, or clumsily pitched balls to one another. Allegra clearly recalls getting through that period after children's early suppers, waiting for the daddies to drive up and provide a change of scenery. Recalls her husband Dal and Susan's husband George coming home and teasing them both about starting without them. When had that glass of wine become glasses, plural, poured at 4:30 instead of 5:30, and then at 3:30 and 3:00, when the children didn't play outside as much anymore, or were at school, or it was easier, all in all, just to stay indoors? She's missed a year or two somewhere, the way she's missed Libba these last nine months.

But why *should* she remember? Alice thinks. According to those lists of questions regularly published in newspaper ads paid for by private dry-out clinics—clinics such as Blair—alcoholics are famous for their blackouts.

But Allegra hadn't been drunk that terrible Sunday morning five weeks earlier.

She closes her eyes to the scene she can't black out. She's wretched with guilt and fear, yet stubborn with anger. She wonders how her children view her–with fear? sorrowfully?—and can't decide whether their pity is worse than their fear. Every time she looks at Sasha and Brent, Allegra wants to take them in her arms and kneel before them and say, *I love you so. Do you love me? Do you even like me?* She wants to tell them everything, but most of all, that she's sorry.

Brent begins closing his mother's door. Allegra almost tells him to leave it open, but Brent's too accustomed to her door being closed; four weeks haven't broken Brent's habit as it has supposedly broken hers.

"Close the door, please, Alley-oop," Frances had said, too afternoons when she and Libba lay on the bed, flipping through magazines, talking. Allegra stood outside holding pencil-smeared pages of an undialogued, unparagraphed, unending story about a little girl the same age as Allegra herself who ran away from home and lived in a hollow tree in the forest, existing on nuts and squirrel meat, whose furry hides she slept on. Allegra wanted to ask Libba, a Real Live Writer, to read her story.

"Derivative," Libba had said. "Too *Boxcar Children*. Too *Little House on the Prairie*." She'd tilted her head and studied Allegra, who reddened with embarrassment. "Isn't that Mary Ingalls a pain?"

"Yes," Allegra had breathed, amazed, charmed, that Libba knew the Ingallses. Relieved that she, like Allegra herself, liked Laura, the misbehaving, oft-punished sister, better.

"You know why Mary is a pain?" Libba asked.

"No."

"Because the author—who just happened to be little old Laura herself—made sure the reader sympathized with Laura. Make a note of it. And keep reading." She'd waved the papers at Allegra and turned back to Frances, asking her about a book Allegra had never heard of, but privately vowed to read when she was a grown-up.

"I'm a little afraid of Libba," Allegra had later told her mother, hoping she'd confess this to Libba, who'd instantly become tender, solicitous, devoted. "Are you going to tell her I said so?"

But Allegra had been mistaken. "Oh, no, baby," Frances had immediately answered. "Libba would be so hurt if she knew that. She's big bark no bite; tough on the outside, mush on the inside."

Allegra used to talk about books with her friend Susan. "Make new friends," Allegra was directed at Blair. But since her return from Blair, Allegra hasn't seen Susan. Hasn't seen her, hasn't called her, and hasn't forgiven her. A real friend, a friend like Libba had been to Frances, wouldn't have done what Susan did.

"Thanks for letting Travis come play, Mommy," Brent says in a tone so grateful that Allegra's fingers go weak on the mirror's handle.

Allegra reads Libba's letter again and decides she might as well go to Vade Mecum. She might as well suffer through sobriety and writer's block with Libba at Creek Cabin as anywhere else.

Whatever their troubles, the sisters are drawn to Vade Mecum like metal to magnet. What could be harder than having been replaced, usurped, supplanted by Libba Charles all their lives? Besides, this is not about Libba. Libba was Frances's friend, not theirs, and now that their mother is gone, there's no need for Libba. What they do need is Vade Mecum, and Creek Cabin. They haven't crossed the Creek Cabin threshold for the two long years of Frances's dying, and this, each convinces herself, is the reason she's going. Because if there's a single setting, one place that Alice and Allegra and Edie identify most strongly with their mother, it's the summer cottage she loved. If Libba Charles wants to meet them there and give them whatever she has that belongs to Frances, fine. It's about time. For most of her life, *Frances* belonged to Libba.

The trouble is that neither Alice nor Allegra nor Edie can picture Creek Cabin without Libba Charles in the picture. Libba, after all, had discovered it.

April 18, 1953

"How's Alice?"

"Drooling. Cutting teeth. Where are you?"

"At a pay phone outside Stockton, a fading artist's enclave in the North Carolina mountains."

"What are you doing in North Carolina?"

"Sam and I are visiting fading artist friends of his. They make dulcimers. Large market, you know, for dulcimers."

Frances laughed. "Never mind the dulcimers, you've dropped that name 'Sam' in our last five conversations. Do I get to meet him? Are you going to marry him?"

"I might. He thinks I'm 'fey.' How can you not marry someone who uses the word 'fey'?"

"Do you love him?"

"You have to love poets. They're so noble and broke. But he moves his lips when he reads. I'm calling from a roadside joint complete with hoop cheese under glass and gallon buckets labeled LARD. This place is so down and out and out of the way that I'm not wearing underwear."

"Oh you are soooo bohemian," Frances taunted. "Big deal. I'm not wearing a bra either."

"Oh you are soooo bohemian," Libba returned in the same tone. "I mean no under*pants*."

Frances giggled. "Easy access for Sam?"

"Details later. He's buying pickled eggs. Besides, I'm calling for another reason. I've found a divine hovel that you have to wear deerskin moccasins to get to. In a previous incarnation it was a girl's summer camp. Place called Vade Mecum. You'll love it."

"Divine hovel is an oxymoron."

"Not in this case. Give the drooler a kiss for me."

June 10, 1953

"Can't you just see them," Libba said, showing Frances around the cottage, "ten girls wearing flowy long dresses and hairbows in their genteel and oh-so-ladylike pursuits: drama presentations, recitations, flora and fauna identification. When they weren't chopping wood and scrubbing floors," she added wryly.

Frances *had* loved it. Loved the idea of it. Loved the cottage itself, its three upstairs bedrooms and ladders to lofts where the girls had slept. Loved the sinks in each room and the flattened tin numerals nailed above the doors—1, 2, 3—and the flowing painted script over the front door: Safe Haven. Along with a scorched campfire circle behind the cottage, they were all that remained of the camp, and even during a brief remodeling stint, Frances had insisted they stay. She herself had settled on a simpler name: Creek Cabin.

"It's . . ." Frances searched for words to explain Vade Mecum to John. Like Libba, Vade Mecum resisted categorization. At the turn of the century it was a forested hollow like a hundred others in the Blue Ridge Mountains, situated on the outskirts of a village named Stockton. Stockton enjoyed some fame—or notoriety—as an artist's colony in the thirties and was still home to a thriving bunch of nonconformists who eked out a living with their potter's wheels or looms or paintbrushes.

Summer visitors to Stockton had found the high-altitude coolness and the remove from urban demands appealing. Along a single-lane road some miles beyond the town they'd built a nest of primitive cottages as vacation escapes. Additional roads appeared over the decades and more cottages were built. Some were stilted on ledges up steep hillsides, with no visible evidence of their existence but for narrow rock steps in the dense undergrowth, or a motorized cable that churned groceries or luggage upward to the solitary houses. Some, like Creek Cabin, were nestled near Shoals Stream, the more-than-creek but not-quite-river that wound through the community.

Though community wasn't quite apt, even if Vade Mecum had its own zip code. It was more than a settlement, but less than an enclave. "You don't have to see anyone unless you want to," Frances assured John. Neither was it a *compound*, or *resort*. Lacking amenities of golf course or clubhouse or members-only facilities, there was no sense of status, no feel of wealth.

"Retreat," Frances finally landed on, as close as it came. For the church discovered Vade Mecum in the forties, possibly because of its Latin name but probably because of a nearby Presbyterian mission for Appalachian orphans. On Vade Mecum's most level area the Presbyterians built a large assembly hall, an outdoor chapel, and various offices and meeting rooms that over the years acquired names of dead patrons or good Presbyterians or both. They dammed Shoals Creek to create a small lake, and constructed housing and a dining hall. Thus Vade Mecum became a religious conference center, opening its arms and facilities to church youth groups and congregations, sabbaticals and scholars, and other kinds of spiritual fellowship.

All of which affected the longtime summer residents not in the slightest. Indeed, the secular colony benefitted. There was a small store selling toiletries, Vade Mecum–themed apparel for visitors who arrive unprepared for the colder—or hotter—weather, and the predictable religious plaques and pamphlets. There was a nature hut that provided hiking maps, a library stocked with God-topic books, and a swimming pool shocked clear with chlorine. The Presbys thought of everything, even day camps to entertain the children. Meanwhile, the roads continued to creep up the mountainside, and new houses sprouted among the rocks and rhododendron.

But John couldn't appreciate the finer points of Vade Mecum, much less those of a dilapidated cottage. "It's awfully far away from New York," he'd said, jiggling a fussy Alice against his shoulder. "And what would I do?"

"Just be," Frances said.

He sneezed violently four times. "I don't know if my allergies can take it." He smiled, shifted the baby to the other shoulder. "But you take it," he said. "And take Alice, while you're at it. I saw an old swing out by the woodpile. If it's not rotten I'll hang it on the front porch."

Frances kissed him, and bought the cottage with money she'd inherited from her father. Not much, but in a state of disrepair and neglect, Creek Cabin hadn't cost much either. "It's mine right down to the name on the deed," she told Libba over the phone. "Come be my writer-in-residence."

July 9, 1954

Frances peeled an egg, unwrapped a wax paper square of salt and pepper mix. "I feel guilty about leaving Alice."

Libba shifted, trying to find a more comfortable position on the sun-warmed rock at her back. She closed her eyes to the glare. "Alice isn't even two years old. If she remembers, I'll pay the analyst fees. Besides, it's a nursery, Frances. That's what nurseries are *for*."

"Vade Mecum nurseries are for parents to go to, well, whatever they do here. Pray. Sing. Be holy. Not so the parents can hike Graybeard."

"I could never be a mother. All that omnipresent guilt with you wherever you are. Like God."

"You'd be a great mother," Frances said, then added, laughing, "You're the most instructive person I know."

Libba sat up. Twinkling with a million pinpricks of reflected sunlight, Mt. Graybeard's massive granite outcropping jutted like a chin above the Vade Mecum valley. A landscape of forest green chenille seemed to undulate beneath them, broken only by snipped ribbons of curving grey roads. No humans, no houses. She drew the bandanna from around her neck and gestured to the wide vista surrounding them. "If you don't think that's religion, you need to examine your faith," Libba said. "Now it's summer. It's not summer until we've hiked Graybeard."

Frances ruffled her cap of fair hair, recently shorn for hot weather. "Oh, I know," she sighed.

"How can summer possibly make you sad?"

"I was hoping to be pregnant again by now."

"It's amazing anyone ever gets pregnant at all given the million and one circumstances—single egg, single sperm, whatnot—that have to be *just right*. I'm stunned the planets line up as accidentally often as they do. Give it time." Libba chuckled. "Give *John* time."

"It's not John, it's me. The cyst I had to have removed last winter—"

"—was benign as a wart."

"But the entire ovary had to come out "too."

"That's why God gave us two ovaries. Besides, who knows? Maybe you're pregnant as we speak. All those busily dividing little cells. Want to count the days since . . ." Libba raised her eyebrows suggestively.

Frances shook her head. "Unfortunately, I'm having one of my regular irregular periods. Spotty stuff. I always worry John thinks I'm lying when I tell him."

Libba laughed. "Only you. Seems like just yesterday you were taking Dramamine for morning sickness, then chasing it with an upper to keep from falling asleep. Ready for that again so soon?"

"I want my children close enough in age to be best friends."

"Siblings and best friends are mutually exclusive. That combination doesn't exist in nature."

"Hush," Frances said. "You told me that was God out there. I'm praying. Dear God," she said to the rock, to the sky, to the fleecy clouds above them, and to Libba, "Thank you for my other ovary. Let me get pregnant. Let it be another girl."

CHAPTER 4

Through fate or coincidence, the sisters arrive simultaneously mid-afternoon, carefully crossing under the rock arch entrance spelling VADE MECUM in lighter stones overhead and wide enough for only a single vehicle.

Alice brakes to let a group of people pass, no doubt on their way to some kind of worship, and tries to call Rob on her cell phone. At the blaring sound of a car horn she looks in the rearview mirror.

"Hang up and drive," Allegra plainly mouths.

Aromas of the dinner being prepared at the conference center waft through the car windows. Even now Alice and Allegra and Edie still have no idea where the cafeteria actually is. The buildings that comprise the conference center are mysteries to them but for the ones that directly and occasionally affect them: the boathouse, the nature hut, the commissary.

Nothing seems to have changed with two years' absence. They drive by the lower fields where grassless diagonal paths mark a baseball diamond, and by the Rec Wreck, a hollow tin behemoth of a building where a sagging banner advertises ROLLER SKATING TONIGHT 7:30, just as it did on Saturday nights when they were children. On rainy evenings, the combined cacophony of drumming rain on the tin roof and rolling metal ball bearings of old-fashioned skates was deafening.

A child's shriek rings out. Or perhaps it's a teenager being ducked into the stream by a friend. Or perhaps it was an adult's, getting saved. Because for that matter, Alice and Allegra and Edie have never really, specifically, known what happens inside the conference center buildings either.

For eight weeks every summer Vade Mecum is overrun with cheerful strangers who've driven days to reach their destination. They fill the retreat's buildings, which, constructed of stone and left unlandscaped beyond established trees and plants, blend unobtrusively into the natural environs. You'd never know anyone was inside at all unless you wandered within earshot of singing or worshiping or whatever it is they do.

Sure enough, the parking lots are filled with cars and vans bearing out-of-state license plates the sisters can't help but read as they pass. As children they kept a running tally of each state represented. Next comes the dam and spillway, the boathouse, and the glorified pond boringly—or biblically—named Lake Sarah. Two resident swans glide near the far banks of the lake, and paddle boats bob alongside the dock as day camp counselors strap children into life preservers. With a climb of another hundred yards, they are there: Creek Cabin.

"If you don't look hard, you'll miss it," Frances always cautioned visitors, and indeed, the cottage seems to merge with the evergreen trees and shrubs—delicate mountain laurel, sturdy conifers, and bushy rhododendron—that surround and conceal it; tall deciduous trees spread above it. The front porch looms from shade so deep it's nearly blue.

Stray fallen leaves littering the porch floor are brushed back as Edie opens the screen door to the cabin's dimness. Sunlight scarcely reaches the interior, and slants across the open area of the front and back porches for only a single morning hour. Half bubbles of sky-lights swell from roofs of some sun-starved residents, along with the occasional stark circle of a satellite dish, but Frances had resisted the trends. Like their mother, Alice and Allegra and Edie have always found the cottage's darkness not gloomy, but reassuringly cozy.

Inside, they breathe deeply of the smoky smell rising from the two fireplaces. The cabin isn't only dim, but perpetually damp as well, given the proximity of Shoals Stream, twenty feet from the rear of the house. But for the fireplaces the cottage is unheated; for many years there wasn't a phone; multi-legged insects occasionally roam the bathtub.

"Earwigs," Frances had explained, prompting Alice to stuff her ears with cotton balls before bed every night one summer. But the three sisters wouldn't trade the woodsy, watery, lushly green intimacy that is Creek Cabin for a sleekly contemporary, fully functional home with a mile-high view of the entire Blue Ridge. All three have spent some portion of every summer of their lives—even if only a week, only a weekend—at Vade Mecum. Until and except for last summer, when their mother was so wretchedly ill. Beyond ill: dying.

They move slowly through the cottage as if trying it on again for size. In the same patterns their feet traced for years, they tentatively, silently, cross oval rag rugs and a threadbare oriental carpet toward kitchen and back porch and single downstairs bedroom. Despite her absence Frances, Wilson emanates from the knot-holed wooden walls and the needlepointed pillows and the rush basket of old *Southern Living* magazines no one ever picks up unless it rains all day. Her perfume still permeates the chenille slipcovers and the folded quilt on the sofa's back. Frances Wilson's daughters feel her presence so strongly that it wouldn't surprise them to find strands of her hair caught in the caned backs of chairs clustered round the game table where they worked puzzles, played Hearts and Yahtzee. They expect to hear the bell bolted on the back stoop clang as she calls them from the creek to supper.

On the staircase wall Frances smiles at Allegra. She grins from pictures in five-and-dime frames, in Lucite box frames, in home-made collages. Frances hiking. Frances lighting candles. Frances filling the porch planters with dusty miller and begonias and lobelia. Frances in Shoals Stream, shorts rolled high on her thighs. Frances with John. Frances with Alice and Allegra and Edie. Frances with Catherine and Luke and Thomas and Frannie. Frances with Brent and Sasha, with Teddy. And of course Frances with Libba. Smiling, healthy, her face unrecognizable from the papery death-mask visage melting into the hospital sheets nine months earlier.

Edie pretends to study the glass-paned corner cupboard whose shelves hold crafts the sisters brought from summer camp: a basket made of wooden reeds Alice had soaked for hours to bend into curving submission, Allegra's baby-food-jar terrarium whose contents have long since perished, a clay vase that resembles a coiled snake and whose unfired bottom leaks. Leaning against the cabinet's back wall are Edie's products: two wood-burned plywood pieces crookedly lettered #1 DAD and IF LIFE GIVES YOU LEMONS, MAKE LEMONADE. Edie still remembers how hard it was to force the straight beveled nib to make a curve. "Anybody home?" she finally says.

The game table in the corner of the room is cluttered with spiral-bound notebooks and legal pads, tabbed dividers and file folders and a terra-cotta flowerpot filled with scissors and white-out and ballpoint pens bearing motel logos left over from book publicity tours. To Allegra, who helplessly covets the mess of her writing, it's clear she's there. For like the sisters, Libba has spent some portion of every summer at Creek Cabin, too. Frances gave it to her friend and Libba sequestered herself with her work, shaping or creating or revising, depending upon publisher's deadline or editor's whim.

When the screen rasps on the porch floorboards as the door opens again, three women look up. Unlike their mother at sixty-three, this woman at sixty-four is beautiful still. The frizzy nimbus of her silver-shot black hair frames chiseled features and eyes like iced pewter. The flesh at the jaw is still firm, and it lifts when she smiles that confident, casual smile. "Look who's here," she says, as if she never doubted they would come. "Grave Alice and laughing Allegra, and Edith with golden hair."

Alice puts her shaking hands into her pockets. She won't cry. She *won't*. "What do you know. You've managed to remember our names."

"Sure," Libba says. "Still making your grocery lists in the order the food comes on the store aisles?"

With her unerring aim, Libba has struck a bull's-eye. "You never forget anything, do you?" Alice says.

"Nothing that Frances told me."

For a long moment the two women's eyes lock over something unsaid, unforgiven, then Libba leans over and reties a tennis shoe.

"Well. You've already been through this once. How did it go? But then you three have always *claimed* things: the last Popsicle, the front seat of the car, to be first down the steps on Christmas morning—"

"Been through what?" Allegra interrupts.

"Dividing Frances's things."

"How did you know?"

"John told me."

"You've talked to Daddy?"

"Sure."

Before they can ask more—Why? When?—Libba opens a small paper bag and pulls out pads of colored Post-its. "I thought these might be handy for tagging whatever you want. Just leave me something to eat and cook with." She hands a pack each to Alice and Allegra and Edie, who stare at them, puzzled. Libba points to the wall of pictures flanking the staircase. When she speaks her voice has lost its usual briskness. "And just a few of these. So. Maybe I should go flag down a day camp counselor to help lift some of these bigger pieces. The hutch and the sofa."

"What are you talking about?" Allegra asks.

"Creek Cabin," Libba says.

"What about it?"

"John didn't tell you?"

"Didn't tell us what?"

Libba gazes resignedly out the window. "Well," she says again, "Opening in the aftermath of trouble is always a good place to begin a story."

"What?"

"Frances left Creek Cabin to me."

The papery scrape of crickets is the only audible sound as three pair of eyes fix mutely on the woman before them, film over with the realization that they've been shut out once again from something they believed was theirs. Shock, blame, sorrow, and resentment fuse. And something else as well: envy.

"We had no idea . . ." Edie begins, trails away.

Libba sighs, though perhaps it's more silent laugh, and presses knuckles to her chin. "You have no idea of the things you have no idea about."

• • •

July 19, 1954

Libba searched through cabinets, taking inventory. "What do you feel like for supper? Not soup again, it's too hot. No canned vegetables. Gerber's strained spinach?" She made a face. "I realize it's why we're here, but sometimes I wish Vade Mecum weren't *such* a wilderness. What I'd give for some Chinese take-out about now, though I have a theory that it all comes from the same vat in the kitchen and the cook just ladles a different sauce over— Frances? Are you listening to my fascinating theorizing or is this just a worthless soliloquy along the same lines as poor Hamlet's—Frances?"

She stood in front of the closed bedroom door. "Listen, pal, it's not fair that you get the convenient downstairs bedroom and I'm consigned to the upstairs with the bogeymen and ghosts. Granted, your name's on the deed but don't I get some kind of privilege too, a finder's fee?" She put her ear to the door, heard nothing, and stood back, crossing her arms over her chest. "Mother—which Mother was that?—lectured me to *always knock* when the door was closed. Everybody else learns about sex at school. *I* learned because of the 'always knock' rule. A closed door equaled Doing It when I was growing up. How will you teach Alice?" Libba rambled on, and opened the door, surprised to find the bedroom empty, and the adjoining bathroom door shut as well. "Reverted to the old Em Sem modesty days, Frances?" She put her ear to the door and heard nothing but the sound of running water.

"Another Nair session?" Libba called through the door. "That stuff stinks to high heaven and John isn't even coming this weekend to appreciate your hairlessness."

And then, a muted groan.

Libba brusquely opened the door into the sudden brightness of the small room. Frances was bent over the sink rapidly filling with water tinted rust. "I'm still spotting, so I was washing out some underwear."

"Damn being female and all that goes with it. If men alternated with women in having children, there'd never be more than one child in a family. Come sit down. I'll make some tea."

Frances made an unsteady path to the sofa. "Hiking Graybeard probably made things worse. The exercise."

"Want the heating pad?" Libba called from the kitchen.

"God!" The cry was one of such acute pain that Libba stiffened, dropped the kettle. "Libba!" Frances cried. "I've never felt anything so—! My God, the gush—" She curled fetuslike, mashed a hand against her crotch and held it up. Her palm was a bright red flag of blood. Frances's eyes closed and she groaned in misery.

Libba snatched the Vade Mecum directory, swiftly scanned the names. She grabbed a towel from the bathroom, pried open Frances's thighs grown rigid with pain. "Hold this between your legs," she said, panicked by the sight of underwear stained dark red, soaked and warm with blood. "I'll be right back."

"Don't leave me," Frances pleaded, then clutched her abdomen. "It hurts. Not... period pain," she grunted, then cried out piteously.

"I'll be right back." Libba quietly shut the screen door, afraid her terror would communicate itself to Frances. The stone path to the street was black, and in her haste she fell, scraping her knee. The creek's gurgle, usually so comforting, mocked her passage, as did the knot of teenagers lazily making their way up the street on their way back from a conference event.

"Watch it, lady," one snapped as Libba pushed him aside. She broke into a sprint up the hill, the noise of their laughter a backdrop of adolescent ridicule, and cursed the absence of streetlights, house numbers, sidewalks, the multitude of Vade Mecum's advantages that, with a single situation, had become barriers. And then began a litany of thanks, that a car was in the driveway of the cabin name she'd found in the directory. The door stood ajar, only a bowed screen between her and the single entry in the directory prefaced with "Dr."

A deeply tanned brunette woman of her own age answered Libba's frantic knocking. "Is Dr. Chandler here?"

"Who—"

"Is he here?"

The woman turned, called behind her. "Dennis? There's someone—"

Not waiting for an answer, Libba opened the door. "I'm Libba Charles, please come."

His face was square, lightly freckled to match his ginger hair, his blue eyes bright with question. He looked her up and down, searching for an obvious injury. "Your knee?" he smiled, as though accustomed to paltry ailments.

"Not me. My friend, down the road, she's—" Libba glanced at the woman, his wife, minced no words "—bleeding, from, she thought it was her period, but this is—it's very heavy and painful and—" Libba gestured for the door, "— please! Please come."

"Where," he said, not question but statement, and was out the door before Libba could even direct him.

In the short distance, six cottages down the hill, Libba told him what she knew of Frances's irregular periods, the benign ovarian cyst and oophorectomy. Frances hadn't moved from the sofa. The doctor stroked her forehead, one sympathetic gesture, then removed the wadded towel from between her legs. Frances's flesh was pale. She murmured unintelligible answers to his questions, groaning.

"I'll call an ambulance," Libba said.

He stood abruptly. "No, there isn't time. Get your car."

"But it's twenty minutes to the nearest—"

"I said get the car."

"There's a baby—"

His eyes flashed. "She's pregnant?"

Libba's hands fluttered in confusion. "Asleep upstairs."

He picked up the telephone, dialed. "Joan. I need you to stay with a child while I go to the hospital." He glanced at Libba while his wife responded. "I suspect . . ." he turned, spoke inaudibly though Libba strained to hear from Frances's side, so fearfully still. He craned his neck, shot a question to Libba. "What's the baby's name?"

"Alice."

"Hear that?" he said into the receiver, then hung up the phone and in a single movement lifted Frances from the sofa, her legs dangling against his forearms, her head cradled against his chest. "My wife is on her way." Libba followed him to the car, where he laid Frances's body, alternately limp then tensed with pain, across the back seat. "I'll drive. You talk to her. *Talk to her.*"

"Frances," Libba said, "we're going to the hospital. You'll be alright. A doctor is here. He's your neighbor, did you know? Isn't that lucky? We should have gotten out more, made a few friends and—"

"Go on," he said.

"What's wrong with her?" Libba cried. "Tell me."

"Who are you? Sister?" Ignoring the solid yellow line, the curve of the road, he swerved into the left lane, honked at the sedan moving slowly on the right.

"Friend."

He flicked the headlight to high beams and mashed the accelerator.

"I'm almost finished with my new book, Frances, called *Small Doses*. Know where I got that title, Frances? From you. Remember how you said you can take anything in small doses?" she blathered, ignoring the physician's questioning glances. "No gerunds, Frances. You told me never to have a title with gerunds, how you hated them."

Streetlights winked in the distance. The doctor slowed for a stoplight, quickly scanned oncoming traffic, and sped through it as Libba gasped. His voice bordered on harshness. "This is an emergency—what did you say your name was?"

"Libba."

"Libba. Well, Libba, you seem like the type who's accustomed to breaking rules. Your friend is very sick." He squealed around a corner, the brick bulk of Asheville Community Hospital loomed, and he braked at the emergency entrance. "Get inside and tell the desk."

Libba raised her fist to strike the glass door a fraction of a second before it sighed electronically open. "Frances Wilson is coming in with Dr. Chandler from Vade Mecum, and she—"

The doctor pushed past her to an examining room, trailing bright crimson droplets to the floor. By the time Libba had satisfied the registration nurse and found her way to the room, Frances's legs were hoisted and spread into stirrups, her head lolling pathetically to the side. Harsh fluorescent overhead lights cast her ashen skin even paler. Dr. Chandler spit rapid-fire instructions to a nurse, a resident. "No rectal bleeding, the friend doesn't know whether there might have been bleeding from the bladder—"

"What?" Libba asked, frantic with incomprehension.

"Well, was there?"

"I don't—"

"Page a surgeon. She's ruptured a tube. Get a transfusion tray, STAT." The attendants jumped, scurried, and the doctor lifted Frances's ankles from the stirrups, cold and sterile as instruments of torture in the unremitting glare. Metal clattered as he dropped them. Tears squeezed from Frances's eyes, rolled down her temples and into her hair.

"What are you doing? Libba asked, her voice quavering with panic and indignation. "What's wrong with her?"

"Is there a husband?"

"Yes, he's—"

"Get him."

Libba blindly, robotically headed for the pay-phone booth huddled in a waiting-room corner. She dialed, got no answer. "John," she whispered, "John," then dialed again, waiting, her palms sweating against the greasy black receiver where a thousand frightened calls had been placed.

From four doors down the hall Dennis Chandler's voice rang out. "Who's on call? No resident, I want a surgeon." Like a slow-motion film, Libba glimpsed a nurse leaning around the door frame, signaling for another nurse. "Yes, I'm a GP! No, I'm not from this area, or even this state. Screw your administrative dithering! There's so much blood sloshing around in there it's difficult to make an accurate diagnosis, but I know what I see. Which is the point!" he shouted. "I don't care *what time* it is or *what night* it is, or how statistically rare they are or who she is, this woman is hemorrhaging with an ectopic pregnancy and we'll *lose* her," he thundered. "Do you understand?"

His voice reached Libba through the folding glass doors and she dropped the phone ringing in the vacant White Plains house. Her legs moved bonelessly toward the examining room where she saw bloody towels in the white sink, saw crumpled paper on the table, saw a sheeted bed wheeled into the room, saw white-coated strangers lift Frances's body onto the gurney.

Frances's lids lifted, the eyes beneath them glassy and unfocused. "Libba," she whispered calmly, "am I going to die?"

The men disappeared into the elevator. Libba reeled, roared at Dennis Chandler's chest, her fists flailing against his sweatshirt, her voice high and shrill and demented, no match for the doctor's. "Do something, do you hear me? *Don't you goddamn let her die!*"

CHAPTER 5

Allegra slowly sits down in the ladderback chair at Libba's work table. Edie's eyes drop to a rush basket that holds plastic blocks and a xylophone, outdated toys her sisters' children played with in years past. Only Alice moves immediately, surely: turns away and climbs the stairs. Without looking or stopping she flicks a switch at the landing and the attic fan instantly gushes on with a roar, drowning out the shrill keening in her ears.

Creek Cabin belongs to Libba Charles.

"Leave it to Libba," her father used to laugh. Which is precisely what Frances did. How could she? Why would she?

Alice opens the door to the first room on the right, which has always been hers. Until now. From the second-story rear window she can just glimpse Shoals Stream overhung with rhododendron. Fallen logs and smooth boulders form plashy waterfalls and the occasional pool deep enough to duck your head. Beneath smaller stones hide orange newts whose spatulate toes stick pleasantly on open palms. Rocks trail velvety algae in the current like drowned Ophelia's hair in a painting Alice has seen somewhere. She knows the floating green strands melt to nothing but jellylike threads if plucked from their natural environment because she's tried it a hundred times, convinced that if she only picked the *right* jeweled tendril it would last, remain the same as it looked while she leaned over it.

Alice can make out the rounded rocks ideal for scrambling over, leaping across. As a child she'd left Creek Cabin early one morning, intent on finding not where the river went, but where it began, certain that if she walked long enough and far enough she'd discover its source, revealed to her as reward for being determined. She should have realized then there were no absolutes, Alice reflects; no pure openings and closures, beginnings and endings, blacks and whites. Not as long as there's Libba.

She's even there in the bookshelf beneath the window's sill, ten volumes stacked neatly as soldiers in order of publication: *It Came With the House, Small Doses, Necessary Concessions, Loose Ends, Father of Girls, Fairly Frantic, This Go Round, Very Married, Relative Sorrow*, and *Built to Last*. Books authored by Libba Charles in which, despite the standard disclaimer on the copyright page, she unstintingly utilized Alices, Allegras, and Edie's lives.

Woven throughout the novels are scenes of piano recitals and baton-twirling lessons, art shows and birthday parties and impromptu dramas on the terrace. And darker depictions: of Allegra wrecking a competitor's science project, Edie's school phobia, Alice's thrall to a charismatic classmate. Despite different names assigned to the characters, within the pages are Alice's desperation to be chosen for sixth-grade class representative, the afternoon Allegra told Edie in crude terms where babies came from, Alice's despair at being dumped by a boyfriend, and countless other trivial snippets or full-blown episodes of humiliation or comedy.

The fan drones, sucking in air from the open window. A mile upriver, Alice had given up her quest to find the stream's source. Cold and wet, she'd sat on a river boulder and cried, unwilling to make the long trek back to Creek Cabin, unwilling to admit she'd failed. Frances had come to find her, bedraggled and soggy as Alice herself, and hoarse from shouting her daughter's name, frantic with worry. Alice thinks of her mother, who will not, cannot, rescue her now, and is swamped by sadness again.

The bed, with its soft blossomy comforter, beckons. She'd loved those comforters as a child, delighted in the unaccustomed necessity of sleeping with blankets in the summer, the pleasant heaviness over her body. Curled beneath them she'd pretended to be a Nordic child, or perhaps Dutch—her fantasy included wooden clogs and striped stockings placed neatly beside the bed—snug under layers of eiderdown. It's so easy to lie down, yield to grief, and there are trees here to watch, just as there are from her bedroom window at home. Alice sinks to the bed. She turns her head from the breeze at the window and the bookshelf beneath it, and the titles that mock her: *Relative Sorrow* and *Necessary Concessions*. Feet on the pillow and head at the window, she succumbs: swaddles herself and her misery and her anger in the comforter's quilted warmth.

She wakes in the dark with a sense of dislocation, then remembers where she is. Her face is cold from the night air drifting though the open window. Someone has turned off the fan and in the silence she's able now to hear the distinct changeless gurgle of Shoals Stream, and another sound as well: singing. She follows the voice down the steps and through the dark downstairs and onto the back porch that spans the entire width of the cottage. Enclosed by screens whose occasional holes are plugged with pine cones, the porch is open, unevenly floored in fieldstone, and is deep enough for a rug, tables, lamps, chairs and a sagging wicker sofa. All of which is arranged around a raised hearth, ideal for feet to the fire, which Alice loves more than any other feature of Creek Cabin.

In a rocking chair before the hearth is Libba, wrapped in a plaid flannel robe with her head turban'd in a towel. "Sshh," she says when she sees Alice, "the orchestra comes in here." Sure enough, in seconds Marion Pou's lullaby solo of "Goodnight My Someone" is sweetly, softly joined by instruments. "But you knew that, didn't you?"

Alice unnecessarily pokes the fire. Until she was well past ten she could squeeze her entire body into the triangular space of the three-foot-tall stereo speaker cabinet. Closing the hinged door, she'd snuggle against the scratchy, gold-threaded fabric and surround herself with the music until she knew the words, the order of the songs, even the records' scratches. Records Libba had brought.

"The best thing John ever did for Creek Cabin was wire this porch for music from the hi-fi. Back when they were hi-fis."

"Seems to me you'd have used some of the song lyrics in your books. Like you used our lives."

"Too hard to get permission," Libba says matter-of-factly and unwinds the taupe-colored towel woven with Frances's initials in fading navy. "Your mother got engaged thanks to these towels. I was with Frances when she bought them. So was John. On a lark, we'd all gone to New York during spring vacation. Saks was having a sale on monogrammed towels and Frances decided to buy some. When the salesclerk asked her what initials she wanted, she looked at John and asked, 'Should I get married or maiden?'"

"Mother wasn't that forward. She'd never do that."

"What you need to know is there's a lot about your mother you don't know."

Alice is silent. She'd taken the same towels to swimming pools and camps and college, never suspecting their role in her mother's marriage. Yet Libba has always known.

Libba shakes her damp hair, black-and-silver streaked, before the ember'd fire. "But I'd already reassured Frances that John planned to marry her. He was correcting her tennis serve, which requires serious intimacy." Libba laughs, a low throaty gurgle. "That was before your father had developed the knack for knowing when to make the ask."

John Wilson made money by getting it out of others, had a talent for "knowing when to make the ask," as he phrased it. *Fundraiser*, the girls had always written beside "Father's Occupation"on standardized forms. *The Shuns* the three sisters termed the vague faceless entities who employed their father: Founda*tion*, Institu*tion*, Convoca*tion*, Conven*tion*.

The silence is nearly palpable. There's no hum of air conditioning, only the trickling creek, the discordant chirping of tree frogs. Nor is there light but for the fire's tangerine glow, though glass votives that Frances lit for dinner parties line the mantel. She'd used quilts as tablecloths, surrounding the plywood-slab table with an assortment of caned chairs. Alice shuts her eyes and sees those suppers, the flowering roadside weeds in pitchers, the mismatched crockery plates, her mother cooking, talking. She sees herself and her sisters in their good-girl nightgowns, the shadows of limbs illuminated behind eyelet and batiste. She sees them crouching before this hearth with board games, playing cards, marshmallows, and she wants to weep again.

"Do you wear your mother's pearls?" Libba asks and raises her feet, clad in thick heathery socks, to the hearth.

Alice startles. "How did you know she left me the pearls?"

Libba's steady gaze suffices as answer. A log dissolves into hissing chunks. She rises, pulls the robe's belt more tightly around her slender figure and looks up at the night sky. "Oh moon, oh pale inconstant platter."

"And who said that?" Alice asks sarcastically.

"Me. A line I never found a place for."

Alice sits down on the sofa whose cushions are exhausted with age, spotted with mildew from creek-drift and slanting rain and morning mist. "Unlike other things. Such as my coming home from school and telling Mother that I'd decided people who had eat-up socks and scabs on their legs were always dumb. Such as me spending my allowance on red-dye tablets to see how well I was brushing my teeth. Such as Allegra stabbing me with her kilt pin, though you named her 'Emily.'"

"Always liked that name, Emily."

"You have no shame, do you, about taking literary license with people's lives. Such incredible . . ."

"Temerity? Unmitigated gall?" Libba finishes. "'If a writer has to rob his mother, he will not hesitate. The 'Ode to a Grecian Urn' is worth any number of old ladies.'"

"I can't believe you have the nerve to even utter such a thing."

"I didn't. William Faulkner did. Harper Lee made Truman Capote famous. He was Dill in *To Kill a Mockingbird*." Libba sits, her head against the rocker's back. "You were never the plot. Only the minutiae."

"But it was *my* minutiae. The letters I wrote home about crushes, having my wisdom teeth pulled. Trying to pee like a boy, starting my period while I was still wearing feet pajamas. How could you write about those things? You never had a child so you had to feed off us. What did Mother think of your using us—her—like that?" Alice doesn't wait for Libba's response. "For forty years you've lived off our lives like a parasite, and I'll never forgive you."

"Careful with the nevers," Libba says. She leans forward, plucks a long wooden match from a brass bucket near the hearth. "Seriously, Alice, cut to the chase because I find score-settling drama tiring." The slender stick snaps in her fingers. "Which is it? Do you resent me for using details of your life, or Frances for telling me details of your life? Is it that you don't have Creek Cabin, or that it's me who does?"

Alice rises resolutely and stabs remaining coals into white ash. Who she didn't forgive was Libba for loving Frances more than she, Alice, did. No, because Libba couldn't possibly love Frances more than Alice did. No, for . . . for . . .

Libba tosses the matchsticks onto the crumbled coals and walks into the blackened cabin, calling behind her, "That's a stumper, isn't it?"

In the morning Alice makes the bed, plumps the pillow and comforter. "I doubt Daddy wants anything," she hears Edie say downstairs. "He said he was going minimal."

"Minimalism isn't so charming when it's mandatory," Libba says. "John and Frances's first Christmas tree was a fake rubber plant decorated with red ribbon bows."

"How do you—" Edie begins, then stops. She knows how Libba knows: Libba was *there*.

"They ate canned spaghetti three times a week. A dinner party was chicken salad with more celery than chicken. One weekend someone dropped a fifth of liquor in the kitchen and all of us dropped to the linoleum like a sniper was after us, frantically soaking up scotch with paper towels and wringing them out over a bowl."

Alice picks up the phone on the bedside table as Libba's voice floats up the stairs. "When there was enough money to go to a restaurant, Frances was so excited that she'd fill up on the basket of crackers and be too full for her entree," Libba says, and goes outside.

Where was her family? Alice thinks, hearing only her own voice on the answering machine. Had Rob found the slice-and-bake cinnamon rolls she'd made a special trip to the grocery store to buy, to make her absence easier on him? If he went out for bagels I hope he remembers to slice them, Alice thinks, or they'll be rocks by the time I get home.

Downstairs Edie and Allegra hold the gummed notepads. Pink for Edie, blue for Allegra, green for Alice.

"Are you going to just let her get away with this?" Alice asks. "Possession is nine-tenths of the law and so forth?"

"Mother gave Creek Cabin to her," Allegra says.

"She writes fiction. How do we know she hasn't made it up? *Libba Charles has something that belongs to us!* She has—" Alice looks around her at Granny's heavy Victorian chest with its lavish flourishes, drawer pulls deep enough to fit four fingers into, carved to resemble leaves. She looks at a wormy pine end table keeping strange company with a breakfront secretary. She looks at her sisters: Edie, who's never made a conscious decision in her life, and Allegra, who's always idolized Libba anyway.

"Fine," Alice says. Duffel dangling from her shoulder, she slaps a green paper flag on a spindly straight-back chair, a cider jug lamp, a painted box, a mounted checkerboard so primitive that it looks as though a child has painted it. "I want this," she says, "and this." Though she doesn't want lamps or boxes or anything else; she wants only her mother.

Allegra pulls a blanket of crocheted brown, and, orange octagons from Frances's Em Sem trunk utilized as a coffee table. "Who wants this hideous afghan?"

From the porch swing Libba's voice comes through the window. "Alice lay under that afghan for four days when she had red measles, a fever of a hundred and three." The swing chains creak with Libba's steady rocking. "Her eyes were so scabbed that Frances had to soften the crust with a warm washcloth just so Alice could see."

Alice stands just inside the screened door and looks at Libba in the swing. One leg is tucked beneath her and one thin, bare, aristocratic foot dangles to the floor, moving the swing slowly back and forth. Alice can barely remember having the measles, scabbed eyes, raging fever. She barely remembers her mother's ministering.

Without looking up from her book Libba says, "Has it ever occurred to you that your mother had something that belonged to *me?*"

Alice opens the door, crosses her arms, and faces Libba. "Such as what?"

Libba uncharacteristically falters at the challenge and says, "There was a vaccine for measles by the time Edie came along."

Alice waits for a church van to pass, arms waving from its open windows, then carefully reverses from the semicircular gravel driveway perilously close to a trickling creek running parallel to the road. She deliberately points her thoughts toward what needs to be done at home. Flashlight batteries and stamps for Frannie and Catherine. She hopes Rob ordered two large pizzas last night. Luke takes leftover slices to work for his lunch. Maybe her friend Margaret has finally found time to call.

Ten miles outside Stockton, Alice slows to steer around a half dozen old model sedans, cars of country folk parked unsafely on the shoulder near a mailbox draped with a tight spray of red carnations. Against the mailbox's listing pole is propped a whitewashed plywood sign. As though its painter had miscalculated the space, stark black crudely lettered words slant across the board in one unbroken, unpunctuated phrase:

SLOW DEATH IN FAMILY

Even on the other side, even in her rearview mirror, SLOW DEATH IN FAMILY it reads, coming and going.

Alice begins to cry.

Even as she cries Alice knows she'll come back to Vade Mecum. She'll return to the cottage for more than just the chair or the quilt or the checkerboard. Because not only does Libba have Creek Cabin, she has something more that Alice needs. In her memories and her stories, Libba has Frances, too.

July 22, 1954

"Here's the funny thing," Frances said wonderingly, her voice a small bleat. "I thought about it. Worried about it. Ever since I read that conception occurs in the fallopian tubes, I knew I'd have an ectopic pregnancy."

"You read too much."

"You're always telling me to read *more*." She listlessly pushed away the tray, the compartments of applesauce, mashed potatoes, green beans, breaded cutlet. "I didn't even know I was pregnant, Libba," she said, a clotted cry. "I didn't get to tell John. I didn't even get to be *glad*."

"Be glad that you're alive. I am." Libba unwrapped the fork. "You can't go home if you don't eat."

Frances touched the tube taped to the crook of her elbow, then pointed at the bag above her head. "I am eating. Involuntarily. Want to see my scar?" She pulled up the thin rumpled gown, touched the patch of gauze. "I have to do something to thank Dennis Chandler."

"Stop with the obligations. It's his job."

A radio laugh track blared from another room. "Let me see *your* scar."

"It's not a scar."

"It is to me."

Libba held out her arm, the criss-cross of tape in the elbow crook. "Don't ever say I didn't give you anything," she said lightly. "Handy, being a universal donor. Probably went to some redneck who got in a knife fight."

"You saved my life. Getting the doctor. Giving blood."

Libba raised the window blinds. "There's your knight in shining armor and the princess, right on schedule. Can you lean?"

Frances inched to the side of the bed. Two stories below, John stood in the parking lot with Alice on his shoulders. Libba cranked open the window. "Alice! Mommy's here!"

Frances waved, too weak to call out.

"She's eating her applesauce! Just like you! Yum!"

John flapped Alice's wrist. "We'll be back tomorrow," he shouted. "You still okay with closing up Creek Cabin, Libba?" She shot him a thumb's up.

"Bye, baby," Frances said behind her and Libba cranked the window shut. "John's told everyone I have 'female troubles.' Remember how we made fun of anyone at Em Sem who skipped gym class because of 'female troubles'? You said it was the worst euphemism you knew."

Libba stood. "Where's that list of no-nos? No driving, no euphemisms, no climbing stairs, no—"

But Frances had retreated into her private misery again. "I have a ruined, ruptured, fallopian tube on one side. And I have a missing ovary on the other side. And I have scar tissue everywhere else. Those are all the things I *have*. But what I'll never have is another child. One plus one is zero. Is there a euphemism for that, Libba?" She covered her face with her hands and began to cry softly.

August 29, 1954

"Let me hold her. I can almost stand up straight again."

"No dice. No heavy lifting. And this—" Libba leaned over the side of the playpen and hoisted Alice to her hip—"qualifies as heavy lifting." She settled the toddler on the bed beside Frances.

"Hello, fatty," Frances murmured. But her chin quivered and she blinked back tears. "She'll be an only child. What's worse, Libba? Trying and trying to have a baby, always hoping, always checking and counting and believing it will eventually happen and living on hope, or knowing beforehand that all the checking and counting and believing and hoping is pointless?" She twisted the sheet in her fingers. "And then I hate myself for being so selfish and self-pitying, because I *do* have a child." Alice stared at her mother's tears. "Only-child Alice," Frances said and opened her arms. Alice immediately scrambled for her mother's lap.

Libba was just as swift, scooping her up and away. "Let's play keep away from Mommy's tummy. It hurts."

"Not as badly, no, better every day." Frances gazed out the window. "I want to be well, Libba. I want this to be over."

"It *is* over."

Frances touched her chest. "Not here. Some of me wants to be up and playing with Alice, taking her to the park, strolling, fixing her meals, reading her stories. But most of me can't do anything. I don't care. Like the anesthesia hasn't worn off. Nothing matters."

"Your only job is taking care of yourself. I'm taking care of Alice."

Frances tried to smile. "And how are you finding motherhood?"

"I hope I'm a better writer than mother. Let's leave it at that. All you have to do right now is be."

"What?"

"Just be." Their eyes locked a long moment, until the sound of an opening door reached them. "There's John," Libba said, and closed the door to the bedroom, taking Alice with her.

In the kitchen, Alice squirmed from Libba's arms and toddled over to her father. "How's my girl?" he asked, swinging her into the air, then looked over her head at Libba. "And how's my other girl? Did she smile today?"

Libba rinsed Alice's supper dishes. "It's going to take time."

John came to stand beside her, his shoulder touching hers. "Libba," he said in a low voice. "Suppose she never, she can't . . . We both wanted children, and I can be happy, *am* happy. But Frances . . . she's so fragile on the inside now, can't shake the despondency . . . She's lost her joy, too. I'm scared for her, and for us."

"She's *alive*, John. A lot of women with tubal pregnancies die. You can't think beyond that right now."

"I am thinking beyond that. I'm looking for a new job. Somewhere away, back South. Maybe being closer to home will cheer her, help her start over." He resolutely shut off the faucet. "In the meantime, you don't know how much it means to both of us to have you here." Alice pulled at his earlobe and he gently loosened the toddler's grasp. "All three of us. Get any writing done today?"

"I'm not here to write. I'm here to look after someone. Several someones." She glanced up at John. "We have a deal, see?" She reached for Alice. "Come here you, time for a bedtime story And you," she said, jabbing John, "go see your wife." He turned in the doorway. "Go on," Libba said. "I know her. She'll be alright."

"I think it'll take a miracle."

Libba pointed to the book whose cover Alice was busily chewing, *The Little Engine That Could.* "Miracles happen."

CHAPTER 6

Edie debates whom to call first. She always calls her father over the weekend. But if she calls Teddy first, and then her father, he'll ask about Teddy and if she hasn't called him yet, she'll be able to truthfully tell her father she doesn't know how Teddy is. Her father doesn't exactly approve of Teddy. Teddy doesn't care what John Wilson thinks and Edie wants not to care either, but she does. Her father has always been both her hero and her best-loved parent.

The phone rings and as often happens to Edie, the decision is made for her. "Hey, babe," Teddy says.

Edie's heart goes runny with love, or lust, or something. When she and Teddy went through one of their phases apart from each other, sometimes they'd meet solely for sex, including one freezing winter night in the car, her legs tangled around the gear shift, heater blowing against her thighs. She'd been embarrassed afterward, modest as a virgin, which made Teddy only love her more.

"What are you doing?" she asks.

"Tying my shoes. Going for a run."

Edie can picture him stooping, sees the curly calf hairs above the white socks, on his thighs below the nylon shorts, and on his wrist around the complicated workings of his watch.

"Was the shrimp good?"

The vision vanishes. Edie's hand flies to her mouth. She'd brought two pounds of fresh shrimp from Charleston to Vade Mecum, thinking they could have it for dinner. Last night's dinner. "I—" she's incapable of lying, "forgot. There was a lot of—" Edie grapples for an excuse, "confusion, and things didn't go quite as expected, and—"

"And you forgot to reserve staff for the Turner catering job last night. I had to recruit students at the last minute."

Edie looks out the window at her ancient Toyota, which no doubt stinks of rotting seafood. The gas cap is missing because she'd driven away from a pump with the cap lying where she'd left it—on the car roof. She's stuck a potato in the hole as a temporary plug. She's the one who leaves the car windows down on the night it rains. The Toyota's rear is sticking awkwardly into the street, and the crummy parking job was her fault too.

"Are you wearing underpants?" Teddy suddenly asks, and Edie smiles, flushes. One stifling day Teddy had squeezed her fanny and discovered to his delight that she hadn't bothered with underwear. He's never stopped testing since.

"I'll bet it's nice to be panted after, no?" Libba says when Edie hangs up. "Russell panted after me. And others like me, unfortunately. Sam, though, was intense and squirrelly. Every social gesture was an act of bravery for Sam-I-am."

Edie dials her father's condominium number. Libba's ex-husband recollections have nothing to do with her. She's so focused on hearing her father's voice that when the phone is answered on the fifth ring she says, "It's me," before she realizes the voice is female. "May I—is John Wilson there?"

"Hold on. He's grilling on the hibachi."

Hibachi? Edie hasn't heard the word *hibachi* since she had her own first-apartment minuscule terrace. Grilling? At lunch?

"Hello?"

"Daddy?"

"Hey, Peedie. Was that you calling before? Sorry we couldn't get it. I was wrestling the—what is it, Bree?" A woman's voice answers indistinctly and he turns back to the phone— "kielbasa."

We? Edie thinks, *Kielbasa?* "Who . . . who was that?"

"Bree Michaelove. She's helping me with a New Hampshire account."

Edie thinks she might have had a toy horse named Bree, a plastic stallion with a fiercely pink tale and curly mane, part of a princess fantasy set.

"How's Teddy?" her father predictably asks.

"He's in Charleston. I'm at Creek Cabin. With . . . Libba." John Wilson is quiet. "Daddy, did you know Mother gave Creek Cabin to Libba before . . . before she died?"

The pause before her father answers is so prolonged that Edie thinks she can hear the telephone wires vibrating. But perhaps it's only the kiddie kazoo band outside, the ragtag parade of day camp children filing by the cottage toward Lake Sarah, blowing tunelessly but enthusiastically on tissue-covered combs. "She'd mentioned it," he says finally, lamely. "I guess I did know."

Edie's surprised into silence.

"Your mother and Libba . . ." He seems to grope for words. "They had a lot of history between them at Creek Cabin. It was the setting for some . . . happy reunions."

Edie scrunches next to the wall, addresses a knothole in a low voice. "Alice thinks we should fight it, or whatever you do. Contest."

"Ah, Ede, no. Your mother fought so long there just isn't any fight left in me."

Edie is newly taken aback. This from a man so orderly that when his daughters were children he'd painted the handles of lawn tools orange, so if they were left in the yard—left usually by Edie—they wouldn't be accidentally mangled by the lawn mower blades. After Edie dented the car fender by pulling in too closely to the garage wall, he'd hung a tennis ball on a string from an overhead beam. "Watch the string," he'd told Edie. "When it moves, brake."

"Can you just take my word, Ede?" he asks. "Libba deserves to have the cottage." Sensing Libba's eyes on her, Edie speaks hurriedly. "I thought I might come see you this afternoon on my way home."

"Bree and I need to get this proposal ready for presentation. Another time, okay?"

"Oh."

"How's Libba?" he asks suddenly, then softly, surprisingly: "Give her my love."

Children's voices float through the window, six-year-olds following counselors slung shoulder to hip with hula hoops. If Teddy were here, Edie knows, he'd speak to each child: "Hello, pardner." "Hey, pal." "Gimme five." He can't resist. She watches a pigtailed child straggling at the rear. "I don't want to come," the little girl whimpers, using her kazoo tissue to wipe away tears. "I want my mommy."

Edie had wanted her mommy too. When Edie was three, Frances left with Libba for a two-week writing conference. By the time Frances returned Edie was calling every mother in the neighborhood "Mommy." She'd imprinted like a gosling on anyone who'd fed her a cookie or a sandwich. Libba had used the incident in *Fairly Frantic*, and though Libba's readers found the scene humorous, Edie, who knows it's true, doesn't find it funny at all.

"How's John?" Libba asks.

"He's . . . busy." Edie's as inept at lying as she is at making decisions, so she doesn't even try. "A lady's helping him with a project."

"Good. John needs a woman. When he was home on weekends he'd follow Frances around the house while she folded laundry or emptied the dishwasher. He adored her." She runs her fingers down a stack of records. "Frances made camellias bloom in the mud for him."

"What?"

"*Mame*," Libba answers, and places the needle on the soundtrack.

"I needed Mother to pick me up from movies or a birthday party. I needed her to bring lemonade or potato salad for Field Day or Teacher Appreciation Day. I needed her to order my gym uniform so I wasn't the only one without it at the first game. Everyone else looked after me because Mother was with you."

"Or maybe that's just the way you remember it," Libba responds.

"You and Tennessee Williams, depending on the kindness of strangers. And when did you become the poster child for marital convention?"

"Like you were? Whatever happened to Sam and Russell? Nothing left of those, is there?"

"They were infatuations, not relationships. Sexual romps. We didn't adore each other enough. Strong verb, 'adore.' And they weren't as tolerant as John about putting up with my visits to your mother. Sam and Russell wanted exclusive rights." Her gaze is level. "Know what I mean?"

"Libba?" A ruddy-faced older man holding a damp paper bag opens the door. "I brought you the paper and some trout. I've been shooting fish in a barrel at the stocked lake down the road."

Something about the man is familiar to Edie. The square lined face and full head of snowy white hair lend him a leonine appearance.

"Edie, you remember Dennis Chandler."

Placing him, Edie reddens yet again. The last time she'd seen him, he'd had gingery hair and she'd had a raging yeast infection. Dennis Chandler was a widowed physician from Chattanooga, one of the Vade Mecum summer people that fell into the friend-of-my-parents category. A frequent guest at Creek Cabin for casual suppers, dropping by to chat on the walk up the hill to his own cottage, Dr. Chandler was a kindly, gentlemanly doctor of the old school. Over Edie's objections, Frances had called him for a prescription.

Libba's eyes hold Dennis's. "We were talking about Frances."

"Oh," he says, understanding. "I miss your mother. Please tell your sisters I said so."

Edie only nods, shoulders her quilted bag, and brushes past him in the doorway.

Through the screen, Dennis watches Edie open her car door. "She seems . . . disgruntled. Did you—"

"No," Libba interrupts. "I didn't then, and I won't now." She takes the sodden bag. "Thank you for dinner." She touches his shoulder. "It's just that Edie's memories are different from mine. And yours."

Even after a stop at the Dumpster, where Edie pitched in the entire cooler, the stench of rotted shrimp is suffocating. Breathing through her mouth, she rolls down all four windows and slows to navigate the six-lane highway leading from Stockton to Asheville, a stretch she's never stopped dreading. The road drops two thousand feet in only eight miles, a dizzying descent in which fifty miles per hour feels like ninety. Eighteen-wheeled rigs seem to bend with the curves, their massive loads threatening to topple over. Mudflaps warn "Back Off," a message emphasized by swashbuckling mustachio'd midget Confederate rebels; others sport silvery silhouettes of perky-boobed nymphs. "What are you doing?" she'd ask her father when he pumped his forearm to a passing truck driver seated high in the cab.

"Listen. He'll toot the horn," and the *blat-blat* blared, just as he'd predicted.

At the crest of the hill, a green highway sign reads EASTERN CONTINENTAL DIVIDE: 2786 FEET. "At this very place," her father had said, "all the rivers flow toward the Atlantic Ocean instead of the

Mississippi." Edie still loves this idea, an absolute of nature she somehow can believe in and attach to, the way she can't quite attach herself to anything else.

Every hundred feet on the steep downhill route, signs reading RUNAWAY TRUCK RAMP alarm Edie now as much as they did when she was a child. Like stumpy thumbs, abbreviated exits of raised, coarsely chopped dirt veer away from the curving descent, and end in a blunt mound. "Those are in case the brakes fail on those big trucks," her father had explained. "Their brakes burn out on the incline." Edie seems to recall, in fact, that it was just that sort of accident that left Dr. Chandler a widower.

"Why is the truck behind us flashing his headlights?"

"To tell me I can come back into the lane."

"Why does that one have its lights on during the day?"

"Because it's a holiday weekend." Her father knew all the answers.

Outside the open windows the gas-cap potato plug breaks off as Edie rounds another wide curve. One potato half bounces along the interstate pavement, but the other half falls into the gas tank itself. A dozen miles beyond the Eastern Continental Divide and the runaway truck ramps, the potato chunk works its way to the mouth of the fuel hose and stops the car engine dead.

Parked on the shoulder, Edie opens the hood with no idea what she's looking for, and giving up, leans her rump against the warm car. Traffic passes: station wagons and SUVs and pickups and sedans and trucks and trucks and trucks. A flatbed lumbers toward her and she thinks it might stop. Instead, it only slows, as if the driver is studying the stranded waif that is Edie. This truck doesn't carry logs lashed to the flatbed, or chickens in cages, or new automobiles. It carries only one item, a dully gleaming stippled copper container, rectangular, with a rounded lid. Thick, wide, webbed straps securely hold the coffin vault to the platform.

Edie watches the truck pass, turns and drops her head into her forearms on the roof of the car, and not for the first time wonders, like Alice, whether Libba loved Frances more than Edie did, or whether Frances loved Libba more than she did Edie. No one can answer this question. Except perhaps Libba herself.

An old jeep slows to a stop on the shoulder fifty yards beyond Edie's car, as though its driver had second thoughts about passing her. The zippered plastic window flaps open and a baseball-capped head sticks out. "Need a lift?"

Edie decides maniac highway rapists do not drive jeeps faded more orange than red, trots toward it, and climbs in. The hem of her long loose dress catches on a protruding bolt, rips, and gapes limply open. She's unsurprised.

"Hate to tell you this, but the closest garage is back in Stockton, near Vade Mecum," the driver says. The plastic nametag pinned to his shirt reads CLARK.

This doesn't surprise Edie either. Another decision has been made for her. "It's alright, Clark," she sighs. "I'm going back there anyway."

● ● ●

June 11, 1955

Frances parked the carriage beside the railing of the bridge over the
spillway dam and unrolled a bag of bread heels. "See the duckies,
Alice? Hungry duckies, watch." She tossed crumbs into the water
and the half dozen ducks bobbed greedily. "Quack," Frances said.
"What does the duck say?"

Alice clutched a crust, put it in her own mouth. "Me."

A stout woman wearing a name tag blazoned with a cross
passed behind them, reached to touch Alice's hair and said, "Hello,
sweetie." Libba watched silently.

"Nobody can resist a baby," Frances said, then laughed. "Except
you."

"Maybe it just seems that way because having a child has never
been a goal of mine."

"'Goal'?" Frances laughed again.

"I mean," Libba struggled, "the idea, the possibility, just hasn't
been part of my plans. My own childhood was so disruptive I never
wanted to inflict that likelihood on another life."

Frances straightened. "Don't get defensive, I'm not criticizing you."

"Joosh," Alice said.

"Okay, honey." Frances steered the stroller toward the hill, and Creek Cabin. "This time last year, *I* had a baby."

Libba shook her head. "You can't think of it that way. It was . . . tissue, not a baby. There was absolutely no possibility of a fetus surviving. You were lucky *you* survived."

"Oh, but Libba," Frances said, "when you want a child, it *is* a baby, a hope, a love, the world . . ." She set Alice on the porch strewn with toys. "Watch her a minute while I get the juice."

Libba hoisted Alice to her hip, but the child swatted at her. "Wok," she said, impatient to escape.

Libba let her down, picked up a xylophone stick. "I know just how you feel, kid."

Frances pushed open the screen door with her hip and handed a glass of orange juice to Alice, and Libba. "You know how she feels about what?"

Libba placed the glass on the porch railing. "And what is it if you don't want it?"

"Fine. Don't drink it."

"Not the juice."

"What then?"

"What if you don't want the baby? What happens then?"

"Fictional hypotheticals are your job. Why, are you writing a novel about an unwed mother's home?"

Libba picked at the rail's flaking paint. "Or what if you don't *know* whether you want it?" She turned to face Frances. "Another week and I'll be two months late."

Frances's arms dropped. "Libba, oh Libba."

"No one pronounces my name the way you do: '*Lubba*.'" She passed her hands over her abdomen, then cupped each breast. "Doesn't take long, does it? They're already . . . heavier."

A range of emotions swiftly crossed Frances's face: shock. Joy. Jealousy. Libba saw them all. "Who's—"

"Does it matter?"

Frances tried to control her voice. "It might to him."

"A teacher at the Ellis School where I was writer-in-residence this spring." Libba laughed tiredly. "Seemed like the ideal job: free meals, free lodging with a pretty view, no obligations but one class of students scratching out Emily Dickinson imitations, and solitude. Plenty of solitude. A little too much, as it turns out." Alice banged the metal slats of the xylophone. "His name is—was—Robert. English teacher, and object of every senior girl's crush. I know; I read their journals. *We* read their journals. In bed."

Now stun played over Frances's features and Libba braced for disgust. "Does he know?"

"He's a Henry James aficionado. *Portrait of a Lady* is his favorite book."

"Do you love him?"

"I love the way he traces my collarbone and my chin and the inside of my wrist." She looked at her fingernails, added flatly, "Wanting isn't loving. And he's married."

"Does Sam—"

"No."

"You could . . . couldn't you tell Sam that it's his, and, well, you love each other, you could get married—"

"You have it all plotted out, don't you?" Libba said. "Except for a few significant discrepancies. I haven't been with Sam in the last two months. And answer me this: Would John have married you if you were pregnant with another man's child?"

"He—"

"Even poets have their pride. Besides, this is an inconceivable to you, but Sam doesn't want a child. He wants fame, not . . . domestic bondage."

Frances's eyes misted with hurt, but Libba plunged on. "Sam wouldn't marry me, and I don't *want* to be married. I need my independence."

Fierceness replaced pain in Frances's expression. "And maybe independence is just a form of selfishness. Damn you," she said, grabbing Libba's arm. "Why have you waited until now to tell me?"

Shaking off the grasp, Libba mildly said, "I didn't have to tell you at all."

Instantly, Frances slapped her, shoving her against the railing. The juice glass toppled and fell, crinkling into shards on the rocks below.

Alice poked her head between her mother's legs to look. "Uh-oh," she said, pointing.

Libba rubbed her cheek, looked at the broken glass pieces, the juice-splattered stones. Finally she said, "I can't think of it as a baby. I can think 'pregnant,' and I can think 'it,' but I can't think 'baby', because then—because then I can't do—"

"No," Frances said. "*No*."

"But here's the thing, you're my friend, and I need a friend to . . ."

"To help you locate some illegal backroom quack?"

"I'll do the locating. I just need someone to come with me, stay with me a day or two." Libba set her mouth, toed the rough floor-boards. "Are you going to make me beg? I have one book out and one under contract, and sixty pages of notes on the new one, and two taking shape in my head and—"

"You could bleed to death, get septic poisoning, you could die, Libba, die!"

"I might as well be dead as be pregnant. I'm trying to conform for a change, Frances, to be more conventional, and having a—"

"You are *not* trying to be conventional. You're trying to get rid of some inconvenient *tissue*."

"I won't let biology—"

"Biology!"

"Or economics, or time interfere—"

"While you're throwing nouns around, call it selfishness. Or pre-meditated murder." Frances took two steps toward her. "Look at me," she said. "But never mind you." She grabbed the collar of Libba's shirt. "*Look at me!* You think books are on a par with a *child*?"

Libba reached for Frances's clenched fingers. "'Unwed mother' is the kindest term I'd be branded with. Try 'banished.' Try on 'slut'and 'whore' for size. Writing is what I was born to do. It's what I want to do. This isn't a planned, wanted child . . . this is a love child."

Frances knelt beside Alice. "And what do you think she is, a timely and economically convenient child?" She kissed her daughter's forehead. "And at least you were 'born' to do your writing," Frances hissed. "Abortion is immoral, if it doesn't kill you first."

"And what else is immoral? Bringing an unwanted baby into the world? Is having an illegitimate child immoral? Is not telling the father immoral? I'm not asking you to act immorally, Frances, I'm asking for help. Two or three days of your time. Is that too much to ask of a friend?"

"You think you're entitled you to some reciprocal *favor*? That because you saved my life I'll help you destroy one? Me, who would give anything, anything on earth, to be in your *unfortunate* predicament? You're insensitive and selfish, and you're damn right it's too much to ask." Indoors, the phone rang, but Frances ignored it, her eyes locking onto into Libba's silver ones. "And you have grossly overestimated our *friendship*."

The phone rang shrilly on. Frances glanced at Alice, who was absorbed in a wicker bucket of toys. "Don't you even touch her."

The door slammed and the ringing abruptly ceased. "John, hi." Frances's voice broke. "No, we're fine, I just . . . caught my finger in the door. It's beautiful here, I miss you. Libba? She's going back to New York. Something to do with a book."

"Baby," Alice said from the floor, and held up a Raggedy Ann doll for inspection. Libba reached for one of the striped stuffed legs. "No no," the child said, drawing back. "*My* baby."

CHAPTER 7

"And then there were two," Libba says to Allegra. "When do you have to go home?" she laughs. "See this *Go Round*."

Allegra knows the reference. "When do you have to go home?" she asked playmates as a child when she'd grown tired of them, thinking herself clever not to insult them by saying *When are you going home?* One Saturday she'd called one classmate after another to come play and had opened the final phone call with, "I've called everybody else, so can you come over?" While Libba laughed, Frances made Allegra call the child back to apologize.

Allegra's head hurts. The person she most wanted to apologize to was dead.

"Soon," Allegra answers. Like Edie and Alice, she'd phoned home, too. But no one had answered and now it's nearly time for supper. Where are they? She stares at the phone. *Ring now*, she thinks, the way she'd tried mental telepathy on boys as a teenager. It hadn't worked then, either.

"What a little pain you were," Libba says. "The report cards came home with a big fat D, and your excuse was 'The teacher's a prick.' 'I wrecked the car, I got kicked out of school,' but it was never *your* fault. You wore Frances out."

Allegra flinches. She hates to remember herself those years, when the only way to get her to do something was to tell her not to. "No wonder Mother and Daddy sent me away to boarding school."

"'Sent'?" Libba sharply echoes, snapping open the Sunday paper Dennis Chandler brought by with the trout. "Boarding school is a privilege." Her voice gentles. "Never mind. 'Bad children are harder to endure than good ones, but they are easier to read about.' Flannery O'Connor. But I'm accustomed to unruly children: novels go feral if you don't watch them carefully. Besides," she adds, "I always pull for the underdog, the—" she points to an article headlined MANHUNT FOR MILLER– "'elusive fugitive.' Bert Miller, the fellow who bombed the Alabama abortion clinic, has been tracked to our very own mountains. But even with dozens of FBI and local lawmen and tracking dogs and infrared, it's all for naught. Bertie's holed up in a cave somewhere. I'm on his side."

"Naturally," Allegra says. Again she looks at the phone, which remains stubbornly silent. She'd meant to check the Vade Mecum phone directory to see if an AA meeting was being held somewhere. Ninety meetings in ninety days.

When Libba begins clattering pans in the kitchen, Allegra wanders over to the writing table, irresistibly drawn to the papers, the corkboard propped between the typewriter and the wall. The clutter takes her mind off her headache, and her fear of sobriety. She hadn't expected the fear. Her foot stubs something beneath the card table, one of three cardboard boxes bearing the word SEAGRAM'S, and she kneels, lifts a lid. "If you're looking for liquor, it's in the cabinet under the sink," Libba says, and Allegra straightens, brusquely shutting the lid. "Those are albums and books," Libba says, "the only worldly possessions I care about, so be careful."

One corner of the table is stacked with novels and short-story collections: Updike, Evelyn Waugh, Munro, Cheever, the quoted Flannery O'Connor, even *Charlotte's Web*. When Allegra fans the pages, bright yellow blocks of highlighted paragraphs and sentences blur by. Allegra lifts scattered papers—stapled, clipped, loose. A magazine article on infidelity, a newspaper survey detailing what people consider sins. She picks up two notebooks labeled *Fresh Out of Comfort* and *Make Me Safe*. "Are these new novels?"

"One's a lump of fiction and the other is a car on blocks that needs a new engine. But I've lost my muse."

Allegra's silent. "Can't I be your muse?" Dal had teased her once. But they're hardly sharing meals together now, much less jokes. Laughing Allegra. Ha ha hardly. "If I were writing," Allegra begins, though she isn't, wasn't, couldn't, "what advice would you give me?"

"Show, don't tell," Libba replies. "Avoid clichés, exclamation points, and needless dialogue tag lines."

Allegra's sorry she asked.

Beneath a *New Yorker* is a copy of *Loose Ends*, the book that, Allegra knows, was roundly panned. It's also the only book in which Libba Charles included a dedication. Allegra reads the peculiar wording aloud. *"'For Frances from your friend with whom up you put.'"*

Noise from the kitchen ceases and Libba appears, frying pan in hand.

"You never dedicated any of your books to us," Allegra says lightly. Libba returns to the counter, dusts the trout fillets with flour. "Designating things is a tricky business."

"Like Creek Cabin?"

But Libba doesn't rise to the bait. "My books weren't for you."

"I know," Allegra says. "Not age-appropriate, though that term wasn't around when I was thumbing through your books, looking for the 'fucks'."

"No," Libba says, repeating the phrase as though speaking to a four-year-old. "They weren't for you." She slices butter pats into the pan. "That was my favorite book, but . . ." Except for the sizzle of heated grease there's a long silence from the kitchen until finally she says, *"Loose Ends* is about compromise, and compromise isn't satisfying to readers. It isn't . . . tidy and conclusive."

"We were raised on your compromises. Mother used to tell us about them. That you'd help her be brave at Em Sem, and she'd help you be accepted by all those judgmental Southern belles, that she'd be the married anchor and you'd give her stories."

"They weren't compromises, they were promises."

"Compromise, promise, same root, same thing."

Again Libba comes to the doorway. "Here's some advice: write what you know about. And that is something you know absolutely *zero* about."

The steely, definite tone of Libba's voice makes Allegra look up.

"Here's another cardinal rule," Libba says. "You should be able to reduce a novel to a one-sentence synopsis, like the television movie section in a newspaper. A family's vacation with another family's gone awry, *Fairly Frantic*. An estrangement between son and grandfather, *Father of Girls*. The aftermath of a child's anapha-leptic seizure, *Small Doses*. Someone who remarries her first hus-band, *Relative Sorrow*. Divided loyalties when a family business goes under, *Necessary Concessions*. A young wife being lorded over by her in-laws, *It Came with the House*. Et cetera."

Again, Allegra calls home. Again, no answer. Simultaneously perplexed and alarmed, she replaces the receiver.

Libba brings two plates to the sofa before the television. "Now you know how it feels when no one answers. I wrote letters to Alice and Edie, but I called you. Or tried to."

"There's a message machine."

"I don't like message machines."

Allegra avoids the silvery eyes.

"Why don't you answer the phone?"

Allegra thinks of Susan, who betrayed her, and witnessed her children's . . . pleading. "Because I don't know who my friends are anymore."

From the television, Alex Trebek reads *Jeopardy!* answers.

"What is the Nile," Libba says.

"Cool Hand Luke," Allegra says.

"Question form. Who is Catherine the Great."

"What is Sicily."

Libba rises, takes a bottle of white wine from the refrigerator, and pours herself a glass. Allegra tries to focus on Double Jeop-ardy. There will always be white wine, always. "What is Monti-cello." She glances at the silent phone again, murmurs, "I have to get on the road," and wonders what her children are having for din-ner. She swallows hard in a throat so sore from withheld tears over the last few weeks that she's sure her gullet has callouses. She leans forward to put her plate on the floor and *Loose Ends* drops from her lap. Two slender pieces of paper fall out, newsprint columns. "What are these?"

Libba eyes them. "Bookmarks."

But Allegra's holding a copy of her mother's obituary. Libba had sat at the dining room table that warm September evening of Frances's death and written it. It had seemed only natural, given Libba's lifetime of composing words. What hadn't seemed natural was her vanishing after the funeral. "Why did you disappear for nine months after Mother died?" Allegra asks.

"I could ask the same of you," Libba says. "We have a lot in common, you and me and Bertie the bomber."

Allegra reads the obituary. When and where Frances was born, and when and where she died. Allegra closes her eyes. *I'm sorry*, she thinks, *for the way I behaved*, as though the same mental telepathy that failed with her high school boyfriends and her husband might work on her dead mother. *I'm sorry*, she thinks when she reads Sasha's and Brent's names among the grandchildren. Food curdles in her stomach and, stripped of her liquid security blanket, Allegra has a sudden impulse to get something of her own back. "You left something out. You should have included yourself under 'survived by.'"

Libba folds the newspaper to the television schedule. "Are you always this contentious or only when you're sober? 'Girl falls under spell of traveling salesman,'" she reads. "*Picnic*. Now you give me one. Give me a one-sentence synopsis about whiskey school."

Allegra's head jerks up. "How did you know?"

The phone suddenly shrills and Allegra jumps for it, smiles at the familiar voice on the other end. "Hey, pal. Hey Brent-buddy," she says eagerly. "Where have you been all day? I've been trying to call." She listens. "Where?" Her eyes widen. "Oh. How long?" She nods. "Was it fun? I see. I bet you will. Be good. Can I speak to Sash?" Allegra turns to face the wall, murmurs softly into the receiver then listens, saying nothing.

Finally she hangs up the phone. "That was Dal."

"Was it."

"He's in . . . Birmingham." Allegra can't fix her thoughts around this fact: Dal has taken the children on a trip, away from her, without so much as telling, asking. "They're . . . visiting his mother." She stands. "Sasha and Brent." Her limbs feel unaccountably numb, heavy, as if she's moving through water. "Birmingham," she repeats, and moves unsteadily, touching objects about her as though blinded—the curved back of a chair, the warm parchment of a lampshade—anything that's a firmer reality than what she's just heard her children happily tell her, and her husband dispassionately inform her. "He's flying back day after tomorrow, but Sasha and Brent are—staying. For a while. Dal's . . . can he do that? Just because I . . ." Her eyes fill.

"What happens next."

As though her sight has been restored, and she must adjust to light again, Allegra's head swivels slowly in Libba's direction. "What?"

"Creative Writing 101: Always leave the reader asking what happens next."

Through her dazed misery Allegra stares at Libba. "I don't know." She cradles her face in her palms. "Do you know any plots about disgraced recovering functional alcoholics with questionable maternal instincts and floundering marriages?"

It's grown dark. Here and there a voice calls throughout Vade Mecum, a mother or youth leader calling someone home for the night. "Watch semicolons and dangling participles and nobody wants to read about dreams or dogs."

Allegra lifts her head, looks dully, disbelievingly, at Libba. "What?"

"Writing advice." A radio blares from the youth hostel four cabins down. "Sometimes the best thing a writer does in one day—sometimes the *only* thing a writer does all day that's worth anything, that's a single step forward, is to make one decision. To use a first-person voice, to move a scene. To keep a character in one place for a while. For a writer, one personal epiphany is progress enough."

Allegra looks at her bag, at the phone, at the sticky notes on chairs with speckled patinas from having spent too much time under open windows during thunderstorms. She thinks of Brent and Sasha four states away, the empty house in Charlotte, the walls that will close her in, alone. "Maybe I'll just . . . stay here until they . . ." she begins, "Maybe I'll just be . . . an elusive fugitive, too."

Libba runs her finger down stacked books on her table, chooses one, and hands it to Allegra. "Go to bed and do what I do, which to Frances's everlasting chagrin, you always have. Take a book instead of a drink."

Upstairs, Allegra puts on pajamas and brushes her teeth. Knees raised beneath the comforter, spine against the hard wooden headboard, she thinks of Sasha and Brent, wonders if Dal is saying their prayers, blessing people in the right order, the way she does. Even when she was woozy with drink she always said her children's prayers. She wonders if they are blessing her, too, and her lower lip trembles as she opens the book, a old, jacketless collection of John Updike stories.

"Write what you know about," Libba had said. Again Allegra thumbs the pages. The volume's unevenly cut pages resist fanning, fall open in chunks. The near-blank page of a story's conclusion startles her with its sudden emptiness, and the last sentence leaps out at Allegra, a single line that, years earlier, Libba had underlined. "'. . . I felt how hard the world was going to be to me hereafter.'" This is something Allegra knows about.

Downstairs, Libba stoops to retrieve the other slip of newsprint that had fallen from the pages of *Loose Ends*. The Help Wanted notice looks like nothing more than a yellowed ragged scrap. A scrap she's meant to laminate for almost forty years.

September 1, 1955

"John."

He inhaled sharply into the telephone.

"Is she home?"

For a long moment he said nothing. Then, "Libba."

"Don't hang up, John, please."

Finally he said, "She misses you."

"Can I speak to her?"

"She isn't here."

"Isn't there or isn't speaking to me?"

"It's her bridge night."

Libba looked out the window at umbrellas like mushroom caps on the wet city sidewalks that looked oily beneath the streetlights. She waited, straining to hear evidence that Frances was home, that John was lying.

"It's done, then," John said.

Libba waited. "I don't begin a story until I know how it's going to end."

"I see. And how are your . . . stories going?"

"Slowly. Badly."

"Not surprised."

Libba drew herself up. "I need a change of venue, to get out of New York. Away from . . . away. That's why I was calling. Vade Mecum will be beautiful soon, with the leaves. I was hoping I could go there."

"With Sam?"

"Sam's teaching in Ohio."

"Where?"

"It doesn't matter where. I don't do small talk well."

"Did you tell him?" His voice was taut. "That's not small talk, is it?"

"No. And no."

"So you'd be there alone, then."

"But that's what writing *is*, John. Alone. Unless Frances would come and visit."

"We have a two-year-old, Libba. Frances isn't quite as *free* as you are. Besides, we're thinking of moving South again, want to raise Alice there. I've got some feelers out. It's a busy time."

"That's fine. I understand. Dennis and Joan are coming for all of December. I've talked to him."

"'December'? How long were you planning on staying at Vade Mecum?"

"Until . . . I have a January deadline."

John was silent.

"Safe Haven is exactly what I need now."

"She's renamed it," he said abruptly.

"What?"

"It's Creek Cabin now."

"Oh. Please. Will you ask her? It's very . . . it would mean a lot to me."

"Go ahead and go. She won't care."

Stung, Libba said, "Thank you and tell Frances that I'll . . ." But she can't call. There wasn't a phone. "Tell Frances that I . . ."

"What, Libba?"

The dry impatience of his tone was cauterizing. "Nothing."

CHAPTER  8

"That's how a ruler rules a queen!'" Libba exclaims with King Arthur. Creek Cabin smells of boiled eggs and sounds like Richard Burton. Allegra and Edie take turns trying to hear Alice on the phone over *Camelot* blasting from the speakers.

"After I take Catherine and Frannie to camp today, I'm detouring through Vade Mecum to pick up what's mine," Alice says.

Allegra looks at the colored squares flagging Creek Cabin's furniture. Only pink and green are left, and some of those have already floated to the floor. The yellow notes are gone. Teddy had taken Edie's picks with him in a mini U-Haul, and the patchy absences make the remaining furnishings less pathetic than simply more eclectic.

"What about your plans, Edie?" Alice goes on. "Didn't Teddy come with you to pick up your stuff?"

"We're hiking Graybeard," says Allegra.

"Teddy's gone back," says Edie. "I brought a separate car."

"'Back'? 'Graybeard'? Who's 'we'? When?"

"Yesterday," says Edie.

Allegra disposes of Alice's staccato questions. "Back to Charleston. Yes, Graybeard. Libba, me, and Edie. In a few minutes."

"Wait."

"No," says Allegra, "she won't wait any longer."

"I mean *you* wait. I mean *why* can't she wait?"

Allegra shrugs, and leaves the phone and the remainder of the conversation to Edie, who says, "I'm going back tomorrow, and hiking Graybeard is . . . kind of a bon voyage."

"Bon voyage?" Alice repeats with amazement, thinking that if she herself is a double A-type personality, and Allegra is an AA—Alcoholics Anonymous—personality, Edie is a POLER personality: the path of least resistance.

"Dennis reminded us that nobody should hike alone."

"Who's Dennis?"

"Remember that doctor who took care of our summer earaches? Besides, who knows when we'll be at—" Edie almost says "Creek Cabin" and then amends her answer "—Vade Mecum again?"

"Why do Graybeard today of all days?" Alice presses. "It's July Fourth. The trail will be mobbed."

"Libba claims everyone will be at the Vade Mecum games," Edie says.

Olympics of a sort, retreat wide competitions, are always scheduled for July Fourth. Three-legged races and sack races, eggs on spoons and greasy balloon relays, softball and volleyball and ultimate Frisbee followed by a cookout, fireworks and general patriotic melee. "Libba says it's not officially summer until she hikes Graybeard," Edie goes on, "and that she's going come hell or high water."

"Oh, right," Alice says. "I forgot about She Who Must Be Obeyed."

Edie's looking forward to the day, and deflects her sister's criticism. "Maybe we'll see you later."

The hike to Graybeard and back is more than eight miles, a five-hour round-trip that covers a variety of terrains, beginning with the banal blacktop running parallel to Shoals Stream. They walk abreast until it narrows to a gravel cart road. With two hundred more yards the gravel becomes a footpath, open space leads into forest, and the climb begins in earnest.

For a mile or more the trail follows the creek, and the women walk silently through speckled gloom, dense woods that had seemed an enchanted forest when Allegra was a child, mossy and dripping, home to trolls and fairies. Roots hump from the earth like lion's paws, and the trees themselves hang over the trail as though they might speak threateningly to Allegra like Dorothy in *The Wizard of Oz*, or protectively enfold her like Snow White. But the same trees turned on Snow White at night, Allegra thinks. Dreams, all.

Walking sideways up the hills, as though invisible switchbacks are chalked on the trail, Edie drifts and lags. Going sideways is easier on the muscles, Edie knows, but she's always approached issues from the side, so differently from head-on Alice, who is likely making Frannie's and Catherine's bunks about now, sweet-talking the cabin counselors, and lining toiletries on wall studs that serve as shelves. Edie stubs a rotting log beside the path and it crumbles into soft splintery shreds, instant humus.

The trail has grown narrower, steeper, rockier, and they climb for half an hour. Knees lift and calves tauten, and breathing becomes panting with the ever-ascending trudge uphill. The path has rejoined Shoals Stream now, though it's less creek than rivulet.

"How much longer to the top?" Allegra asks.

"Mile or so."

As rivulet yields to bog the terrain grows temporarily flatter, spongy. They cross an old spring-fed lake bed dotted with shallow pools and muck. Weathered boards are laid across the marsh, and they tightrope the bowed, springy planks. In the open, it's grown warm, nearly hot.

"It clears out up ahead. Chop-chop." Singing, Libba sets off for drier land through wild grasses flattened by previous hikers. "Val de ri. Val de ra. Val de ra ha ha ha ha ha."

The landscape itself forecasts their nearness to the summit, for they're beyond the tree line now, and indeed, the royal blue directional stripes painted by Vade Mecum nature hut employees on tree trunks and stones have vanished, as though hikers should know there's no further need for markers. The trail straightens across a low broad rise through scrubby undergrowth, shrubs dense as an English hedgerow with intertwining branches. Libba and Edie and Allegra cross a field so crowned with boulders that the path is wide enough for only a single foot, then break suddenly onto a slanting plateau of granite crusted with lichen and pillowy chartreuse moss. The ledge is scored with seams of white quartz. Narrow crevices hold pockets of water, and compact juniper bushes with silvery blue berries have found purchase in wider fissures.

In exhausted satisfaction the women fall silent, savoring the tranquility, the view around and above and below them, one hundred eighty degrees of horizon. This is what they've come for; this is why the strenuous climb is worth it. The outcropping overlooks sooty distant mountains, gradations of blues and greens, the entire Vade Mecum valley. High harmless clouds ripple the skies, a chinchilla fringe against azure.

Cross-legged on slaty boulders, they halve sandwiches and pass chunks of cheese. The sunlight is strong in the shadeless open, and Allegra unbuttons her shirt and lies back, her bra a white glare across her chest.

"The last time I hiked Graybeard was with Frances," Libba says. Neither Allegra nor Edie are surprised; wasn't it always the two of them? "Frances got so hot she took off her shorts and hiked in her underwear."

"I don't believe it."

"Then don't." Libba pulls the red bandanna from her hair, which springs out in a peppery nimbus.

"I want your hair," Edie says from behind the pale drape of her straight, no-style cut somewhere between shag and grunge that only emphasizes her waifishness.

"Frances had straight hair until she gave birth," Libba says.

Her mother's Em Sem senior picture flashes through Edie's mind as she considers the implication. Maybe childbirth would alter the texture of *her* hair. Maybe that was a good enough reason to have a baby. It's as good a time as any; Edie sorts the appropriate words. "I think . . . I think Daddy's seeing someone." She can't manage to utter the term *dating*. "Just a hunch," she adds hurriedly, as if afraid she might recant.

Allegra stops chewing. "A woman?"

"When I went by to see him two weeks ago he introduced me to someone named Bree."

"*Klute*," Libba says.

"Jane Fonda," Allegra says.

Edie has no idea what they're talking about. "She owns a garden store."

"Concrete frogs," Allegra guesses.

"Topiary bunnies," Libba says.

"They seemed to know each other pretty well." Edie speaks slowly, testing her own reaction to a situation she's been examining, turning over in her mind. Until she'd said it aloud, her father's involvement with a woman other than her mother hadn't seemed definite or even possible. But having stated it, Edie now realizes it's not only possible, but probable, and true. "And then there's his new condo. I had a feeling a woman had been there. Cuisinart, copper pans. Even the food in the cabinets, twirly pastas and balsamic vinegar and—"

Allegra's jokey manner is replaced with astonishment. "Daddy seeing someone? What was she like?"

"She's . . ." Edie pictures Bree: dark-eyed and straight-spined, an athletic build at odds with her chirpy, feminine demeanor. "Alice's age."

"*Alice's* age? With a sixty-five-year-old man?"

Edie crumples tinfoil into a ball, relieved that her sister is aghast. She herself had only felt concerned, and anxious, and . . . jealous?

Allegra scrambles to a stand. "Let's go. From here it's all downhill."

"*Au contraire*," Libba says. "The toughest part of a story is wrapping things up, the denouement."

The descent is quieter than the climb, silent but for the sound of twigs crackling underfoot. Breathing is easier, inaudible. Eventually the burble of Shoals Stream signals they're nearing Vade Mecum. Sap oozes down pine trunks like melting candle wax, and the path is prettily strewn with rust-colored fallen needles that conceal roots gnarled across the trail like skeleton fingers.

Perhaps she trips on one such root. Perhaps the fallen needles are slick. Perhaps it's that she's winded, or that she's holding a nosegay of galax and hasn't the extra hand to balance herself. Whatever the reason, Libba stumbles, and not until she curses sharply do Edie and Allegra realize she's sitting on the path, eyes shut to the pain, rubbing her ankle.

"What happened?"

"Tripped. Nothing that a soak and one of Frances's worn-out Ace bandages in the bathroom cabinet won't take care of." She rises unsteadily, grimaces. "Go on, go on. We're almost there." She'll have none of their offers of a shoulder or hand, will only allow them to take her backpack. But by the time they reach the blacktop Libba's face is drawn, and she collapses heavily on the wicker settee of the back porch.

Upstairs, where she's already writing a letter to Frannie, Alice hears the back door open and close, hears Allegra say, "Face it, someone needs to look at that. That Dr. What's-his-face. Chandler."

"Don't bother Dennis."

"Is it swelling?" Edie says.

Libba waves away the ministrations. "If you need to do something useful, put on a record, *My Fair Lady*. Bring me my sweater and the newspaper so I can check on Bertie's unknown whereabouts."

Upstairs, where Alice takes her old place at the open window, the voices rise from the porch as clearly as if she were sitting there. She flicks carcasses of long-dead June bugs scattered like pecans on the sill inside the screen, the glittery green of their carapaces grown brown and crisp. She thinks of Libba and what she knows, and turns for the stairs. From the landing she can see Libba on the porch in her Henry Higgins cardigan, silverygray cashmere that matches her eyes. The same sweater, Alice knows and remembers, that Libba was wearing the night Frances died. The night she and Edie and Allegra went home to eat dinner, leaving Libba by Frances's side. No different then than it had been all their lives, Libba and Frances together.

"... *her smiles, her frowns, her ups, her downs,*" Henry Higgins agonizes with bewildered and belated realization. Violins play mournfully, questioningly, and Alice knows this is where Eliza Doolittle returns to him. The ending to *My Fair Lady* has always bothered her, not knowing if Henry and Eliza married, or stayed together, or precisely what happened. Bothered her the way something undecided and unknown has bothered Alice, eaten at her since that warm September night Frances died. Nagged Alice throughout Divvy Day and the first-after holidays, through hours she's spent lying across her bed, grieving, weeping.

"Put the galax in water," Libba says.

Alice halts beside a framed picture of their mother on the staircase wall and thinks of the pall of galax leaves, no larger than a powder room face towel, that had covered her mother's cremation urn. She thinks of the obituary Libba wrote, and Libba's absence for the past nine months, and unresolved endings, and, wholly certain of one specific conclusion, walks onto the porch.

"Alice," Edie says, "when did you get here?"

Alice ignores her sister. "You were the last one to see her alive."

"Alice?" Allegra asks, confused. Libba shakes open the paper.

"It was you. While we were at home. You—you killed her."

Edie sinks to the hearth, twines one leg around the other, the body language of pain. Rooted, riveted, Allegra's eyes flash toward Libba, her idol, her—

"Did you. Didn't you. Our mother."

The record ends and through the speakers the needle ticks repetitively around the ungrooved vinyl.

Libba massages her ankle. "Yes," she says. "I let her go."

With a swift *stit*, a pocket seam tears beneath the weight of Edie's fists.

"How?" Alice demands.

"Is that really what you want to know?"

"Yes."

"Painlessly."

"How."

Shouts thinned by distance reach them from the playing fields near Vade Mecum's entrance. "I closed her nostrils with one hand and covered her mouth with the other."

Allegra trembles, clasps her elbows in her hands to stop the shaking.

"Ask me why," Libba says.

But Edie can't ask anything. Her breath is shorter than it was during eight miles of hiking.

"Frances had earned her death. I did it for her."

"*To* her, you mean," Allegra chokes. "You did it *to* her, not *for* her."

"She'd have died so much earlier, except that we couldn't stand to lose her. Isn't that true?"

Edie fights to listen, to concentrate. Claps hands to her eyes, fighting off the vision of Libba's hands upon her mother's face. Fighting off the vision of the wraith in the hospital bed, not speaking, barely breathing, but struggling nevertheless, beneath—a body must surely physically struggle against—Allegra slams the back door, heads for the creek, with Edie on her heels.

"Looks like I'm the only one left to take you to the doctor," Alice says brusquely to Libba. "Let's go."

February 7, 1957

Libba tacked the photograph to her bulletin board, a colorful splotch against the black-and-white clippings. Her own face beside Alice's four-year-old one grinned from the kitchen table at the Wilsons' Raleigh home. The glossy dustjacket of *Small Doses* was eradicated by the flashbulb's glare, and Alice's chubby fists, clutching the squished results of Frances's failed attempt at something called a red velvet cake, looked bloody. They'd been belatedly celebrating both the publication of Libba's second book and Allegra's first birthday, but the younger honoree had been fast asleep.

Libba turned back to her typewriter, positioned her fingers on the keys. But nothing came, not a single *the*. Her eyes fell on the slender strip of newsprint she'd scissored from the paper's want ads.

GOVERNESS it read in bold, followed by a job description that would have been laughable if it weren't so deadly credible, so piercingly ironic. Libba glanced at her watch, hesitated, then picked up the phone.

"Hello, you," Frances answered, laughing. "I knew it would be you. ESP."

"How are things?"

"'Things'?" Frances laughed again. "You're always preaching about being specific in writing, not using generalities. Everything and every*one* is fine. Did you get the birthday picture?"

"Already on my bulletin board." Libba picked up the column of small print. "Do you ever read the classifieds?"

"Honey, I don't even have time to read the headlines. And that includes at eleven o'clock at night. I have to hang up because Allegra's a little croupy."

"Shouldn't you call the doctor?"

"Libba," Frances said, "I'm in charge here. You do what you do best and I'll do what I do best. The water's gotten hot in the shower, so we're going to stand in the steam. You write."

Libba put down the phone, picked up the Help Wanted advertisement, and read it again.

GOVERNESS
Position includes primary duties
of supervision, education and
habilitation of two children,
three and one years old, with
sole responsibility during regular
work hours, evening and some
additional; must be available as
needed, if parents are required
to work at night. Secondary
responsibilities include management
of large household, meal preparation,

household tasks and preparation
at anytime for showing of house.
Weekday begins when children
get up or parents, leave for work,
based on parents need. Primary
child care duties: dressing, feeding all meals and snacks, morning and afternoon activities, assist with bath and bedtime (as
needed), assist mother after
birth of additional children, take
children to medical appointments, develop daily learning
activities, take children to church,
teach Bible stories, prayers and Bible
songs, attend church with family
during work hours. Household
management includes running errands,
budgeting household funds, reporting
repairs and maintenance, maintaining
family car (servicing), purchase
groceries, household supplies, etc.
Requirements: must be literate, have
two years, full-time child care experience
equivalent to Child Development
Associate, good driving record with
no serious infractions, no criminal
record/child abuse/neglect. 8am–6pm,

40 hrs/wk. 10 hrs overtime, $150 per week. All résumés must include social security number. Apply at nearest Job Service office or send résumé to 151 Bergen St, Brooklyn NY 11217.

CHAPTER 9

"Fine," Libba says to Alice, "You're the perfect person to escort me." She hobbles through the cottage and out to the car.

With a single movement Alice sweeps the front seat free of road trip detritus—fast-food wrappers, magazines, loose cassettes. "Even nonwriters recognize irony when we see it. You took my mother away from me all my life, and you took her away from me at the end of her life, too " She jams the key into the ignition and roars the engine into life.

Libba rolls down the window. "I've always thought the corollary of long strong grudges is long strong love. The greater the anger, the greater the love. True?"

"Save the motherly advice for Allegra. She's the one who currently needs it." Alice steers up the hill. "Even though you have no maternal credentials."

"You've never seen my résumé."

"Does it say 'Playing God'?" In her anger Alice overshoots the Chandler driveway. She flings an arm over the back seat and reverses. "It's immoral!"

"'Immoral,'" Libba repeats wonderingly, and grasps the door

handle. "You're your mother's child in a hundred ways."

Alice doesn't hear her. "You appropriated our lives fictionally and you appropriated her life literally. How does it feel to kill somebody? How does it feel to watch someone die? Will we read about it in the next book you've come up here to . . . to—regurgitate? Or maybe you'd call what you did 'a blessing.'" Warmed to her tirade, Alice answers herself. "But no, that would be coming close to compassion, something Libba Charles wouldn't recognize served up on a platter."

"*Au contraire.* Compassion is the reason I did what I did."

"Like putting down a horse? Of course *you'd* say that. But how about Mother? How about the person who had no part in the decision?"

"Righteous indignation feels good, doesn't it, Alice? Feels good just to *say* it, those jaw-grinding teeth-gnashing syllables."

For a long moment Alice's rapid breathing, the exhaustion of anger, is the only sound in the car. "It wasn't your choice to make." Alice's stare is riveting. "She was *our* mother. To you she was only a friend, a straight man, a second-in-command at that. What's a friend? Everybody has friends."

Libba grabs the seat belt stretched across Alice's chest, tightening it, forcing her to look into the icy eyes. "Don't you even dare." She releases it and it snaps back, a slick-threaded slingshot.

The street is unnaturally deserted in the gathering dusk. Most Vade Mecum residents are at the holiday games and the cookout. The fireworks will begin as soon as it's night proper, early enough for toddlers to enjoy yet not past their bedtime. Alice knows; she's taken her own toddlers. Years ago, so long ago. They'd clung to her then, afraid of the whizzing Roman candles. "How can you live with yourself?"

"I couldn't live otherwise."

"Mother was always there for you. And at the end you weren't there for her."

"That's just it: I was."

Alice is beyond caring what she says. Within the hour she's leaving for home. "You're a killer, pure and simple." Suddenly, shockingly, the horn blares in the silence and Alice jumps, startled; her tensed fingers have inadvertently pressed it.

The screen door of the cottage opens and a man emerges to inspect the source of the noise. Hands in the pockets of his khakis, he peers curiously at a car he doesn't recognize.

"I don't need a doctor," Libba says. "Let's leave." As Dennis Chandler approaches the driver's window Libba cranes her head from her own.

"Libba," he says. "Are you—"

She cuts him off. "I didn't want to come, but they insisted."

He brings his palm down they length of his jaw. "How very wise of them."

Alice gets out of the car. "Dr. Chandler, I'm—"

"I know who you are, Alice." He shakes her hand tightly though his eyes are soft.

Libba opens the car door and displays her foot like a child with a splinter. "It's my ankle. Or maybe my Achilles heel."

Though the physician's expression is wary, his appraisal is less of

Libba's foot than her face as he takes her arm, guides her up the four steps, directs her to a chair and sits on a hassock before her. "You're looking jaunty this evening."

"Terrific." She tugs at the bandanna around her neck, pushes the knot higher. "I always wanted to be jaunty."

"What were you doing?"

"Hiking Graybeard."

His eyebrows lift. "Hot day like this?"

"Nobody can tell Libba anything," Alice puts in, taking in the cabin's interior. It's no more up-to-date than Creek Cabin, but the furnishings are masculine, clearly the residence of a man long widowed. A television so elderly that it sprouts antenna rods topped with foil sits on a braided oval rug in blues and reds. The furniture is heavy and substantial, upholstered in cracked leather with dull brass nailheads. On two wagon-wheel end-tables are a pair of dusty lamps whose shades are tea-stained with age.

"I'm well aware of that," he answers Alice, and reaching for Libba's foot, probes and kneads the flesh. From a coffee table he brushes away beige specks, the dusty filigreed droppings of Queen Anne's lace blossoms arranged in a small hand-thrown vase, to gently place Libba's foot upon it.

Alice stares at the vase's deep royal glaze. She has one like it. Her mother had bought a dozen such vases from a local potter one summer, kept them among other items in what she referred to as her "inventory closet" at Creek Cabin, thoughtful gifts at the ready for a sick friend, a hostess present, a last-minute birthday remembrance.

Dennis takes Libba's pulse, pull down the skin beneath her eyes. When his hands drop to her abdomen, she pushes him away. "Tell me to take some aspirin and let's be done with it."

"Libba."

Doctor and patient lock eyes in a staredown. "Criminy, Dennis, not now. Your timing's all wrong. Don't you know anything about story arcs and revelations?" Her tone is simultaneously teasing and pleading.

He leans his head into a wide palm. "I know medicine."

She raps her knuckles against his knee. "Don't tell other people your problems. Eighty percent don't care and the other twenty per cent are glad."

He looks toward an open window, and the last haze of sunset gilds the pale strands of his eyebrows. The brief shrieking zip of a bottle rocket and the staccato snapping of a firecracker string puncture the twilight's stillness.

"And on a national holiday, for chrisssakes," Libba adds.

A look passes between them. "Libba . . ." he says again in a tone that is both sorrowful command and gentle reprimand. He stands and turns to Alice. "You and your sisters should know that—"

Instantly Libba rises, pushing him aside. "Oh no, that's *my* line. If anyone's going to do the telling, I will." Dennis takes her elbow, but she lifts it away and crosses her arms on her chest. "I have a pathological process, Alice. Isn't that what you called it, Dennis? Or," she gestures to a bookshelf, "did I get that out of one of the books you gave me?"

"Not enough," he answers, as though the conversation belongs only to the pair of them, as though Alice isn't even present.

"I have ad-eno-car-cin-oma. Commonly known as cancer." She turns back to Dennis. "Satisfied?"

Unsure what she's heard, Alice's countenance is blank and uncomprehending. Then a range of expressions crosses her face: puzzlement, surprise. And doubt. She suspects some kind of sick joke on Libba's part. "I don't—"

"The bad kind," Libba says, then asks, "or is there a good kind?"

Dennis Chandler's arms dangle at his sides. "You are the most stubborn person I've ever known."

"You have—" Alice begins. Stun replaces stun. Her mouth has gone dry.

"Of course, some people say '*my* cancer,'" Libba says, putting a finger to her cheek in dramatic self-debate, "as though cancer is a pet. Others say '*thuh* cancer,' but I don't like that, sounds like 'She's out with *thuh high blood*' or 'She's down with *thuh pneumonia.*'" Ignoring Alice's shocked expression, Libba plays out her riff. "And you can always say just '*cancer,*' but that's kind of nonspecific and writers need to avoid generalities, so I'm still formulating the exact term. Meanwhile, let's just leave it at pancreatic. That specific enough?"

Alice's knee involuntarily jerks as if she's been standing too long. As if those numerous trips up the hills of Camp Rockglen, laden with laundry baskets and duffels and trunks and tennis rackets and sleeping bags have only now begun to affect her. But it's Libba. Libba, who is standing there before her. Libba, who has cancer.

"It's probably the *perfect* example of irony, but then again irony, has always been one of those literary tropes that's the devil to define."

Alice looks to Dennis for confirmation, or explanation, or help. He simply nods.

"No one knows but the good doctor here," Libba says. "Retired, but still bound by physician-patient confidentiality. Dennis is friend first, as I was to Frances. As Frances was to me. Which you attach little significance to." She takes Dennis's hand and squeezes it affectionately, then turns back to Alice. "I'm of the don't-tell-me-till-I'm-eaten-up-with-it school of thought. Which is convenient, since I am."

Libba shoves her swollen foot into her shoe, leaving the laces untied. "Confession *is* good for what ails you. I'll just shuffle back down the hill to Creek Cabin by myself, so I can begin shuffling off my mortal coil." She taps Dennis on the shoulder, pauses at the door. "Alice was wondering what it feels like to watch someone die. You tell her."

August 4, 1962

Frances twined one wiry stem around the small nosegay of glossy circular leaves she'd found growing beside Shoals Stream on their climb up Graybeard. "Know what this is? Galax. Lasts forever in water. I've tried to get it to root, but it only grows in its natural habitat." She glanced at Libba. "My book club is dying for you to come talk to us."

"Ugh."

"So is my Arts and Antiques group."

"Double ugh."

Frances put the galax cluster in a natural vase formed by pooled rainwater in a narrow crevasse. "It's against the law to pick galax."

"Your illegalities are safe with me. All of them."

Frances reached for her sandwich. "I'd arrange a special date, get three or four clubs to meet together on one day. There would probably be fifty people, a good crowd."

"I'm like galax. Girl gatherings aren't my natural habitat. You know that, too."

Frances was undeterred. "They buy books, they give books as presents. People ask me about you all the time. They're curious, interested. They want to know—" She broke off.

"Know what?"

"Beth Thomas asked me how I put up with you."

Libba pressed her lips together. "Did you bite back? I thought I'd taught you that during Em Sem days."

Frances laughed, relieved. "Why should I bite back when I have you to do it for me?"

Libba didn't laugh. She plicked her fingernail across the rough rock surface. "But that's just it. You should have bitten back on my behalf."

"You're right. I'm sorry."

"Never mind. Tell Beth Thomas I'm an incorrigible introverted codger."

"You aren't an introvert and codgers are male."

"A curmudgeon, then. A cute curmudgeon."

"You can't be cute and curmudgeonly."

"Crusty, then. I'd make a good crusty curmudgeon."

"I'm going to keep asking you to come."

"Asking's not against the law." Libba stood. "Ready to go? Don't forget your galax. Shall we have a verse of 'Edelweiss'?"

March 14, 1964

Nudging her baby fingertip between swollen nipple and the raised blister on the baby's upper lip, Frances carefully, gently broke the nursing vacuum. "Ouch."

"Does it hurt?" Libba asked. "More than it hurts not to?"

Frances nodded. "I wish I'd nursed Alice. I was still listening to my mother then." Frances looked over the warm head at her shoulder to Libba. "But it's the good kind of hurt. Like the good kind of tired."

"Have the girls come yet?"

"John's bringing them tonight."

"They won't like it that I had the first viewing."

"Stop. They're in school. Besides, Alice is mortified that I'm breast-feeding." She tugged the pink flannel blanket more tightly around the baby. "Does this blanket look familiar?"

"I thought I recognized it."

"I had John bring it from home. Oh, Libba, I saved everything, hoping even while I convinced myself there was no reason to hope. Sometimes I'd be in the attic for Christmas decorations or the suitcases, and there they'd be, the receiving blankets and crib sheets and daygowns. I'd sit down right in the halfdark, push aside the dusty magazine stacks and pretend like the baby things needed refolding just to touch them." She wrinkled her nose, lowered her voice with confession. "Sometimes I brought them downstairs to launder them, as if . . . The rattles, the mobile, the little brush-and-comb set, all stacked in the bassinet like . . . like a store display. I couldn't let them go. And now—" She looked at Libba with shining eyes. "She's the real thing, a miracle."

"I'll bet you say that about all the babies."

"But this one *is*. She wasn't supposed to happen."

Libba reached to touch Frances's hand. "I know."

Frances pressed her lips to the soft fuzzy scalp. "I love bald-headed babies. She'll be blonde."

"That's good," Libba teased. "No questions about paternity."

Frances tensed with some inaudible alarm. "Libba," she said suddenly. "My parents are ancient. John's one of four. If anything ever happens to me, to us, I want you to, will you—look after them."

"Surely there's someone more capable, more . . . *maternal*, than me. I don't know anything about children. They don't come with instructions."

"You know everything. Even when you weren't there, I've told you about the children. Whatever else they need to know, you're the one to tell them."

"Can I start small, by holding the miracle?" She carefully clasped the bundle to her chest. "Do you have any idea, baby girl, what you've put your mother through? Do you have any idea what it's like to lie still for eight months while Libba Charles bothers you, baby Edith with golden hair?" She touched her index finger to the newborn's pink palm and watched as the fingers closed instinctively around it. "Rounds out the poetic trio."

"Not Edith. Edie."

"Why not Peedie, while we're at it?" The baby had fallen asleep. "Here. I'm not skilled at cooing and I can feel your fingers itching."

Frances reached for the bundle. "Why Peedie?"

"P. D. Precious darling."

Frances covered the baby with kisses. "Miracle, yes, but no more precious than the other two."

CHAPTER 10

Jeopardy! squawks before Allegra and Edie, collected but red-eyed. "What is Caspian," a contestant says.

Alice slams the front door. "Where's Libba?"

"Taking a bath. She . . ." Edie switches on a lamp and looks at Alice as though like always, she'll tell her what to do next. "She hardly spoke to us and no wonder. What do we do now? Now that we know about what she did to Mother?"

"She's . . ." Alice falters, unable to convey what she knows; unable to condense the brief conversation with Dr. Chandler after Libba left. "*Backache,*" he'd said. "*General fluey feel. Weight loss, which most people view as a gift, so they don't suspect a problem. Mixed symptoms people pay no attention to, and damnably difficult to diagnose.*" The abdominal pain that had eventually driven her to a doctor. "*Usually mistaken for any number of other conditions: ulcer, gallstones.*" The upper and lower GI series, the blocked bile duct, the CAT scan biopsy in May, not two months ago. The facts were minimal, and incontrovertible. "*Her cancer is beyond malignant,*" he'd concluded grimly, "*it's malevolent.*" How to couch it, how to phrase it—"Libba's sick."

"She ought to die of shame," Allegra says.

Alice's mouth falls open.

"You knew all along, didn't you, Alice. It just made sense. Libba, and Mother. Alone together. Alone together at the end." Allegra rifles through the wooden bowl where car keys accumulate. "What are we doing here?" she asks dully of no one. "Why did I stay?"

"Dr. Chandler says, I mean Libba said . . ." Alice twines her fingers. "She has cancer."

The studio audience applauds the day's champion, his four-thousand dollar winnings.

"Pancreatic."

Allegra clicks off the television so quickly that Edie's gasp is audible.

"She wasn't going to tell us," Alice says. "He forced her to."

"No." Allegra squeezes her eyes shut. "Not again. Not possible. Not fair."

"What did he, she—" Edie gropes in bewilderment and disbelief "—say?"

"Just that . . . we ought to know."

"'Ought to know'?" Allegra's mimic is less laugh than sputter.

"There aren't any early detection methods and people think it's gas or arthritis. Not until ultrasound picks up a mass. And then it's too late."

"Cancer," Edie says. "Again. Not even a year since—"

The door to Libba's bedroom opens. "Nasty shock, isn't it?" she says. "An interviewer once asked me if I wasn't afraid that some fictional situation I'd concocted might actually happen, come true." She smiles slightly. "But I never wrote about cancer. It seemed too *predictable* a disease, too easy." She smooths the ridged fabric of her chenille robe over her hips. "Why couldn't I contract something literature-worthy, something dramatic like Lou Gehrig's or Parkinson's or AIDS. I mean, *cancer*. How banal." She looks at the three women. "Though I suppose this may be dramatic enough before it's over. You should take notes, Allegra, might be something you can use."

Horrified by the black humor, still trying to process the information, the sisters can only stare at her, the thick hair waving back from the yellow shawl collar, the bare feet, the gray eyes fierce in the beautiful face they've admired, envied, resented. "It's too much," she says, "just too much to digest, I know. Revelations unfold gradually for characters in books. Reality is so much sloppier than fiction. I prefer outlines, never write a word until I know how a story's going to end."

"Libba!" Edie exclaims, teetering between awe-struck and anguish. "Why didn't you tell us?"

"Don't be appalled," Libba says. "People who act appalled make me want to appall them more."

"How long have you known?" Allegra says. "Why were you keeping it secret?"

"Whatever my secrets, they're *mine*," Libba says; then, mildly, "Or wasn't your drinking done in secret?" She twirls a pencil on her table, a compass point gone haywire. "Have you ever noticed how people with cancer are fine until it's public knowledge?"

"What?" Edie's hands flutter, as though waving away the ad-lib, Libba's calm non-sequitur.

"Think about it. Not until everyone else knows someone has cancer does the victim actually get sick. When the treatments starts she gets that cancer *look*. Cancer has a definite *appearance*. Besides, why tell you?"

"So we could go into action. Get specialists. Take you to—"

Libba interrupts. "And have you stay at Vade Mecum out of pity? You can't help me. I'm going to die. No," she says, pointing a finger at Allegra, "don't be coy with your readers. Am dying. What John would call a 'done deal.'"

"What about surgery? And radiation and chemotherapy and—"

"And all the weapons in the cancer arsenal?" Libba says. She sits on the small day bed under the slant of the stairs, a quilt-covered single mattress where each sister has snugged herself on some rainy afternoon as a child, burrowing in its cozy crowded intimacy. "Because it's too late and too big and too far gone and whatever other *too* you want to attach. The mortality rate for pancreatic cancer is ninety-nine percent and I'll be one of those statistics, too." Her voice is neutral. "By the time you—I—find out you've got it—" She interrupts herself. "What *is* the verb, anyway, do you *catch* cancer, or *contract* it or *develop* it or what? Remind me to ask Dennis—it's too late. What I have is virulent. No, that word goes with plague."

Allegra nearly shrieks. "Enough with the word dissection!"

"Exactly," Libba answers. "I have no intention of wasting my last months learning a new language. Medicines and treatments and diagnoses and tumor types and surgery options, no thanks." She plumps one of the needlepoint pillows lined across the knot-holed wall beside the day bed. "This is very simple. Pancreatic cancer is the deadliest cancer. Or 'pancan,' as it's affectionately termed by those of us in the club. Not that I know any other members, or care to."

"But there's no hospital anywhere for thirty miles. Barely a doctor. Why stay at Creek Cabin?"

"Where else, the rest home out on the interstate?" Libba retorts. Alice and Allegra and Edie know the institution she refers to, have shuddered as they passed the long brick box of a building not twenty yards from four lanes of highway. Behind a chain-link fence-aged residents sit in webbed lawn chairs on a concrete slab, their only view the traffic hurtling past.

"But you could have the finest facilities and the most advanced therapies and the best care somewhere else."

"And support groups and biofeedback and homeopathy? I don't think you understood me," Libba says. "ETD is eight weeks." Her words are slow, deliberate. "I. Have. Until. September." Her glance sweeps the room. "Creek Cabin is my last stop, like Granny's furniture and Frances's afghan."

"Don't you have any hope?"

"Know what the two necessary ingredients are in any story?" Libba asks. "Surprise but inevitability."

"Is that an answer?"

"It's enough of an answer for me."

"But you don't know what strides they're making. Experimental drugs and new treatments and—"

Libba's voice rises with the first instance of vehemence. "Don't know? *Don't know?* I know Mitomycin and Adriamycin and

Pancrease and Phyzyme and Restoril and Sinequan. Who do you think you're talking to? I'm a reader. There're more books about cancer than there are about diets and celebrities put together! Shelf after shelf of volumes, reams of paper devoted to the subject. Any keystroke on any computer in any library under Cancer with a capital C will give you a hundred titles. All of which only convinced me of something that I knew already: nonfiction is dull."

She picks up the thread of her monologue, rolls her eyes. "Though I must say, the down and dirty, the physical description, is skimpy. In my business that's known as 'cheating the reader.' But there's plenty on courage and dignity and any other synonym you can come up with. All you have to do is reach back to *Death, Be Not Proud*—which I remember you weeping through for summer reading, Allegra." Libba snaps her fingers. "Author?"

"Who is John Gunther," Allegra says quietly.

"Good."

"So where are you?" Edie asks.

"What do you mean, where am I?"

"In the . . . process."

"Process?" Libba parrots. "Which part of the 'process' are you referring to? The endless doctor appointments? The vomiting, the raw throat, the hair loss, the constipation, the diarrhea, the high fevers, or the mouth sores?" She ticks them off on her fingers, begins with a new hand. "Or, let's see, the weakness, the hospital stays, the needles and tubes and bedpans? *That* process? No, you must mean being tethered to an oxygen tank, or a chemo porta-cath." She cocks her head. "Or do you mean little nothings such as no driving, bathing, dressing. Or do you mean a refrigerator full of waxy suppositories like bullets," she snaps, "and having to slit them open sideways before insertion because you aren't sure where the medicine is? Not only illness, but every humiliation that accompanies it, indignities the books overlook that I just happen to remember from the not-too-distant past. From Frances. My friend. *Your mother.* That process?"

Libba crosses her arms over her chest. Not protectively, but as though daring the sisters to contradict her. Which, vividly and starkly confronted with the frail specter of their mother, they cannot.

"You have to fight it," Allegra says. "You have to be determined. I'll force you to."

"You and whose army? I cut my teeth on the word determined. Why aren't you at alkie association? That's determined." Libba goes on relentlessly, fixing a gaze on each sister in turn. "Maybe I just assumed you'd grasp this fact: I am not seeking treatment of any kind. Is that clear? Nada, none, zero, zilch."

"But don't you want to live?" Edie asks as simply as a six-year-old.

"Do I want to live?" Libba smiles, but her voice is tremulous. "More than anything. But I won't. And I won't go down the same path as your mother. That will not be me. I want to know the last time I drink a milkshake. That's what I need to *know.*

"And there's only one way to do that. Look at me because I'm only going to say this once. I have declined any and all 'aggressive therapy.' After I die it will be said— you can say—she steadfastly refused all treatment.' I lived through Frances's suffering and that . . . nonlife she endured, and I will not do that or be that. I do not choose to submit myself to that kind of saving."

The sisters know that kind of saving. They remember the first tumor and the first surgery, the year of outpatient therapy, the grinding life of chemotherapy. They still see the person transformed from vibrant mother and wife and woman to exhausted victim of malignant illness and its treatment. They see her bald, pale, frail. See her confused, desiccated, incontinent. They see her captive to tubing and monitors, prisoner to technology and the disease technology battled. They see twitching, see the arms, even the finger pads, bruised by needles, her veins like cords. They remember twenty-nine months of their mother living with terminal illness, and can't contradict this woman, their mother's friend.

Edie leans forward, forehead to knees. Alice turns, stares out the front door screen at darkness but for bits of illumination laced by trees, lights winking from cottages throughout the hillsides. The fireworks, and the holiday, are over.

Libba strokes her cheek. "It's oddly comforting, knowing you're going to die. Knowing I'll never turn into one of those doddering old ladies who obsess about sleep and food."

"So you're going to do *nothing*," Alice says.

"Poor Alice," Libba says, "who can't conceive of doing nothing." Her eyes grow soft. "What I plan to do is not 'nothing.'" She stands, straightens the quilt over the cot. "When you're waiting to get a revision back from the editor, dying—pardon the pun—to know if this version will pass muster, you just have to go on with things as though the manuscript didn't exist. Go on with writing the next book, or taking your walks, or going to movies or seeing friends, any ordinary thing, and forget about the manuscript. Forget that someone's scrutinizing and judging it. You go crazy if you build your days around the waiting. Cancer— *my* cancer—is the same way. Live out what days are left to me in doctors' offices, hospital halls, and a haze of side effects? No, thank you. Nor am I going to be downharded and depresst and een a speen."

"*Gigi*," Edie says softly, recognizing the lyric. *Downhearted and depressed and in a spin.*

"Correct again. And I don't want anyone around me who is. No grand gestures, no histrionics. I'm going to just live. Quality, not quantity, if you'll excuse a cliché. Everything I need to be content is here at Creek Cabin, including the soundtrack of *Gigi*. Can't you understand? I want to be *aware*. This is my last Fourth of July. This is the last time I'll hike Graybeard. This is the last time I'll pick galax. This is the last time I'll shave my legs." She looks up, her eyes brimming. "Frances always said nothing in the world felt better than shaved legs on clean sheets. Frances . . ." Libba rakes her hair back from her forehead. Silvery streaks glint in the upslant of the table lamp. "But for Dennis, I wouldn't have told you at all, and now I find myself in the disadvantaged position of having to seek your mercy. To keep a secret." Another wry smile. "I wanted to wait until I started showing, like being pregnant." She strikes through *Hike Graybeard* on a list that lies on the cluttered card table, then pauses at the door to her room, the only bedroom door lacking a number nailed to its frame, a remnant of Creek Cabin's history. "Tomorrow morning I will get up," she says briskly. "I will eat breakfast and read the newspaper to find out what my old outlaw Bertie the Bomber is up to. Then we'll help Alice load up to go back to Raleigh. Leave a light on."

Later, by the light left burning, Allegra hovers about the notebooks and pads, the files and clippings. There's nothing there, no hint of what Libba has known about herself, what she's living with, what she's facing. No, what I face too, Allegra thinks, because, *Look after Libba,* her mother had said; *Promise.* Her mother whom Libba had not killed, but only helped to die.

Allegra picks up the Dictaphone, a recorder no larger than a deck of cards. She presses the Rewind button, then Play. With no catch of stutter, no emotion, no fear, Libba's voice speaks from the black box. *"What's better?"* She asks herself. *"Being senile and physically able, or cognizant and physically worthless?"* The tone is curious, not self-pitying. *"What's worse?"*

Later still, by the same light, Alice tries to finish the letter she'd been writing that afternoon—could it have been only that afternoon, a few hours earlier?— when her sisters and Libba returned from Graybeard. To make sure her children will have mail as soon as possible, Alice always sends letters the same day they arrive at camp. She says little—to have fun, that she misses them already—a mother's usual words. But this time she adds a P. S. Because regardless of what Libba said, Alice does owe her something: *Look after Libba.*

When you write, the P.S. reads, *send your letters to Creek Cabin. This is where I'll be.*

April 1, 1966

Frances's voice was breathy with happiness. "It's one of those weeks you never want to end, when all's right with the world. John got an account he's been coveting. Alice got her Gold award in scouting. Allegra petitioned her principal to allow the sixth grade to make a creative writing magazine. Edie plays so hard she's exhausted every night, and just listening to her talk to herself in the bathtub makes me smile. And yesterday I nailed Allegra for April Fool's—when I woke her up I told her it had snowed during the night and school had been called off. You should have seen her spring out of that bed for the blinds! I swear, I get her every year!" Frances laughed. "Libba?" she says into the silence. "You there? I've got to run."

"But we've hardly had a chance to talk."

"I need to get Alice to her piano lesson and Allegra to get a haircut."

"Can't John take them so we can visit?"

Frances laughed again. "You've no idea what being a mother is like."

The line crackles with long-distance static. "No," Libba slowly answered, "for a very good reason."

Frances's laughter, her litany of achievements and pleasant obligations, died.

Into the strained silence Libba spoke, her tone low and pained. "That was . . . beneath me. Sometimes I feel left out of your lives. Cruelty is even worse than self-pity."

"No, it was my fault. I was thoughtless, with that hymn to busyness. How smug I sounded."

"I *do* want to know about them. You can't spend your life censoring what you tell me. We'd grow to hate each other. And we can't ever, ever let that happen. Promise."

"Promise."

"Besides, I *need* all those details," Libba finally laughed. "What else would I write about? Now go on. Take them to—wherever. Drive them, feed them, bathe them. Then call me back and tell me everything. Always."

June 17, 1966

Frances picked up her tray, looked helplessly around the crowded cafeteria, and waited for Libba, grinning at her friend's baffled, nervous expression. "You wanted to know what writing conferences and teaching seminars are like. Here it is. There's no substitute for experience."

"Did I ask to come? Remind me."

Libba scooped ice into a glass. "I've forgotten how many times you've asked."

"It's like grade school all over again, thinking 'Who will I sit with?'"

"Oh no, it's worse. In grade school you know everyone's going home to sleep in their own beds. People aren't here just for the *learning experience*," Libba drawled. "They're here for the fol-de-rol and fooling around. A Shriner's convention for *artistes*."

Frances whimpered and Libba laughed.

They navigated through throngs of people, bearded, blue-jeaned men leaning forward over tables in earnest conversation, jabbing a pencil for emphasis. Women with shapeless sweaters or tight T-shirts wore serious, steely expressions on their faces as they leafed through spiral notebooks and bound manuscripts. "Actually it's more like high school," Libba said, "where everyone's out to impress. The same old leaders and losers, sycophants and suckups. And the smokers in the parking lot who might beat you up at the slightest provocation."

Frances set down her tray and gave a cautious smile to the person beside her, unsure what gender, with the short curly hair, glasses, and oversized overalls, her tablemate was. "I'm Frances." She'd already learned that last names were of no importance.

"WASPy name."

Frances stared.

"I'm Pat."

"WASPy name," Libba echoed, as unfazed as Frances had been speechless.

The girl shrugged. "Androgenous. You poet or proser?"

"I'm just auditing," Frances said.

Libba rescued her. "She's with me. I'm teaching."

Across the table, a man with auburn hair and a square chin pulled a mimeo from a folder. Frances watched while Libba, who apparently knew exactly what she was doing, reached over her tray. "That one," she said, pointing to the list of teachers, "with the four titles in the biographical sketch."

Convinced, the man spooned sugar into coffee and introduced himself. "Troy."

Frances looked at the distinctly orange meat-and-noodle casserole on her plate. "Pass the salt, please."

Troy snickered. "'Please.' You Southerners slay me."

Frances started. "We're in *Tennessee*," she whispered to Libba, and when she'd somehow gotten through another meal, said, "I'd rather starve. How do you do this twice a year?"

"When all else fails, I think of the money. And so should you. But I know what you mean. Which is why now and then I open the closet and look at my clothes and say to myself: these are mine. I am me."

Talking to John on the hall pay phone after the evening reading, Frances leaned against the wall, feeling naked without a booth surrounding her. "The place reeks of incense. And you should see the posters on the walls in the room Libba and I share! Rock groups I've never heard of. And people are constantly peeling off and pairing off, disappearing together."

John groaned.

"Libba's looking after me."

"Where is she?"

"Having a beer with some of her students."

"Come home. Please?"

"No one says 'please' here, honey."

"What do they say?"

"They say, 'Chekhov is a master,'" Frances replied, and laughed. Being wanted shored up her confidence. "How is everyone? What did you do for dinner? Edie's in the bath? Hang up this minute, John, go check on her! Kiss them, love you, 'bye."

Dawn was just breaking through the dusty institutional shutters when the dorm room door slowly opened and Libba crept into the room. "Where have you been all night?" Frances asked.

"Um," Libba fell on her bed, reached up and idly picked at a piece of tape holding down a poster of the Jefferson Airplane. "Not much like our Em Sem room, is it? No oranges. No extra chest. No dressing in the closet." She giggled.

"Where have you *been*?"

"With the book reviewer who was at the reading last night. Did you see him? Kind of graying at the temples, suede patches on the blazer elbows, sort of a . . . unibrow. Named Russell."

"But you're not finished with a book. What do you need a book reviewer for?"

Libba casually rolled over to her side, propped her head on a palm. "Think hard."

"I can't think. I'm too busy being anxious."

"About what?"

"That I'm not smart as other people here. That I'm not . . . *groovy* as other people here. That I'm not sleeping with someone here. That

I'm married. That I don't have a bona fide job. I want to go home. I miss my girls. And John. They need me. What was I thinking? My baby Peedie, thinking her mommy's abandoned her—"

"There are only two days left in the conference. You can make it."

Frances threw back the thin blue blanket, the coarse rented sheets. "It's not whether I can. It's whether I want to." She opened the closet and pulled her clothes from among the peasant shirts and tie-dyed garments and fringed shawls belonging to the room's absent owner. "These are mine. I am me. Tell Pat and Troy and Russell and Chekhov I'm neither a poet nor a proser. Tell them I'm just a mother."

CHAPTER 11

They've been commanded, charged, dictated to, directed. "Issue-skirting, hushed tones, and worried glances are *verboten*," Libba said in her best *Cabaret* accent. "And don't bother Dennis." She craned her neck around the card table leg where she'd stooped to fish through one of her cartons. "Yes, as a matter of fact I *do* know what you're thinking."

But they had nevertheless; called on Dr. Chandler like a trio of delegates, emissaries. Expressed dismay, mystification.

"We're adults," he said. "I'm not going to pretend. This is a fatal illness and Libba wasn't hedging. She's dying."

We know that, they'd said impatiently. But what about cancer-treating drugs at the very least?

He placed a toolbox on the railing and picked out a hammer. "Sometimes the side effects are caused as much by anxiety as the toxicity of the drugs. Pancreatic cancer is an orphan cancer, besides. It's so lethal that research money goes to treatable cancers. What you'll do is called palliative care, providing comfort, not a cure. I'm here for house calls and pain control." He regarded the three sisters sternly. "She's at a plateau of feeling well, but she'll go downhill, very soon. She'll crash."

But this staunch refusal of treatment. Hadn't studies proved that people who deny they have a disease survive longer than those who surrender to it? Edie protested.

He tacked a rectangle of new screen, bright silver against the older, rusted panel of his front door. "Your mother's friend doesn't fall into either of those categories. She's not in denial. And she's not depressed."

"Satisfied?" Libba asked when they returned.

"This is not an if/then situation," Libba had said. "This is a so/ now situation."

And it's sadly amazing how easily the days arrange themselves; amazing how simple it is to fill a day with everyday excursions, small diversions. One or two or three together they walk, take out a paddle boat, throw pebbles over the spillway dam, toss crumbs to the swans, keep up with Bertie-the-Bomber's unknown whereabouts, read, listen to musicals, check the silvered wall of mailboxes in the basement of the rock-walled Great Hall. "Was that all the mail?" Edie asks the plump Vade Mecum postmistress. She knows her father's condo doesn't have an answering machine; she's already tried.

And it's as though with the telling, Libba's allowed herself to deteriorate, to grow actively ill. They can't help but notice the small signs: increasing fatigue, decreasing appetite. She accompanies Edie into Stockton to buy groceries on what has become a near-daily trip to try to satisfy her changeable food cravings, or to more often, lack of.

While Libba browses, Edie lingers by the deli counter where a black Lab lies in his usual place on the floor, unfazed by the proximity of roasts and chops behind the slanted glass, a carnivore's paradise. She kneels to stroke the animal, fur soft and thick as mink. He's huge, gorgeous, docile. A pair of sneakers comes to rest at the dog's back and she looks up at their owner, finds herself smiling at the same young clerk who's waited on her before. The same young clerk who drives an orange jeep and offers rides to damsels in roadside distress.

"Your dog?" He nods. "What's his name?" But she knows the dog's name; Cobey is as much a store staple in the deli as bread.

"Killer."

Edie laughs. "I guess we'd all be this content if someone fed us Vienna sausages."

"I don't know what you're talking about," he says innocently.

Edie laughs again, because she's seen him do it.

"Ready, Edie?" Libba calls from the aisle.

Edie stands. "So long, Cobey. So long, Clark-the-clerk."

Clark-the-clerk adjusts his baseball cap. "See you later, Edie."

"What's Teddy up to in Charleston?" Libba asks on the way back to the cottage. "He's been pretty amenable to your staying up here indefinitely."

Edie isn't sure what Libba's suggesting, and she isn't sure what "amenable" means, but she's sure that she doesn't like the direction of the conversation. "Don't forget the sliced turkey," Libba says when they reach Creek Cabin, and hands her the butcher-paper package.

They don't need turkey. Edie had lingered with Cobey and Clark so long that she'd felt obligated to buy something.

"Octopus!" a child shrieks, and falls backward on the black mesh, trying to trip anyone in the radius of her wildly waving arms and legs. Alice and Libba and Allegra are sitting on a flat expanse of lawn below the tennis courts, watching a dozen children fling themselves upon four trampolines.

"My children have always wanted a trampoline," Alice says. Her friend Margaret gave her children a trampoline as a collective gift from Santa. Fingers numb with cold, Margaret's husband Steve wrestled the contraption together by car headlights, the legs and tarp and forty-four separate springs, on a frigid Christmas Eve midnight. Though morning dawned with a temperature of twenty-nine degrees, weather hadn't stopped the children from jumping in their pajamas until they collapsed from exhaustion, not cold.

"Why don't you get them one?" Allegra says.

"Too dangerous."

"Oh, I forgot," Allegra says. "I'm the family risk-taker."

The trampolines are flush with the ground, bolted to railroad ties outlining hollow pits deep enough for the bounce of heavier bodies. They'd been installed in the spring, donated by a Vade Mecum family in honor of their oldest son, a gymnast. Alice has never driven past the tramps and seen them vacant, ever; a child is always jumping.

"Body slam!" a boy calls and fellow jumpers instantly crash on their backs.

The ebony elastic glistens like obsidian. Alice watches the flying bodies, listens to the gleeful cries and commands and exclamations. Though she's never jumped on a trampoline, she understands why they're never empty. That lack of gravity, loss of control, is appealing. "Double jump!" a child of indeterminate sex—Prince Valiant haircut and shorts—yells from the farthest tramp.

Alice points to the child she's been watching. "She looks like Frannie, don't you think?"

"Have you heard from them?"

"It's about time for another letter. They're required to write every other day during rest hour."

"Only you would send children to a camp where even the rest periods are orchestrated," Allegra says. She knows what she's doing, transferring meanness and blame to her sister because she's been lax with her AA attendance; because the occasional letter from Brent leaves gaps of information and innocently assaults her with fear of the unknown. *Dear Mom, It's hot here. Nannie takes us to the pool. We might go to a day camp.* We? Allegra wonders. Camp?

"Crocodile!" comes a scream from the tramps.

"The whole camp is going to Sliding Rock this week," Alice says. Sliding Rock is a famous expanse of water-slick boulder popular with tourists and numerous summer camps in the area. Thirty feet across and sixty feet of incline, the rock sheet covered with moving water is a nature-made sliding board. At its base is a pool to safely splash into, though the current is strong enough that a thick length of rope spans the stream to catch the incautious. Sliders, though, are generally less incautious than too stunned to swim to safety: the deep water is frigid, so numbingly cold that it snatches away your breath, paralyzes your lungs.

"I forget about Sliding Rock," Libba says. "We should go watch sometime."

Allegra shudders. "I haven't been to Sliding Rock in twenty years. It's the only time in my life I actually thought my heart had stopped."

"They're games!" Libba suddenly says "They're shouting out names of trampoline games." She takes a pad and miniature pen from her pocket and begins writing.

"What are you—" Alice asks.

"Hush, ideas are coming too fast."

Alice and Allegra look at each other, then at Libba, silently taken aback that she thinks she may use—may have time to use—whatever it is she's scribbling.

In even two weeks' time her strength has diminished and her skin has sallowed with jaundice. Pain is evident in the grimaces that pull her lips into a tight slash, leave her perspiring.

"I haven't done anything constructive today," Libba says. There was no need to add *haven't felt well enough to do anything today*; Alice and Allegra and Edie know that. So that they find themselves idly wandering the single street that constitutes Stockton's downtown one afternoon.

The plate glass of a recently refurbished store is covered with posters and placards of smiling faces; folks beaming from hammocks and boats and bicycles. TO YOUR HEALTH reads the sign on the door, and a single bell tinkles primly when they open it.

Frosted with florescence, hundreds of bottles and containers, an alphabet of vitamins, sit neatly and precisely row upon row. Barberry, wild licorice, and yellow jasmine compete with other herbal supplements. CDs hawk mood music of waves and waterfalls and wind.

"Hello!" a young woman chirps. With bright eyes, long brown hair gripped in three toothed clips, water bottle fastened to a belt, she's the picture of health herself. "How are you ladies this morning?"

The array of products is astounding. Alice picks up a bottle labeled "Happy Camper," and opens the cap. The white tablets inside look like aspirin.

"Happy Camper is one of our most popular products," the clerk says. "Attitude adjuster vitamins. Give you the sense you had as a child that all's right with the world. Remember that feeling?"

"Vaguely," Libba says, and sniffs the stuff.

The clerk, however, smells a possible purchase. "Also comes in liquid form."

"Do you have any saltpeter?" Allegra asks. There'd been a perpetual but unproven rumor that the cafeteria food at DeWitt Academy was laced with saltpeter to suppress sexual urges.

The clerk frowns. "I'm not familiar with that."

Libba bends, pretending to study the hieroglyphics of a label. "Snake Oil."

The sisters whirl. "Where?"

"Made you look," Libba says.

Undaunted, the clerk walks to a full skeleton dangling from a hook.

"Kind of a depressing marketing strategy, isn't it?" Alice says.

The girl grins, picks up a bony hand and waves its fingers at them. "Who, Sammy?"

"I used to know a Sammy," Libba says. She stoops at the bony crotch. "How do you know it's a he?"

"You silly gals." The clerk shakes her head. "Seriously though, you're all so slender, but thinness translates into osteoporosis. Now's the time to get started on calcium supplements." She runs her fingers lovingly down a display of bottles with cheery yellow labels. "Now there's calcium carbonate and calcium citrate. Calcium carbonate contains more calcium but doesn't dissolve as easily. Calcium citrate is more acidic so your body absorbs more of it though there's less pure calcium. Of course, spinach and leafy greens are high in calcium too. And naturally you should be cutting down on salt. After all," she says with a knowing, conspiratorial smile, "at your age calcium is an issue, isn't it?"

Libba stands as erect as her pain will allow. "The issue is cancer, actually," she says brightly. "Pancreatic. The symptoms are just *so* similar to arthritis and flu and other pesky little ailments. What a nuisance!" She smiles mechanically, her tone a dead-on mimic of the perky clerk's. "Growing all hidden and cozy and deep inside you until it's just too gosh darn late and what does it matter anyway because by then you only have a month or two left and it's going to kill you one way or the other, and so what do you say, have any vitamins for that? I've got a real problem here—want to feel?—with bloating, and maybe something for the diarrhea and jaundice and the exhaustion, and oh, the pain, I forgot the pain, anything in here for that? Dying is *such* a drag."

The woman stares.

"By the way," Libba asks, following the sisters out the door, "do you work on commission?"

"Libba—" Edie begins.

"What was *that?*" Allegra says.

"That was raging against dying of the light. I'll say this for death as a fait accompli: it makes a lot of prescriptive advice irrelevant. I won't have to spend any of my sleepless nights being sleepless over my calcium intake."

"Can we just go home?" Alice says.

But Libba is already entering a shop featuring apparel guaranteed to fill every outdoor need from lumberjack to farmer. A headless mannequin in the corner wears a battered cowboy hat, and the limp arms of a plain gray sweatshirt dangle from the torso. Libba passes flannel shirts, steel-toed boots, rain slickers. She stops before shelves of denim, runs fingers down the blue stacks, flips size labels, and chooses one. "It's time."

"Time for what?"

She enters a cubicle with a sliding curtain that looks more like a shower stall than a changing closet. A minute later she appears wearing bib overalls—baggy, buckling, big-legged farmer jeans. "Time for a cancer uniform." She stands before a mirror. "Remember staying in your pajamas all day when you were sick as a child? In the morning it felt cozy. But by supper, it felt dirty."

Admiration for Libba's ability to remember and capture a particular, trivial sensation she believed she alone had experienced, overcomes Allegra's speechlessness. "You remember everything."

"It's an affliction, not a talent." She pulls at the loose bib, slides her fingers beneath the straps. "I'm not checking out in a hospital gown and I'm not checking out in a bathrobe either. I intend to die *dressed*."

"Do they fit?" Alice finally asks.

"What's to fit?" Libba says. She rips off the tag and hands it to a salesman. "I'll wear these home." He beams; another satisfied customer.

"Can we stop by the post office?" Edie asks as they cross beneath the Vade Mecum arch.

"Hope springs eternal," Libba says as she and Alice and Allegra stay in the idling car, watching Edie sprint for the basement mailroom.

Alice has no idea what Libba's talking about. "Who's the letter for?" she asks her youngest sister, thinking it might be from Frannie or Catherine.

"It's from Daddy." Edie rips into the envelope. She recognizes the handwriting, the stationery, the letterhead. Her eyes travel slowly from the page to their faces. "He's coming to Vade Mecum for a night. With Bree."

Only Libba is unsurprised. "Ingenious," she says, "the way the story moves forward by the choice of whom to tell what and when. That's a narrative structure I've never considered."

"August fifth," Edie says. "Nine days."

May 22, 1967

"Edie was fretful for a while, but she's asleep now," the elderly woman said.

Frances took a bill from her wallet. "Thanks, Emma. I'll call again soon." She saw the sitter to the front door and went directly to her bedroom.

Libba, though, kicked off her shoes and squinted into the bright glare of the open refrigerator. "How do you exist on that girl food, luncheon dainties? Chicken salad, tomato aspic." She lifted the lid of a plastic container, peeled back the foil on another. "Were you saving this leftover meatloaf for dinner?" She searched for a knife. "I take it silence means no. What about that Sally Whitcomb's get-up? Between the scarf and the shoes and the necklace she was wearing three hundred dollars' worth of accessories. And what's with that Mary Franklin, Frankfurt, Frank-something? Anyone with hair that long after forty years old is bound to be tough."

She opened the breadbox. "Haven't you talked your girls into eating whole wheat bread? This white stuff will kill you." She folded a heel around a chunk of cold meatloaf and called out, "What time do Alice and Allegra get home from school?"

Still dressed in her luncheon clothes, Frances appeared in the doorway.

"There you are," Libba said. She ripped a paper towel from the roll, pointed to the counter and winked, "You missed a spot here next to the sink. Don't let it happen again. Remember the time John wrote 'Dust me' on the dining room table? You let him off too easy for that crime."

"I suppose it's never occurred to you," Frances said quietly, "that the reason for the 'girl food' was that no one wanted to be in the kitchen cooking something hot. They didn't want to miss a word you said because they'd been looking forward to this meeting for so long."

Libba wiped the counter. "And was I worth it? Sit down and let's dissect, like always."

Frances didn't move from the doorway. "We don't need to dissect because you already have."

"Have what?"

"Dissected us."

Libba swivelled. "I talked about writing."

"That you planned to write a satire about a wife who broke her neck coming down the attic stairs carrying the Christmas decorations? Is that about writing?"

"I was being funny."

Frances's lips narrowed. "And that crack about country club housewives."

"I said I'd happily be one except that the pay was terrible."

"Did you hear anyone laughing at that either? And then you

talked about your fondness for—what was it you called them—
'domestic details.' 'I count on you for my stories,' you said. To learn
how many ways to use a can of cream of mushroom soup, or the
best trick to take a lipstick stain out of a linen napkin."

"They laughed when I suggested using sock feet as a dust mop."

"They didn't laugh when you suggested having a party where
everyone came dressed as their Suppressed Desire. Or holding an
hors d'oeuvres Olympics."

"I was teasing."

"That wasn't teasing. That was savage."

"*Au contraire*. They were just offhand comments. What are
your other programs about—bonsai gardening? Silver polishing?
Thanksgiving centerpieces?"

"*Au contraire*," Frances said in bitter imitation. "They were
extremely specific comments. Most of which I'd told you, such as
the scene you mentioned about the husband who always brushed his
hair after sex. What's the matter, the paucity of your own imagina-
tion unable to come up with something better for your novels?"

"Nicely put."

"Jan Dawson told me that about her husband, and she was
there."

"Is it that Jan Dawson heard about herself or that you were afraid
at being caught gossiping about her to me?"

"You and I weren't gossiping. We were telling funny stories."

"And what was this today?"

"This was between me and my . . ." Frances hesitated.

"Your what?"

"My friends."

"Really? And what does that make me?"

Silence hung thick as smoke.

"I know being married and having children has its trivial and laughable aspects," Frances said. "You think we don't realize that, question ourselves? Being a wife and mother is all about ambivalence. But so is religion. So is politics. And so is belonging to a country club. We aren't out there secure and smug about what we do or who we are. A person can subscribe to something and not be wholly part of it."

"Something like a friendship?" Libba slapped her palm on the table.

Frances didn't flinch. "Maybe. Or maybe something like a *child*." She opened the folding doors to the laundry closet, reached into the dryer and pulled handfuls of loose socks from its well. "For years I've wanted you to come speak to us. For years I've wanted my friends to understand how interesting and different you are. And you finally agreed to come. And then ruined it."

"You need those women's approval? Aren't you too old for that? Those are the type of people who put invitations on their refrigerator so everyone can see how many parties they're invited to. They have discussions in the car about the way to get somewhere with the fewest turns and stoplights."

"So what?"

"Your mother did that, Frances!"

"That's not the point."

Libba folds her arms over her chest. "What is the point? That I divulged someone's postcoital grooming habits?"

"The point is how little you think of me."

"I wasn't talking about you. I was talking about them. I sat with four women whose entire lunch discussion was which church service they should go to to accommodate their children's Sunday social schedule. Including a brief interlude on whether the cleaners ruin cotton sheets if you have them finished. What the hell are 'finished' sheets, Frances? One of your *friends* told me she'd gotten the chicken salad recipe from a chain letter, and that she'd gone to three different grocery stores looking for ripe avocados. I politely compliment the flower arrangement and the hostess said she picked the, the—" Libba splutters. "Some damn flower name to look best with her dining room wallpaper."

Frances's lips stretched tautly over her teeth. "But I'm them. They're me."

"You are *not*."

"You didn't just belittle them. You belittled me. There's a huge difference between me cutting down my children, and someone else cutting them. I'm allowed to humorously deride someone I love, but no one else has that privilege. There's a difference between anecdote and attack."

"Frances, this is what those women are fretting over—ripe avocadoes and wrinkled sheets and interior decorating!"

"And what are you fretting over, Libba? What are your all-important decisions? Are your frets more valid than theirs, your plots and cover art and who, oh dear, oh dear—" Frances widened her eyes with mock drama— "will write a jacket blurb?"

"That's a cheap shot."

"Cheap shot? This, from the undisputed master of zingers. Do you know how hard it is to find a daytime babysitter? Has it ever occurred to you that Sally Whitcomb and the others look forward to putting on decent clothes for a change? Is that a crime? Have you ever thought they were dressing up in honor of you?"

"Please. They didn't dress up for me, they dressed up for each other. Have you listened to yourselves lately? You're still complimenting each other on what you're wearing! Come on, Frances, what are you doing with those women?"

Frances abruptly dropped the socks on the kitchen table. Her tone was deadly quiet. "You're adorably incorrigible, aren't you. You're so clever, such a bohemian, so liberal, so intellectually above it all. But you know what? You have nothing to show for it, nothing. Paper with words that no one remembers after it's on the shelf. Who are you to insinuate that what those women do all day—what *I* do all day—is in some way—in any way—inferior to what you do?"

Libba flattened her palms against the tabletop, leaned forward on her elbows and sing-songed, "So maybe I did do a little ribbing, a little goading. Maybe I'm just trying to prod you out of the wifely rut, the duty dance. You've paid your domestic dues."

Frances folded herself into a chair at the table, crossed her arms among the limp shapes of tube socks, white anklets with colored pom-poms at the heels. "And yours."

"I chose not to join that particular club."

"Choice? Whose? Yours? Mine? Hers?" Frances rose, strode across the slick floor, features twisted with pain and fury. "What you can't understand you have to disdain and deride. You're facing down a midlife full of regrets about the life you've chosen. But that's the pretty side of it. The ugly side of it is you taking potshots at people whose life you envy. Because you're jealous."

"Really. When did you get your psychotherapy degree? You might take a minute to consider who's really jealous here. You have plenty of time to do it while you're eating bon-bons and tuna noodle casserole and screwing your man in his gray flannel suit in your little kingdom of hausfrau convention!"

Frances reeled backward as if struck, blindly reaching behind her for the counter.

Libba covered her eyes. "Oh, God, Frances—"

A wheezed rumble signaled the school bus's approach outside and a pitched wail rose from the nursery.

"Get out of here." Frances pulled a pitcher of Kool-Aid from the refrigerator and a box of Arrowroot biscuits from the pantry. "Go away. My domestic dues needs her diaper changed and my other two ruts will be here any minute." She rattled an ice tray.

"'My,' 'my', 'my.'" Libba mimicked, and rose. "Only as long as I want it that way."

Frances whirled. "Is this some kind of sick blackmail? Are you threatening me?" But Libba had vanished.

Allegra slammed her books on the table. "Guess what, my poem was picked to be read at the eighth-grade graduation. I need some bell bottoms. Alice has bell bottoms."

Alice looked at the shoes on the kitchen linoleum. She knew her mother's shoes by heart, and those weren't her mother's. "Is Libba still here?"

"Hurry and eat your snack," Frances said, trying to control the shaking in her voice, the trembling fingers that handed glasses to her children. "You have your last baton lesson this afternoon and I have to change Edie before we go."

June 16, 1967

"Don't answer that," Frances told Alice when the phone rang.

"Mom, it's rung a hundred times since we got to Creek Cabin."

"Someone's trying to sell me something I don't want. Besides, you want to get to camp in time to have the best bunk, don't you?"

"What are you going to do while we're at camp?" Allegra said.

"Libba will be here, won't she," Alice said. "She's *always* here."

"Libba's busy writing a book. And she has lots of speaking engagements."

"Won't you be lonely without us?"

Frances knelt and gave Allegra a quick, swift hug. "I'm never lonely at Creek Cabin. I'll be thinking about you riding horses and canoeing. And writing you letters. And I'll have Edie to keep me company—and busy! And Daddy will come on the weekends."

The phone rang again. "Let it ring," Frances commanded. "Allegra, pick up Edie's diaper bag. It's time to go."

CHAPTER *12*

Creek Cabin smells rich, wintry with the aroma of simmering chicken and raisins and apples. They'd decided on curry, along with rice, asparagus, and strawberry shortcake. "When Mom has a dinner party at home, she, like, puts a big masking tape X across the bathroom door so no one can go in and get it dirty," Frannie says.

Libba's eyebrows rise with mirth when Alice flushes at her daughter's words, but Frannie continues chattering. "My counselor talked about herself like she wasn't, like, there. She'd say, 'Leigh wants everyone to go to rec swim today,' or like 'Don't bother Leigh during rest period.'"

"That's called referring to yourself in the third person," Libba says from the couch.

"Huh?" Frannie says.

"I'll give you five dollars if you can go for an hour without saying 'like,'" Libba challenges her. Frannie regards Libba with interest. Money talks, especially when you've been sequestered at camp, deprived of four weeks' allowance, and the mall.

"Did you use the glow sticks I sent?" Alice asks.

"Yeah," Frannie says. "I broke them apart and we scattered the stuff all over the cabin, like green dust."

Alice sighs. It wasn't what she'd had in mind when she bought them.

Catherine comes indoors from the front porch where she's been sitting on the railing, legs wound around the supports, watching people walk down the blacktop in front of Creek Cabin on their way to meetings, sing-alongs, Bible studies, the forms of fellowship Vade Mecum offer those who care to participate. Adults rounded with age or inactivity or both take long strides to balance themselves on the slope of the hill, a clumsy gait that accentuates extra weight. "Religion makes people fat," Catherine pronounces. "Someone waved to me and said 'Gimme a high five for Christ.' It sucks." She rolls her weary, nine-year-old eyes.

"On the other hand, if you're going to overdose on something, it might as well be God," Libba says. Now Catherine, too, looks at Libba with interest.

Alice watches the old Libba-lure at work. There's not a child alive who doesn't delight in being addressed as an adult, or thrill at hearing an adult speak of topics generally whispered.

"My counselor sprinkled baby powder in our sheets so it was soft and cool when we got in our bunks, Frannie says.

"You're lucky," Catherine says. "*My* counselor kept a chart, and every night she'd ask, 'Did you take a shower today?' 'Did you wash your hair today?' and the *worst*: 'Did you have a bowel movement today?' It was like, heinous."

Libba laughs. "You can't make this stuff up."

Alice remembers how nursery school teachers stood on the sidewalk during morning carpool just to see what Frannie would be wearing. After two sons Alice had finally gotten her girl, and clear into second grade she'd outfitted Frannie in smocked dresses and organdy pinafores. For what? Alice wonders, regarding the Daisy Duke short shorts and slack-necked T-shirt boasting the slogan USED. ABUSED. CONFUSED. that Catherine is wearing. "There was a child in Frannie's cabin that never got a single letter," Alice says softly. "Not one. Frannie said they asked her every day for a week and then stopped asking so she wouldn't have to answer. If I'd known, I'd have written her a letter myself."

Allegra watches Alice's children, too, their temporary presence at Creek Cabin intensifying the absence of her own. She misses Sasha and Brent with visceral pain, and tries to divert the hurt with wondering whether there isn't something illegal in their prolonged stay with their grandmother. She wonders too how she'll ever get through this evening, thinking of the letter upstairs, the fat alphabet lettering of Brent's printing, a determined slant to the words as though he's yearning for cursive.

"Those people are wearing hats that say, like, I'm over forty and this is my new Patagonia cap," Frannie says.

"Hush," Alice says.

"Eggs?" Edie murmurs, who wonders how she's going to get through the evening as well. Not far away, Edie thinks, her father and his girlfriend—date? lady friend? Aren't dates and lady friends supposed to be twenty and look like Audrey Hepburn or Grace Kelly, both of whom are dead, like her mother?—are checking into The Mountaineer Motel, Stockton's only inn. "Don't riced eggs go with curry?" Edie asks to avoid wondering whether her father and Bree are staying in separate rooms.

"Too late," Allegra says. "They'll be here soon." "They" are Dennis, John, and Bree Michaelove. Allegra opens the drawers beneath the counter where an ice bucket, the bowl of lemon slices, and bottles of wine and liquor are neatly aligned, begging to be opened, poured, consumed. She's missing another meeting tonight. It's not her fault that Vade Mecum's AA meetings are only scheduled at night. Besides, she has a good excuse—the party. And Brent's letter. "Where are the beaters?"

"Don't whip the cream yet, it won't hold," Alice says.

"Kitchen Nazi," Allegra says. "I bet you put silverware in the dishwasher basket with the eating end up, too. And use one of those pasta measures with holes."

Alice doesn't, but she'd think nothing of calling a restaurant to ask a chef whether a cake with cream cheese frosting should be refrigerated. She also folds Luke and Thomas's T-shirts exactly how they go into the washing machine to teach her sons to put their clothing in the hamper right side out. With a take-charge, full-throttle efficiency, Alice sprinkles raw rice kernels into salt shakers whose contents are gummed with humidity. "I just want everything to be right," she says.

They've shaken scatter rugs and doormats, bought candles and shaved the ends to fit into candlesticks, turned upholstered cushions so the less worn sides face outward, rinsed dust from unused glasses, made extra ice and stored the cubes in freezer bags, plucked weeds springing among the dusty miller and begonia in the porch planters, fashioned place cards for the table just as Frances used to, and arranged flowers around the cottage, including the bathroom. Alice is doing everything right, and she's doing it for her mother. Yet even as she's worked, even as the ghost of her mother sits upon her shoulder, Alice is haunted by pointlessness, a sense of futility. *What's it for?* she's wondered. *Why bother?* A day from now her preparations will mean nothing. Guests gone, food digested, nothing left but the cleanup. She won't have changed the world in the most minuscule fashion.

"Remember," Libba says from the sofa, "nary a word." She's wearing her overalls spruced up with a different bandanna in gold and royal blue. "My demise is unmentionable," she'd warned the three sisters earlier, while Frannie and Catherine were at Shoals Stream.

"Can you spare us the gallows humor?"

"I prefer to think of it as mordant. No, 'trenchant' is better."

"A vocabulary lesson?" Allegra says. "Now?"

"Yes, literary to the end."

Though Libba hasn't been up to contributing much, she selected the music. And here at twilight the instrumental opening of "Some Enchanted Evening" flows softly through the cottage, and perhaps the evening will be just that. The flurry of preparations has suddenly ceased and Creek Cabin is lovely. Glasses shine, silverware gleams, the colorful chopped condiments glisten in crockery bowls, pink cosmos droop prettily from the mantel. The only movement is the slight flicker of votive flames on the porch sills. Just, Alice thinks, as her mother used to do, and closes her eyes.

"There's nothing quite like a house just before a party," Libba remarks.

"You and Blanche Dubois," Allegra says.

"Wrong crazy Southern female," Libba says. "You mean Amanda Wingfield. *The Glass Menagerie.*" Outside, a car crunches on the driveway's gravel. "And there's our gentleman caller."

Edie's first in her father's arms, pressed to the silvered temples of his narrow face and the broad shoulders from his days as a competitive college swimmer. He's slender, almost bony, still hitching his pants a little comically high on his hips, wearing a tie as always, though it's not one she's seen before, a French blue with bright yellow circles, casual and splashy. Edie steps back and watches her older sisters take their hugs and deliver their kisses. Until the woman standing to one side, holding an oversized handled shopping bag sprouting hunter-green tissue, introduces herself. "I'm Bree Michaelove."

A young forty with streaky blond hair and a pointed chin, Bree Michaelove is wearing taupe linen pants and a sleeveless shirt with large irregular buttons that look as though they're made of bone. Wedged burlap espadrilles tie at her ankles.

"Short for Briana?" Allegra asks, and Edie thinks of her fuchsia plastic pony.

"Brenda."

They stare politely at Bree Michaelove, whose bare shoulders seem to twinkle with her slightest shift in posture. When she turns her head to smile at Alice, Edie notices gold dust at the corner of Bree's eyes as well. Edie's seen the small pots of sparkle gel at cosmetic counters. She thought the product was for teenagers and actresses. She had no idea people actually *used* it.

John Wilson's eyes scan the room, light on the sofa, and Libba. "Here she is," he grins, and sits down beside her, clasping her knee. "Hello, irresistible force," he says, and holds her tightly round the shoulders. "Where have you been keeping yourself?"

Libba puts a palm to his cheek. "After thirty years of having me under your feet I thought you deserved some time off for good behavior."

"Forty," he grins, "but who's counting? How have you been? Still abhorring and ignoring the status quo?"

"Trying. But I've lost my immoveable object. There's no one to push."

"I know," he says. "Push against me."

Libba rolls her forehead back and forth across his chest, reaches to hug him. They smile faintly, ruefully, sharing their own code.

The sisters watch, confounded anew by the obvious intimacy between this man and the woman whom he must surely—*surely*—resent. How could he not? But he introduces Libba to Bree, adding only a soft, oblique explanation: "We go back."

The front door opens again and Dennis Chandler enters, casually dressed in a polo shirt. The two men hesitate a moment, lift hands to shake, then drop them, laughing, and embrace each other. Again the sisters stare, prepared for awkwardness, not this . . . ease, this immediate connection.

"Did you make a lanyard?" John asks his granddaughters, "like your mother?"

"We made candles," Frannie answers. "What can you use lanyards for? Nothing."

Flashlights, Alice thinks, *skate keys*. She moves to the kitchen, checks that the rice has begun steaming, that the curry is warming, that the erratic breeze doesn't extinguish the porch votives; the familiar role of hostess her mother performed. Frannie and Catherine have disappeared upstairs, given permission to call their father to find out if their class lists have arrived in the mail. For the two-hour drive from Camp Rockglen to Creek Cabin Alice had been regaled with tales of cabinmates and activities and awards and songs and performances. Now, though, the summer is past history for Frannie and Catherine. Now they need to know about school, about the future. And they need *things* again—"I need a terry-cloth robe. And I need some new tennis shoes. And I need a new backpack for school." Needs, Alice reflects, which like the food she's fixing now, her daughters' stories of camp, the hospitable atmosphere she's painstakingly effected, will be replaced by new needs and food and stories tomorrow.

Dennis drifts into the kitchen, lifts the lid on the crock of curry, and sniffs appreciatively. "Frances's recipe?" he asks, and Alice smiles gratefully at him, that he knows.

While she fixes trays for the girls to eat in their room, picnic-style, he rinses his hands and reaches for a small beige towel on a hook beneath the sink.

"Use a paper towel," Alice advises. "Those are tea towels, worthless. They were my grandmother's, then Mother's, and I . . ." she stops before saying, *"can't bring myself to throw them out."*

"They used to be white," Dennis says. "Frances soaked them in tea until they were the right shade of beige to fit with Creek Cabin's decor." He refolds the dainty linen. "She took such pains with everything." Alice stares at him. He reddens, recovers. "You must be glad to have Frannie and Catherine home from camp. Your mother missed you when she was here and you girls were off at camp."

"She had Libba," Alice says.

"She had Libba," he echoes. "Luckily."

Across the room Libba answers Bree's question about readings she'd given through the years. "Yes, so glamorous, those trips to Cincinnati and Kansas City. It was always affirming when students came to readings under threats of F's for not attending. Or the ones who wanted to show off, toss around terms around like 'postmodern' and 'metafiction.'"

Allegra's despair widens, that she herself has no idea what *metafiction* means, that she'll never be a writer, never be Libba.

"Has a movie ever been made of any of your books?" Bree asks.

"Oh, no," Libba says. "Women's issues don't have enough cinematic validity. Or bloodshed."

John laughs. "Same Libba. They broke the mold."

Allegra wonders where Frannie and Catherine have gone. If she can't have her children, she'll take Alice's. Frannie is nearing that age where there seems nothing to do at Vade Mecum; she's too old for the juvenile activities of day camp, too young to drive. Allegra remembers that age, when she began sneaking after dark to the outdoor chapel to meet friends, to drink beer. Frannie had stood in the doorway of Allegra's room that afternoon, as she was reading another of Libba's books. "I bet I can predict what you're reading right this minute," Frannie said. "I'm psychic. You're reading *the*, aren't you?"

Allegra had laughed, then. Then, before the mail had brought Brent's letter. *I sassed Granny this morning and daddy told me I had to say I was sorry and I wouldn't and I had to stay in my room all afternoon and I finally did say I'm sorry and I thought about it and I miss you and I am writing you to tell you I'm sorry I made you cry too.* Those earnest *ands*, written the way he speaks, the sincere and heartbreaking message that resurrects for Allegra the devastation and shame of that Sunday morning.

Pain seizes her again, not so different tonight from the way she misses alcohol, and the twin yearnings make her restless with a thick combustible alloy of anger and fear and regret. She goes upstairs and rereads the letter and takes out the bottle and fixes a drink to deaden the hurt.

". . . my own company," Bree is saying to Edie, who hovers by her father's side, a human shield between him and Bree Michaelove. "It began as a mulch business. I went around town and picked up restaurant waste, rented a forklift and warehouse space and—," she smiles, lifts her golden shoulders, "—composted. Then sold it by the truckload. Eventually I got into the gardening accessory business, too, with a retail store." She hands the shopping bag over John's lap to Edie. "Careful, it's fragile."

Fragile is precisely how Edie feels, but she lets go of her father's arm and removes the tissue. Within is a honeydew-sized orb, perfectly round, lilac-colored, shiny as silver. Edie stares at her purple face, distorted like a fun-house mirror.

"A gazing ball," Bree explains. "They were popular in Victorian gardens. From John's description of Creek Cottage, I thought it might look nice outside, near the—what's the name, Shallow-something?"

Edie lifts out the cool sphere. "Shoals Stream."

"Let's take it outside," John says, "find just the right place." He stands and gives his hand to Bree to lift her, then fits it possessively at her back as he steers her toward the rear porch and outside. Edie follows dumbly as a dog.

"All ready," Alice calls and laughs at Dennis, who's stepped back from the cloud of steam rising from the colander of rice. They gather at the wide counter around pottery plates, the pretty diced condiments of peanuts, scallions, coconut, chutney, the fragrant curry and mounded rice, summer lettuces gleaming with vinai-grette and tomato chunks, bits of red onion.

"Smells wonderful," Bree murmurs, and coats her mouth with pinky lip gloss. Edie watches. The only kind of lipstick she's ever used is Chapstick.

"Ladies first," John says, giving Dennis the briefest of smiles. Allegra clasps Libba's elbow, unobtrusively assisting her, and one by one they serve their plates.

"Look, an upholstered table," Bree says of the quilt Alice has, like her mother, arranged as a tablecloth. Edie winces, and when Bree picks up the place card and says, "I love being told what to do," winces again.

Before taking his plate, John walks around the kitchen's perime-ter, keeping count aloud as he closes drawers and cabinets that hang open. "Nine, ten, eleven, a dozen," he says with satisfaction.

Alice falters, her hand on the serving spoon going suddenly

weak, as though memory has a physical power. Her father had always complained about her mother's habit of leaving kitchen cabinets open. Alice bites her lip, tightens her grip, makes herself wonder what Rob is serving for dinner at home. She'd suggested pasta and fruit salad. He'll never go to the trouble of seeding the watermelon.

Conversation drifts, meanders.

"I'm into permaculture," Bree is saying. "It's a landscaping philosophy." She explains permaculture, how every plot of land from suburban yards to organic produce farms is approached from the idea of not *tending*—weeding, mowing—but allowing anything that grows to flourish. No grass, no carefully maintained beds, no chemicals.

The theory is alien to Alice, who can't imagine a yard without order. And to Edie, who spent many happy Saturdays atop her father's shoulders like a human stole while he mowed the grass. Now it's Bree who drapes an arm around John's shoulder, teasing him about his tie. Apparently she picked it out for him. For Father's Day? Edie wonders dully, and stabs a raisin plumped with cooking. She looks at Dennis, who's looking at Libba.

Libba's fork rests across her untouched plate. After all the chopping and dicing, the stewing and simmering; after all the measuring of spices—curry, cumin—she can't eat.

"Bree's been interviewed for an NPR spot about permaculture," John comments as Allegra excuses herself again for the bathroom. And another drink.

"The producer asked me for suggestions," Bree says. "How about you, Libba? They feature a writer every week."

"Libba doesn't do interviews," John says. "Hasn't in twenty-five years."

"Why not?"

He cuts an asparagus spear. "That's not my story to tell."

A pregnant silence falls as diners wonder what topic is forbidden. Because there are any number of forbidden topics hovering invisibly among them, in the candle flames, in the sushing current of the creek, in the lovely Scottish lilt of *Brigadoon* from the stereo.

"Are you still watching *Jeopardy!* religiously?" John asks, and Libba nods. "One time Frances and I argued over who wrote *Death of a Salesman* and we finally called Libba long distance to settle it." Everyone laughs.

"Tell us another story," Edie says.

"Ask Libba," he answers. "She's the best storyteller I know. Then again, she's the only storyteller I know." He shakes his head with both resignation and affection. "Thank God."

Yet even Libba's answer is a story of Frances. "When John took too long to tell a story at a dinner party Frances put a napkin on her head. When *I'd* told a story more than once, she held up two fingers so everyone could see."

Three sisters pause, struck again how, even when they themselves aren't thinking of their mother, Libba was. Bree plucks at the irregular stitching of the tablecloth quilt. "I have a cabin, too, in New Hampshire."

Alice remembers New Hampshire licenses in Vade Mecum parking lots. "Live Free Or Die," she says politely, silently thinking *Yankee.* "What's it like?"

"Small," John says, "cozy."

Suddenly Edie herself feels nauseous. He's been there, slept there.

Bree clears her throat. "So this is what you do on weekends in Vade Mecum?"

As the alcohol flows through Allegra's veins, antagonism has crept into her voice. "We could have gone roller-skating at the Rec Wreck."

Dennis abruptly stands. "Libba," he says, "I meant to bring something to you." Though a look passes between them, he only adds, "It's time for me to be going anyway. If someone comes with me—"

"I will," Alice says.

"We're on our way out, too," John says. Alice and Allegra hug him again, shake Bree's hand, thank her for the gazing ball. They know their manners.

"What about more wine?" Edie asks.

"Thanks, sweetie, but no."

"Daddy," Edie begins, "don't you want to . . ." but she trails off, unsure exactly what it is that she wants him to do. Finally there's nothing left but to follow them out on the porch and wave good-bye as the pair picks their way down the rocky path to the driveway. She follows their silhouettes blurred by darkness, hears the click of the car door opening. "Will you check me for ticks?" Bree says, and giggles, and Edie, who hears her father answer with low laughter, steadies herself against the railing.

At his cottage, Dennis gives Alice a paper bag. "These are pain-killers. Can you handle it? Allegra didn't seem herself tonight, and

Edie was . . . I know Edie the least of you three. Is she . . . married?
I've never been quite sure."

"She's never been sure either. Edie's catnip for men, but the only
one she's permanently attached to is Daddy."

"Like Frances."

Alice looks up at him, wonders at his softly spoken observations,
then pushes intuition aside and picks up a photograph. "Is this your
wife?"

"Yes, Joan."

"I hardly remember her."

"She died years ago in a car accident. You'd have been . . . let's
see, thirteen. No," he corrects himself, "fourteen."

Alice tries to conceal her surprise at his fussiness with dates. But
he takes the picture from her, wipes dust from the glass. "Joan baby-
sat for you once. No, twice."

"She did? When?"

"You were just a baby. Your mother—your mother and Libba
had gone out."

"Naturally. Good times all the time." Though Dennis smiles at
the comment, she only holds out her hand for the paper bag. "I better go. We have to leave for Raleigh at the crack of dawn."

But Dennis holds on to it, carefully folding it over. "It wasn't
good times all the time," he says, adding for a third time, "no."
Finally he hands the sack to her. "Drive safely."

When Alice returns to Creek Cabin, lights burn and dinner

scraps are hardening on plates. Chairs are pushed back from the table where candles still flicker, slowly shrinking. Everyone has apparently gone to bed, leaving Alice to deal with serving dishes cluttering the counters; the limp greasy green mass that was a tossed salad. She looks about her at the mess, listens to the silence, and decides that she's too exhausted to be exasperated.

Alice blows out the candles, climbs the stairs, passes the closed doors where her sisters supposedly slumber, and goes to bed herself. Frannie has claimed the other twin bed; survival of the biggest, oldest, fittest. Alice steps over Catherine in a sleeping bag on the floor.

Sleepless and hurting, Libba rises after three in the morning to a still house. Aware that aspirin is useless, she searches through Creek Cabin's bathroom cabinets for ibuprofren or Nyquil or Tylenol PM, some forgotten, expired prescription cough medicine containing codeine or anything, anything that will dull the pain or put her to sleep. It's Libba who opens the two closed doors upstairs beneath the flattened tin numerals looking for comfort, company, the painkillers Dennis promised her. She's swiftly losing ground in the rapid advance of her illness.

She finds no sleep or pain remedies in Edie's room, only Edie's unmade, but also unslept-in, bed. A pair of shoes, fake crocodile-skin flats that Edie so carelessly selected in a self-serve store that one is dark brown and one is black, lie overturned on the scatter rug. Libba looks out the window. Edie's car is gone as well.

In Allegra's room, the bed is made. Libba finds Brent's letter lying on the sink, whose old-fashioned, easily-stained porcelain still bears the pink traces of cranberry juice Allegra has mixed all evening with vodka.

Libba lies awake on her own bed downstairs and thinks. She hears Alice leave before daybreak with her children. She watches the sky, waits for another day to dawn, waits for the pain to ease. And waits for two sheep to come home, wagging—or dragging—their tails behind them.

June 30, 1967

Frances poured beer into two glasses and took them to the back porch where Dennis was leaning into the hearth, arranging logs. He held a lit match to newspaper crumpled beneath kindling. "She asleep?"

Frances nodded. "Third babies know they have to be good; their mothers have run out of hands." When he stood, satisfied that the flame had caught, she held a glass toward him. "How's Joan?"

"Joan's a student this summer. She's getting her real estate license."

"I wondered why she wasn't here. And how you managed to leave your practice."

Dennis took a long swallow of beer. "The first summer I've ever looked my partners in the eye and said, 'Cover for me,' my wife decides to go back to school." He shrugged. "I traded their Wednesday golf afternoons and all the weekend calls for the entire autumn for a free summer. The cottage needs some work, and I need some time off."

Frances tilted her head, alert for Edie's wakefulness. "Why didn't you two . . . didn't you want children?"

"Like you?" He smiled. "Wanting isn't always getting."

"I know about that."

"Bet those dark days seem like a lifetime ago."

"Sometimes," Frances said. "Other times it seems like yesterday."

"And where's your other half?"

"He's coming this weekend."

"That's your better half. I was talking about your other half."

Frances stiffened slightly. "I'm not sure. Teaching, maybe. I've lost track of her schedule."

"That must be a first."

She lifted her shoulders. "First time for everything."

Dennis turned at the tone, eyed her.

"What?"

"I've known you thirteen years this summer, Frances, you and Libba both."

"Unlucky thirteen," she said lightly.

"Don't be coy. It isn't like you. Neither is not knowing Libba Charles's whereabouts."

Frances reached behind her neck, pulled at a tendril of hair. "Libba and I . . . she threatened to . . . tell . . . or change her mind or . . ."

Dennis shook his head. "She'd never."

"That's what John says. But what Libba always says is, 'Be careful with the nevers.'"

"What happened?"

"She ridiculed me for being . . . for doing what she asked me to do."

Dennis waited, but Frances only slipped a foot from her sandal, folded a leg beneath her. "I don't want to talk about Libba."

"Alright." He placed the mesh screen before the fire and leaned back in the rocker. "Thought I might hike Graybeard next week. Want to come with me?"

July 25, 1967

The cottage was dark but for the dim wattage of the bulb beneath the stove hood. Beside a hunk of greasy-sheened cheddar and an empty bottle of red wine on the kitchen counter were two plates with the pulpy, pinkish remains of tomato sandwiches and melon slices. Their voices were only murmurs, no louder than the rhythmic creaking of the rocking chairs they'd pulled before the raised hearth, the better to prop their feet to the warmth of the orange embers. With each backward rock, they narrowly missed their shoes, a pair of boat moccasins and sandals, overturned, forgotten.

"Has she stopped calling?"

"Yes."

"It's not like Libba to give up." He studied the fire through the curved bowl of his goblet. "Tell me again when Alice and Allegra come home from camp."

"Two days."

"That's what I thought. Two days," he repeated, and tilted the glass, sipped, stared at the fire. "And we'll have missed our opportunity."

"For what?"

"For—to be together." In the dimness, he watched her throat move with swallowing. "You know I want you, Frances. And I can feel you wanting me." When she didn't answer, he reached and stilled her rocking. "Look at me." He drew his hand through her fixed gaze at the fire. "Am I wrong?"

"No," she said quietly, "you're not wrong."

"We could," he said. "Still."

A phrase drifted up unbidden from the past. *Wanting isn't loving.* "Wanting isn't . . . loving." She sensed his flinch. "No, that's not right. I do love you. Next to John, I'm closer to you than any other man on earth. You know why. For two lifesaving circumstances." She couldn't help herself, reached to stroke his cheek. "What we've done together these weeks, spending time—walking together and eating together and talking and . . . flirting, is dangerous. I knew it was dangerous. But it felt good, because I was miserable, *am* miserable."

He reached, too, his fingers grazing the cool gold of her wedding band, and held her wrist.

"I'm unhappy because of what's going on between Libba and me, and I'm available because this is John's busiest summer ever. But those aren't good reasons. Our bond is too special, too rare, and I won't . . . *sully* what's between us, maybe even destroy it. We could never look at each other in the same way again afterward. I want us always to be close, and if things were different . . ." She touched his forehead. "But not that way. Just because we could doesn't mean we should."

He moved her hand to his mouth, kissed the open palm.

"Wanting isn't getting. Again."

"And I'm a lousy liar," Frances said, half complaint, half chuckle. "Even if John didn't know, Libba would. She could look at me and tell. Libba, who could teach these hippies a thing or two about free love." She gently extracted her hand from his clasp. "Have you ever been unfaithful?"

Dennis sighed. "No. How did I do?"

Frances grinned. "I'm too monogamous to be the judge of that."

"Libba could."

"No doubt," she laughed, then picked up her glass, and swirled the liquid lazily. "But let me say for the record that being *wanted* cheers me considerably."

Dennis leaned back, yielded to laughter himself. "I bet Libba would know a more descriptive term."

"No doubt."

August 3, 1967

She checked her watch in the roof light: after ten. The driver had grumbled about the round-trip to Vade Mecum from the airport in Asheville, but she'd flashed a twenty before his eyes, lifted her luggage onto the seat herself, and stared him down. Her bag banged against the front door, but as usual, it was unlocked.

"Dennis?" Frances called. "Is that you?" She appeared in the bedroom doorway, tying the sash of her robe, and peered through the dimness toward the door. The knot dropped from her fingers. "Libba." She lifted her chin. "What are you doing here?"

"I came to . . . Creek Cabin is the devil to get to late at night."

Frances stared at her with hostility, a bedraggled, travel-weary, unwelcome arrival.

"I came to—" Libba began again. She set down the bag. "I came to apologize. I was crazy, and you were right, jealous, I—please, Frances. I'm sorry, and I'm lonely. Forgive me."

August 4, 1967

The first and only bars of the new morning's sunlight were bright lozenges on the double bed downstairs. Frances pulled up her knees into peaks beneath the pieced quilt. "I was so angry at you, and depressed, too. The truth in what you'd said."

"They were cruel, sarcastic, unfair, untrue. Faced with all those women I might have been, the choices I've made, I heard all those bridges burning and crackling behind me and fell apart, terrified. I reacted to fear with bitterness and cynicism, and—are you going to make me go on?"

"For a while," Frances said primly, then laughed.

"Did you ever try to call me? Did the girls ask about me?"

"They did. I . . . didn't."

"Ouch," Libba said. She sat up, bowed her head to her knees. "There are times I've wanted your life, but you've never wanted mine. Sometimes late at night I'm so afraid. Afraid that I'll wake up one day and be fifty and think I've wasted my life writing."

Frances swiped at a suspended sunlit bar, disrupting falling dust motes. "Suppose you wake up one day when you're fifty and wish you *had* wasted your time writing?"

"You cockeyed optimist. Did you tell John how awful I was?"

"Of course I told him. He's my husband."

Libba squeezed the tea bag, picked up her mug. "Did you tell Dennis?"

"I told him . . . enough."

"'Enough'?"

"When your calls stopped he said it wasn't like you to give up."

"So instead I just showed up." Libba sipped the steaming liquid, debated a question. "Was my arrival the deus ex machina?"

"If you'll tell me what that means, I'll tell you if it was."

"A writing device in which something happens at the end to determine the outcome. 'And then I woke up.' Translated, the gods come in and fix things." She looked at her friend. "I arrived at ten o'clock. At night. You thought I was Dennis."

Frances was quiet, Libba's implications not lost on her. She traced a finger around a gingham triangle on the quilt, a diamond daisy print, a square of blue plaid so worn the cotton batting fluffed through. "Sitting across the breakfast table from John, waiting for him to finish using the sink, watching him drive away to work . . . You don't know what it's like to look at someone and think 'Is this the last—the only—man I'll ever sleep with?'" Frances held up a palm. "Don't tell me about choices. We've both made choices, hard ones. But . . . Dennis." She turned her face to the side, away from Libba. "Dennis wasn't a choice. We took hikes, he brought the mail, or tomatoes from the produce stand. We had some suppers, some drinks, some laughs." She reaches blindly behind her, taps Libba's hip. "That's all there was or is. We have a bond, Dennis and I, that's all. A special—

not sexual— relationship. Is that okay? Aren't I allowed to love the *idea* of what might have been?"

Libba said loftily, "As long as that's all it is."

Frances laughed, a throaty eruption. "Oh I see, you're permitted to sleep around indiscriminately—"

"Well, yes, but I don't have standards to set for children. I'm no one's role model."

"Oh you, whenever it's convenient, right?"

"Sure, wasn't that part of the promise?"

"Not as I remember it." Frances laughed.

But Libba grew serious. "I know how it feels to love the idea of what might have been. Any letters from camp around here?"

"In the desk drawer." Frances squeezed her hand. "Are you staying long enough to hike Graybeard? Don't you have speaking engagements?"

"I canceled them. I don't do speaking engagements anymore."

"Since when?"

"Since the last one, in May. You were there, remember?" Libba stood up. "I brought you a hostess present."

"Something to add to my gift inventory closet?" Frances called to Libba's retreating form.

Libba returned holding a ruffled sheaf of papers. "A book I wrote during my . . . exile."

"Is it about me, as usual?"

"It's about—" Libba hesitated. "Ambivalence," she finally said, and pushed the thick pad toward Frances. "And apology. Something I have no talent for."

Frances took the proffered manuscript. "*Loose Ends*," she read aloud.

"Read the dedication."

"You never do dedications."

"Careful with the nevers."

Frances turned to a page with a single line. *For Frances*, it read, *from your friend with whom up you put*. "Oh," she murmured, "but—"

"Never end a sentence with a preposition. See? Careful with the nevers."

Frances smiled. "But, Libba, what you said that day in the kitchen that day—you wouldn't—"

Libba shook her head. "Life or death."

August 5, 1967

Frances sighed. "If I had only months to live, I could be happy with that view alone." From Graybeard's height and distance the only evidence of humanity was Stockton, a cluster of buildings with the proportions of Monopoly houses, nestled far below within the green valley. "What's Russell up to? John refers to him as 'the phantom spouse.'"

Libba scratched her calf. "No point in muddying your day with my mundane facts of life."

"What facts?"

"Sometime while you weren't answering my phone calls Russell and I got a divorce." Libba shrugged, refusing to meet Frances's eyes. "I needed to have a divorce so I can write about it with authority." She looked at greenly lichened boulders humping the slopes. "Everyone should have a bad marriage, don't you think? So after it's over they can be happy."

Frances's fingers paused abruptly on a pop-top ring.

"Do you hear yourself? You're your own worst enemy, Libba. You make it hard to love you."

"If a character's hard to love a reader has no sympathy for her." Libba watched a slowly circling hawk. "Would it make any difference if I mentioned that Russell tended to love every first female novelist he reviewed?"

"I knew he was away a lot, but I didn't know he was—"

"A womanizer?" The bird swooped gracefully, dipped, then glided on an updraft nearly within reach. "Ever notice how hawks are always alone? Maybe it's characteristic of birds of prey. Or maybe I'm just not meant to be married. I want . . . someone who'll pick me up and pull me onto a moving train the way Gary did to Audrey in *Love in the Afternoon*. Maybe I just need an older man." She laughed at her observation, but her voice dropped. "I know I can be hard to love. That's when I have the urge to claim someone who'll love me unconditionally. But suppose she didn't? Then I'd regret ever asking, ever knowing."

"But she already does. Just like I do." Frances pointed to a raw scar of cleared forest, a red clay gash in the landscape. "Look at that eyesore." A strip mall was being constructed just off the interstate, smashed between an elementary school and a heavy machinery rental outlet. "John debated investing in that center. I told him I'd divorce *him* if he did."

"John once said to me, 'If Frances ever dies, I'll never marry you.'"

"That's awful!"

Libba laughed, and tapped each of Frances's knuckles with her finger. "You still smile when he calls. You're a lifer."

"Libba," she said softly. "We'd only known each other seven years. *Do* you ever regret it?"

"Like waking up when I'm fifty? Rue the day, the what-might-have-beens? " Libba shook her head. "Regret is a useless emotion." She shifted, leaned her back against her friend's for support, and shut her eyes to the sun. "Not for a single moment. Only every moment."

CHAPTER *13*

The attic fan is loud, as though paper strips are attached to its blades the way Edie had fastened clackers to the spokes of her bicycle wheels. Her father had taught her to ride a two-wheeler, his fingers clasped behind her on the banana seat as she wobbled tentatively, unsteadily, forward. Why her father? Edie asks some invisible, hypothetical audience. Because her mother was with Libba Charles.

The fan's vacuum sucks lingering aromas from last night's party through the cottage, and pulls the screen door against Edie's calves as she quietly enters.

"Out here," Libba calls from the back porch. She's stretched on the wicker sofa, an arm thrown over her eyes, which she doesn't remove when Edie sits down opposite her and hoists her bare feet to the trunk. "Let me guess," Libba says, "you had breakfast with your father and Bree?"

Edie picks up a magazine whose glossy cover is rippled from sweating glasses and decides the best defense is a good offense. Teddy's always saying so. Thinking of Teddy, she reddens. "That woman isn't like Mother at all."

"*Woh*-man," Libba drawls with a countrified twang. She crosses one ankle over the other, and Edie sees her lips tighten with pain. The movement requires a contraction of muscles in her distended abdomen, a paunch in her otherwise thin body. "Should she be like Frances?" Libba asks.

"Are you going to sit there—"

"Lie here," Libba corrects, her eyes still closed.

"—lie there and tell me you aren't—" Edie searches for the appropriate word "—aghast that Daddy's dating not a year after Mother died? So soon? If nothing else, it's an affront to decency."

"By some definitions, canceling a wedding and eloping two weeks later is an affront to decency. In some circles, living with someone and not being married to them is an affront to decency." Libba languorously turns her head, opens one eye. "As are one-night shack-ups."

Edie abruptly rises.

"But I forgot, you aren't committed. You're not formally tied down. You like to keep things loose and open." The fan rushes on, unchecked.

"He isn't *your* father."

"No, he was my friend's husband. My friend who is dead. So Bree Michaelove has provided a shoulder—and yes, breasts—for John to cry on. Are you going to hold that against him?"

"It isn't a valid reason for getting involved with someone."

"What *is* a valid reason? What's yours? Retaliation?"

"He's twenty years older."

"I hadn't done the math." Libba sighs. "That *is* a shame. I'm waiting for the *wo*-man to be twenty years older than the man."

Edie stares outside at the gazing ball, whose smooth lavender surface reflects the filigree of overhead leaves. "That fucking ball is so hideous. As bad as year-round wreaths of fake flowers on front doors."

"For a leftover hippie, you sure are a snob." Libba sits up and waves her hand to see if the reflecting ball will catch her gesture at this distance. "Yes, Bree should have brought a safer gift, like cocktail napkins. Then you could have scorned her for her unoriginality. No, she should've brought flowers. Then you could have scorned her because flowers don't last. Or—"

"Shut up."

"There's not one objectionable thing about her."

"I object that she's not Mother. Those tie-up gladiator sandals. Gold dust! '*I love being told what to do*,'" Edie parrots in high-pitched imitation.

Libba nods slowly. "That's fair." She stands and walks toward Edie. "Except that you don't really object that she's not Frances. The only thing you object to is that she's not *you*."

Edie stubbornly tilts her chin from Libba's accusation.

"An objection that entitles you to go out and sleep with a near-stranger—"

"— he's not a stranger—"

"Not now, he isn't—in order to get back at your father for marrying someone who's not the mother that you resent for taking trips, being late, forgetting the occasional car pool or brownies? Have I adequately deconstructed the logic here?"

"Maybe I was just lonely last night. Maybe I just wanted someone to hold me."

"Don't we all," Libba says. "Get in line. So does *he* live up to your father?"

Edie rises, tired of painting herself into corners.

"Complicated, isn't it?" Libba goes on. 'Who are you mad at? Who's to blame here? Your father, for having the temerity to love someone other than you? Your mother for having a similar temerity in loving someone other than your father? But that would be me, wouldn't it, because he *graciously* shared Frances with me."

Edie opens the back door and sits down on the uppermost step.

"And sharing someone is hard, isn't it." Edie looks down at her toes and Libba opens the door and sits beside her. "Isn't it." Edie tosses a pebble toward the gazing ball. "Maybe it's not 'other than you,'" Libba says. "Maybe it's just 'in addition to' you. News flash, Edie: no one is exclusive in anyone's heart. Frances had four roles: wife, mother, friend, self."

Edie walks over to the gazing ball, an incongruous juxtaposition of spangle within a circle of blackened stones, the campfire ring dating from Creek Cabin's era of Safe Haven Camp for Girls.

"Bronchitis. The publication party for *Father of Girls* and *This Go Round*. My mother's funeral. To help me move to a new apartment. A witness at my city hall wedding."

"What are you talking about?"

"Reasons Frances left you to be with me. Are they valid?" Libba rests her chin in her palms. "When you were four years old Frances and I planned a long weekend in Denver. "

"One trip I've never heard about."

"Because she didn't go. She fainted in the airplane bathroom before take-off."

"Because she was sick?"

"Because she looked in the mirror. She'd gone into your bedroom the night before and you'd fallen asleep holding a flashlight shining on a picture of her. The whole scene came back to her when she looked in the mirror, and she refused to leave."

"Why?" Edie asks again.

"That dumb act may work on men, but it doesn't work on me. Why do you think? She couldn't leave you. With your pathetic flashlight and photograph. They had to stop the engines, unload the bags. Talk about pathetic—God! I pretended I didn't know her."

Edie turns her back to Libba, ashamed by her neediness. "Tell me something else." Her voice is small. "Is that pathetic?"

"Human nature. So is remembering only what we choose to remember." Libba smiles.

Edie turns, sees the smile. "What are you remembering?"

"I'm remembering Frances being pregnant with you. She *liked* being pregnant. She didn't mind being put to bed for eight months to guarantee your safe arrival. She liked watching herself grow fat, liked touching herself, the skin so taut and stretched—" Libba stops, flattens her hands against her own distended stomach and shivers slightly. "John would cut her toenails for her because she couldn't reach them. Picture that." She shakes her head. "And then when you were born all your terrors and joys became her terrors and joys. Frances upended her life for you, despite a rather . . . ugly effort on my part I'd rather *not* remember. So many times she told me no, turned me down, packed up and left me in the dust at one conference. For you. She went back to school, she cut your sandwiches just so, she—"

"*What?*" Edie laughs.

"You don't know what it's like, waiting and wanting something." Libba measures her words. "Until you, or anyone, has a baby—" She stops herself, points at Edie. "Why *don't* you have a baby?"

"Because I don't know if—-"

"All you need to know is that you never stopped being a gift. She never got over you."

Abashed, Edie leans and examines at her reflected face in the lilac mirrored surface. "This doesn't work as well as Mother's silver goblets. The ones she used on holidays."

Libba watches her. "I know a little something about the convenience of not committing. It gets stale."

Edie grimaces, grins, gapes at her distorted reflection and casually asks. "What's to eat?"

"You didn't bring anything from the deli? Seems you should have gotten a little something from Clark for your, uh, trouble."

Edie tightropes across the pentagon of logs arranged as seats around the old campfire. "*You* didn't have children. Why not?"

Upstairs, the fan's timer finds its slot and sighs off. "But I did," Libba says, "three daughters." The screen door rattles in its frame and someone stumbles across the threshold, cursing. "I hear one now."

November 11, 1967

"Tell me about the girls."

Frances cradled the phone in her neck while she chopped a green pepper. "Need grist for the mill?"

"Among other things."

"If they only knew how often you asked."

Libba was silent, though Frances clearly heard the repetitive taps of pencil against paper. "Alice's latest industry is making envelopes out of magazine ads."

"What?"

"Folding them so the Baby Oil hunk's face is on the front." A sudden grinding drowned out Libba's response. "Damn."

"What was that?"

"I just pulverized a retainer. Instead of wearing it like she's supposed to, Alice keeps it in a glass of water beside the sink and it got pitched in the disposal." Frances's voice grew distant. "No, this is Libba. Wait until I'm finished."

"Who was that?"

"Edie. She's on a grilled cheese sandwich jag, which she'll eat only if it's sliced into triangles and served with ketchup." The phone clattered. "Stop, Edie!"

"Hello?" Libba said. "What happened now?"

"Edie likes to grab me around the knees and wipe her nose across my backside. I'm a human Kleenex! Every skirt in my closet has a snot trail."

Libba laughed. "What else?"

Frances pulled silver wire and gum-tinted plastic chips from the drain. "Yesterday Allegra threw a tantrum at a birthday party because her Password definition was disqualified."

"Sounds like she has a problem with authority."

"Like someone else I know."

July 12, 1968

Libba paused on the path to pick hitchhikers from her shorts. "Alice and Allegra didn't want to hike with us?"

"They're rock hopping in Shoals Creek with friends." Frances knelt, knotted a shoelace. "We should have asked Dennis to come."

"What is this 'we'?"

"He's your friend, too."

"Like Alice and Allegra's 'friends'?" Libba said without glancing at Frances, who smiled. Libba pointed to a pine trunk newly blazoned with a slash of blue paint. "They've changed the trail since the last time we were here."

"It's an alternate route to the top. But I like the old path."

"Ah," Libba said, and playfully poked Frances with her walking stick. "The road not taken."

"Let us not forget that I'm not the only one of us with a road not taken," Frances intoned good-naturedly, and tossed the Sea & Ski lotion at her.

"No," Libba grinned slyly, "mine was the road less traveled by."

"Oh, you and your Robert Frost! Get moving."

June 29, 1969

"Hello?"

"You sound breathless."

"Do I? I ran in from outside. Edie's learned to ride a two-wheeler just in time to plow through my nasturtiums. I was putting her new basket and bell on her bike. "

"Isn't that John's job?"

"He's taken Alice to the drugstore to buy glitter for her posters."

"Posters?"

"She's gone into the babysitting business full tilt. Made her own personal checklist of client questions. Want to hear them?"

"Maybe later. And Allegra?"

"She's roaming the streets delivering a neighborhood newspaper she wrote herself. All four copies of it. What are you doing?"

"What am I doing. Well. Sharpening pencils. Toasting a bagel."

"Oh, Libba," Frances laughed, "your life. But bagels— I wish I could buy them here. Bring some next time you visit."

"I was hoping you might visit *me*. Next weekend?

"Next weekend? Allegra's having a sleepover Friday night, and John has business people in town on Saturday. And Alice's piano recital is on Sunday afternoon, and you know I don't like to leave Edie, who at this moment is—Edie! Stay on the driveway! Libba? What did you say?"

"I said—"

"Edie, put down that screwdriver and hold your horses, I'm coming. Libba? Call me later, okay?"

"Frances, wait, I—Frances?"

September 2, 1970

"What did you do today?"

"First-grade teacher conference. Consoled Edie because she wants to sit in her teacher's lap all day long. Planned Alice's eighteenth birthday dinner. Eighteen! Consoled myself that I have a child old enough to vote and go to college."

"Not to mention legally drink, run away and get married, or have an abortion."

"Cleaned the basement to avoid thinking about that. Discovered Allegra's escaped kangaroo rats, commonly known as Eeny and Meeny, inside a fertilizer bag that they apparently mistook for dog food. Consoled Allegra grieving for dead pets. She thought they'd just get tired of freedom and return to their cage, like the dog in *Hurry Home-Candy*."

"I gave her that book once upon a time."

"You don't need to tell me that. And you? What are you doing up there at Creek Cabin?"

"Decomposing."

Frances laughed.

"I typed for eleven straight hours today, just passed a mirror and didn't recognize myself. Hair stripped back, bloodshot eyes, teeth and lips stained purple from wine. I only left Creek Cabin once, to call my editor and argue whether 'social security' has to be capitalized. I'm in purdah."

"What's 'purdah'?"

"The state of being secluded."

"Then that makes two of us. I'm in purdah from a couple of teenagers who'd prefer that I was invisible. They make fun of me for saying 'slacks' instead of 'pants.' They cringe when I ask pleasantly who's going steady. And it's going 'together,' by the way, not going 'steady.' You can argue with your editor about that."

"It is?"

"Everything is either 'gross' or 'putrid.' They're perpetually 'p.o.'d.' And when I object to the expression they innocently say, 'Why? It's short for 'put out.'"

"A discontented age," Libba said. "One of the many."

CHAPTER *14*

Allegra fumbles, drops a box of coffee filters. Gauzy cupped shapes scatter across the counter and she snorts a giggle, eyes Libba and her sister. "What a dump," she says. "Where's our housekeeper? But I forgot, Alice went home. By now she's probably making sure all her toilet paper rolls are turned the right way."

Edie clears her throat but Libba says, "Good morning. You're drunk."

"Is it? Am I? Instead of being a secret drunk I've decided to be an open drunk." Allegra dramatically swoops up a filter, lurches toward the coffee maker. "Being a drunk didn't stop Hemingway and Fitzgerald from writing."

"No. Being dead drunks stopped them."

The noise abruptly stops. "On second thought, I hate to ruin a buzz with coffee. I'll have another drink instead."

"There's some mouthwash in my bathroom," Libba says. A small squeak escapes Edie.

Allegra fiercely slams shut a cabinet door. "I never drank mouthwash. I was never even *close* to drinking mouthwash."

"What do you want, congratulations? Where have you been?"

"Out. Left my car at the liquor store. Look, Ma, no blackouts. I'm improving!" She giggles. "They have taxis in Stockton, learn something new every day. Or at least *a* taxi, 'cause it brought me back to Vade Mecum, to the outdoor chapel, nice and secluded and dark as hell all night long. Same place we used to drink as teenagers. Correction, where *I* used to drink." She mugs at Edie's back, who's rinsing dishes. "I was the bad one. Sorry grades, sorry life, sorry, sullen, surly, slurry." She laughs again, entertained with her babbling train of thought.

"Who's the bad one at your house, Sasha or Brent?"

Allegra's voice tightens. "Leave Sash and Brent out of it."

"I'll tell you who's going to get left out: you. Know how fast you'll lose your kids?"

"'Kids'?" She wags her finger at Libba. You mean *baby goats?* Like you'd know."

"*Very Married* was a custody story before it was an inheritance story. I did the research. The easiest way to declare a mother unfit is with alcohol abuse."

Allegra wads the filter, affects an expression of bored disgust. "Am I going to get a lecture? Are you going to tell me you're *disappointed* in me? Are you going to be my mommy and make me *apologize* for being so much trouble to everyone all my life? Too late. You're too late, I'm too drunk, my mommy's too dead."

"Allegra," Edie says, reaching for her sister. "Don't."

Libba swats the proffered arm away. "No lectures. I'm just interested in seeing my investment shows a profit."

"What investment?"

"I paid for the Blair Clinic."

Allegra's eyes glint, her mouth a thin slash. "I hope you bought tuition insurance."

"Get your keys, Edie," Libba says evenly. "Allegra needs something to drink and I'm not able to drive and Allegra doesn't want to risk a DUI anyway, do you?"

Allegra glares.

"Watch this, Allegra," Libba says. "People will do anything for you if you're dying." She turns to Edie again. "Go get the car." Edie shuts off the faucet and finds her purse. "I should have gotten terminal a long time ago, during a dry spell," Libba says. "Maybe someone would have published something I'd written because they felt sorry for me. Pity is a powerful motivator, isn't it, Allegra?"

"That's my name, don't wear it out."

"Who taught you that clever comeback, Sasha or Brent?"

The mention of her children's names halts Allegra momentarily, but she stands, swaying slightly. "Why not, let's cruise. Find some hair of the dog. Whoops, euphemism. Shotgun."

"Sorry," Libba says. "Age and death before beauty. Get in the back."

"Good," Allegra says, "More room." She throws herself across the back, stretches out, closes her eyes. "You know the way?"

But the way Libba chooses, quietly telling Edie, takes them beyond Vade Mecum, beyond Stockton, fifteen miles farther northwest and deeper into the mountains. Edie navigates the twisting two-lane, and the car climbs hairpin curves through a tunnel of trees whose leaves career crazily in the window above Allegra. The ride is silent but for her groans as she fights queasiness that worsens with every dizzying curve. Shutting her eyes only intensifies the nausea. "Are we almost there, godammit?"

"You're so *outraged*, aren't you," Libba quietly answers from the front seat, eyes on the road. "Outraged that we're not there yet. Outraged that Alice is organized. Outraged that you can't drink anymore."

Kneading her belly, Allegra hauls herself up, tries to speak. But sickness overwhelms her, and her gorge rises. Saliva floods her mouth. And still the curves keep winding up and around, left and right, sending her from side to side as Libba keeps talking.

"Outrage is a great cover, isn't it. I know all about it."

"Oh, you know. You know-it-all." Allegra rolls down the window, hangs her head outside in the rushing air.

"Outrage numbs all those feelings liquor used to numb for you."

Allegra gags, heaves, and throws up. Vomit splatters on the metal, the door handle, her cheeks, catches in her hair.

"Turn here, Edie," Libba instructs at a dogleg pull-off that fans into a makeshift parking lot. A dozen vehicles crowd clearings between tree stumps.

"Libba—" Edie begins, her expression a mixture of helplessness and unwilling capitulation.

"Park somewhere." When the engine dies, Libba cranes her head over the back seat at Allegra's prone figure, cheeks and chin wet with snot and slobber. "You need a bath."

Edie's round blue eyes cloud with worry, but when Libba opens the door and reaches for Allegra, she can hardly stand by and do nothing. Together they pull Allegra from the car and onto the gravel parking lot and drag her down the short path of trampled weeds through the woods.

Allegra swabs at herself, draws the back of her hand across her mouth, gags again with the taste. "Where are we?" she asks once, and then through her disoriented stupor hears the slush of running water, the breathless shrieks, and knows. By then it's too late to balk, resist, even drag her feet.

They're standing at its crest. The glass-slick surface worn by innumerable years of running water and human rumps glistens in the morning sunlight. Sliding Rock, the nature-made boulder beneath the thin glaze of falling water that had tempted and delighted thousands of tourists, campers, rednecks, and thrill-seekers, the courageous and the chickens alike who can't resist despite the water's shocking chill. Allegra blinks. Bright-eyed children dressed in souvenir T-shirts or cheap fluorescent bathing suits pause midriver to stare at the odd apparition come to share their play, then jump up and down to keep the blood flowing in their feet. Adults holding cameras, canned drinks, or babies in bunched diapers gaze placidly at the trio.

"Oh, God," Edie says.

"Go on, Allegra," Libba says, "you're the family risk taker, remember?" With her fingers firmly clasped around Edie's upper arm for support, Libba maneuvers herself behind Allegra and thrusts her knees against the back of Allegra's own. "Alley-oop," Libba grunts, and Allegra buckles, stumbles, falls into the stream and onto the slick surface where there's no choice of turning back, no opportunity to change your mind. She screams, reaches, grabs at nothing but falling water and polished rock and slips swiftly and inexorably down to the frigid pool.

The shock is instantaneous. Paralyzing cold snatches Allegra's breath. She thinks her chest may cave in, her heart will stop. She surfaces, splashing, flailing at the waving water dotted with slick heads of other sliders shrieking with cold and panic, floundering in a motion that resembles swimming but is more likely a desperate grab for the closest human being to latch on to, and pull under. Allegra's too intent on simply breathing to scream, on moving her arms to struggle shoreward, her legs that feel encased in weighted ice blocks, on getting out, reaching for the swaying rope that spans the river and provides a sagging bannister up the side of the slick rock.

Strangers in loose house dresses or chino shorts watch from their dry positions at the top as Allegra makes her slow, stumbling, dripping way up the rock, straggly hair and running nose, water streaming from tennis shoes and pant legs and shirtsleeves. Until she stands trembling and sober before Libba.

"There's a blanket in the trunk," Edie says finally.

The ride home is twenty long minutes of silence, the higher, hotter sun having little effect on Allegra's audible teethchattering. She's wrapped herself in the scruffy fringed stadium blanket, her wet head within its folds as though to make herself invisible. Once she raises her head, gasping for air. "Stinks."

"It's you," Libba says. "Vomit stinks."

"Shrimp," Edie says.

At Creek Cabin Allegra waddles up the stone steps, through the cottage and out to the screen porch. She huddles in a corner of the settee, a quaking bundle of swaddled wool and wet hair and bowed head, misery incarnate.

"Edie," Libba says. "Could you stick some kindling under those logs? John set a fire last night and never lit it. Our luck, a morning fire."

Edie strikes a match from the box of Christmas matches Frances received regularly from a friend every holiday, and just as regularly, brought to Creek Cabin. She backs away as the fire catches and begins to sit beside her sister shrunk against the cushions. But Libba says, "This is a private pity party."

Edie picks up her raveled string purse. "I could—"

"You could call Teddy while you're gone, too," Libba says, and the tone of the suggestion is enough to propel Edie out the door.

Allegra draws the blanket protectively around her.

"Think you're so tough," Libba says. "Think you don't need a soul. That's what I once wanted to be. Tough with a capital T."

Allegra draws a clump of damp hair across her face, sniffs it, makes a face. "Some people might say I modeled myself after you."

Libba draws a fingernail across her mouth, a tic she's developed to accompany a spasm of pain. "Frances might." She places a full glass of orange juice on the floor. "What happened?"

The fire pops, and a cinder falls smoking to the hearthstones. "I don't know." Allegra touches it, examines the smudge on her finger. "In the morning after the children had gone I'd look at the breakfast dishes and go back to bed. Get up around lunch and see them again and go back to bed. I'd get up again about three when Brent and Sasha got home from school, and have a glass of wine. And then it was cocktail time anyway, and then it just . . . escalated. I don't know how it happened," she says with soft desperation. "I just wanted to be . . . alone. To have some privacy, some solitude. Like you."

"You know what you do with privacy and solitude?" Libba grips Allegra by the shoulders. "You stare out the window at people taking walks—together. You stare at the telephone hoping someone will call with nothing more to say than you've bought a new shirt, or weeded your garden, something, anything. Some days I've longed to hear even the library call telling me I have a book on hold, the seamstress reporting that my skirt is ready. Sometimes I answer the phone so quickly that the cold-call solicitor on the other end isn't even connected yet. Solitude means you don't clean off half the bed at night, means you don't even fold down the spread, means you long for something to eat that's . . . *warm*. Privacy is just a different name for being alone. And solitude has a despair all its own. *I know.*"

Allegra buries her head in the blanket again. "But you *don't* know." She begins to cry soundlessly. "They . . . they *begged*." Her voice is tinny, muffled. "They were *there*."

"Where?"

"Susan was there, my next-door neighbor, in her husband's office. It was Sunday morning, and Sasha and Brent should have been at Sunday School, kneeling there, and instead they were there, *there*, kneeling on the carpet with their hands around my ankles and crying and saying—" Allegra's voice is strangled with the vision "'Mommy, we want you to be well. We want you not to be asleep when we come home from school, Mommy.' I keep seeing them in that huge empty conference room, their hair and foreheads and knees on the rug, hearing them, watching them." *Mommy, please please please, Mommy.*

"That wasn't—" she can barely bring herself to say it "intervention. Intervention is for adults. Sasha and Brent, my babies, my . . . " Allegra drops her head in her palms. *We love you, Mommy. We want you back.*

"I was furious. Am. Furious that the only way I can blot that scene from my mind is to drink myself blind and furious that I can't ever drink again. You can't know how deep that shame is, shipped off like a package wrapped for mailing. A scene you'll never forget. You've never been humiliated like that. You've never been . . . haunted with regret like that."

"'Regret?'" The coin-colored eyes bore into Allegra's. "You know nothing of my regrets." Libba shakes her head. "Maybe he did it *for* you. The way—" she pauses, seems to change her mind, "your mother and I did things for each other."

"Mother," Allegra repeats with fresh pain. "I'm not a good mother. Not one of those mothers that teach their children to dial 911. My friend Susan—" she manages a barky laugh "— ex-friend Susan, made sure the preschool had a defibrillator in each classroom before she'd enroll her daughter. Me, I sent the check. I'm not a hover mother. I never will be."

"Allegra," Libba says. "Be careful with the nevers. You think you're the only person to hit a rough patch in your life, in your marriage? You think Frances never did?"

Allegra leans her head against the rough wicker curves of the sofa's back. The trees outside are still now, no longer the spinning green hallucinations of the car ride. "I was Mother's rough patch. I—I hit her one time."

"I know."

"She told you?" Allegra cries, and draws a wet sleeve across her face.

"That, and everything. Every time any of you said, 'I wish I'd never been born.' If I'd been there I'd have hit *you*. You're your own worst enemy. Like Frances used to tell me." Libba takes Allegra's cheeks between her palms. "What is it you want to say?"

A blinkered horse, Allegra's forced to look only at Libba, though she thinks of Brent's letter. *I'm writing to tell you I'm sorry too.* "I never got to tell her I was sorry!" Allegra cries, blurts. "I want to say I'm sorry. To my mother, to my husband, to my children, to my friend. For being the childhood pest and the adolescent rebel and the adult alcoholic. I miss my mother's rules and my husband's jokes and my children's hugs and my friend's—I miss sitting in the potholes in her driveway with her!" She covers her eyes. "I'm sorry, I'm sorry."

Libba backs away, sits gingerly down on the hearth. "Know what makes a character a hero? When she's in danger of some kind— moral, sexual, spiritual. When something's at stake. Brent and Sasha are at stake here. And Dal. He's the one who called me, asked me to help. Amazing at it may seem, he loves you. Go home and tell them what you've just told me."

"What about you?"

"What about me? You go home to Dal and don't come back here until you've told him."

Allegra stands and walks to the hearth. She licks dry lips, presses index fingers to her temples. "I have a hangover. Maybe it's a good sign, that my tolerance is low enough that I can get a hangover."

"What do you know, the silver lining."

"Pollyanna is not a natural role for me."

"Or for me. But that's the main ingredient of writing fiction."

"What is?"

The fire gasps, sizzles softly. "Characters have to change." Libba looks at the red mist of Allegra's eyes. "I'm sorry, too."

● ● ●

November 1, 1970

"Only you would have had the nerve to be born on All Saints' Day, Frances, along with all those dead goody-goodies. Happy fortieth. What have you done on your birthday besides wail with anguish over your lost youth?"

"In this rain? Nothing."

"Poor poor pitiful you, think I'll go eat worms. Here."

"We don't do presents. Going out to dinner is enough."

"Open it. I'm making up for my childhood. My mother used to give me money on my birthday and say, 'Buy yourself something.'"

Frances unwrapped the present, drew silvery softness from the folds of crisp tissue. "Cashmere!" She held it to her cheek. "It's so soft, luxurious. And the color . . ."

"I thought it was appropriate."

"Why?"

"At Em Sem you told me with absolute sincerity that women under forty shouldn't wear cashmere."

She laughed, and other patrons at the restaurant glanced in their direction. "Because your body gets accustomed to its warmth, and then when you get old, cashmere isn't warm enough. Whatever you are—cold-natured, or talkative, or frugal—increases with age. It's a fact. Thank you."

"Wear it in good health." As they waited for the check an elderly man with a cane hobbled by their table. A young couple who apparently recognized him stopped to speak, and he nodded confusedly.

"There's a scary sight for a birthday night," Libba said.

"Why?"

"The lively adults of your youth who grow stooped and ancient while you aren't noticing." Arms flailing against the satin lining, the gentleman searched for the sleeves of his coat. "Think of us at eighty," Libba continued quietly. "Out to dinner, stopping by a table to speak to a couple we know, friends of Alice or Allegra, or Edie's. And after we shuffle off, they turn to each other and say, `When did they get so old? How sad.'" They watched in silence as the maître d' handed the frail man over to a male nurse holding a dripping umbrella at the door.

The waitress brought their change. "Drive carefully."

"We will," Frances answered. "Thank goodness this gloomy day is almost over."

The waitress smiled. "I'm glad for all the days."

They looked at her. Perhaps she said this to everyone in hope of a bigger tip. But her face was open, soft, puffy with incipient wrinkles. And guileless.

"Yes," Libba said, "so are we."

August 29, 1971

"Let me tell you about being a mother," Frances sighed, and shook open a sheet. "You're only as happy as your unhappiest child."

"What happened?"

"Yesterday Allegra came out wearing a skirt so short her fanny showed and she was braless under a peasant blouse thin as gauze. Mascara like black glue, eye shadow halfway up her forehead. When I told her she couldn't go anywhere looking like that she sneered at me—"

"And no one sneers like Allegra—"

" —and snapped, 'I know what your problem is, Mother. What's wrong with you is that you're going through menopause. You're afraid of not being a woman anymore, aren't you?'"

"Oh, God. The apple doesn't fall far from the tree."

"She shoved me, my child. You don't know what that's like."

"I've had a friend slap me. Does that count?" Libba stretched an elasticized corner of the sheet over the stripped mattress.

Frances fitted a pillow under her chin. "John calls teenagers 'sweese.'"

"What?"

"Neither swans nor geese."

"When I'm reincarnated, I'm marrying John whether he'll have me or not. I know enough blackmail tales and details to force him. Sex, money, shortcomings. In no particular order."

Finally Frances laughed. "Allegra told me you gave her a first edition of *Rebecca*."

"As a going-away-to-school present."

"She carries it around like it's the Hope diamond, while she claims we're banishing her to DeWitt Academy as punishment. She's told everyone that she was a victim of an behavioral intervention. Where does she get those terms, from you? You get to be Glenda the Good Witch dispensing magic and largesse, and I'm the Wicked Witch of the West. Wonder what she'd say if she knew you were the one who insisted on boarding school? John wants to sell Creek Cabin to finance the tuition."

"I told you that I wanted to pay—"

She interrupted. "I convinced him to take out a second mortgage."

"Fifteen is a vicious age for mothers and daughters."

"Except that Allegra wouldn't do that to you."

"She's like a tornado, blows through anything in her path."

Frances smoothed the flimsy summer spread, then dropped to it. "But not you, Libba," Frances finally said, "not you. Her tornado path detours around you."

September 20, 1971

"I hear the first bell," Frances said and pretended to gather up Edie's lunch bag already within easy reach. From the corner of her eye Frances watched her youngest daughter fight the fear, struggle to get out of the car and onto the schoolyard sidewalk and into the second-grade classroom. And watched Edie's eyes fill with tears. Frances scooted across the seat and hugged her. "What is it, honey?"

Edie shook her head, unable to speak.

"Go ahead," Frances whispered in her ear. "Libba knows. Libba knows what it's like to be scared." Frances glanced over the seat at Libba, who knew about the morning litany, too, knew Edie needed the comfort of its repetition like air. "I love you," Frances began.

"I love you more," Edie said.

"I love you most."

"Will you be at home?"

"I'll be at home."

Edie knotted her fingers. "Will I be alright?"

"You will be alright."

Edie gathered her lunchbox and notebook and opened the car door. "Okay."

Frances watched until the heavy door of the elementary school closed behind the small figure of her daughter, then dropped her face in her hands.

"Frances," Libba said from the back seat. "You went to school every day of first grade with Edie because she was so terrified. Every day for a year of your life she sat in your lap for six hours. Edie learned to read with your chin in her hair."

"I know. But . . ."

"It's not your fault that it doesn't snow on Christmas Eve so your children will have a white Christmas. It's not your fault that the child next door makes better grades than yours. It's not your fault that your child doesn't have a pony or didn't get picked for the lead in the play. You apologize when it rains, Frances, and it's not your fault. What you need to know is that—"

"Oh, don't. That's how they started every reading at that awful conference, with some background. 'What you need to know is that this character is, what you need to know is that this takes place in—' Just don't."

Libba was quiet a minute. "Being a mother is the hardest, longest, most hazardous career on earth. Without even knowing the risks, mothers sign on for a lifetime of guilt and anxiety and the never-ending fear of what they've done or not done, or what will be. What you need to know is that you can't take the blame for everything."

"You've left one out," Frances said. "What about the fear of what might have been?"

Libba leaned over the front seat. "But that's just it. You took on that fear for me, too."

CHAPTER 15

Though Alice had explained to her children that she needed to return to Vade Mecum, it hadn't required much of an explanation. Everyone was involved, in a hurry. Thomas had a new job at a pricey restaurant, and he hadn't been half as excited to see his mother as he was to tell her that he'd be working at a local celebrity gala. He needed to learn how to tie a bow tie, and Rob had already taught him. The girls had nonchalantly called their plans over their shoulders as they headed for the mall or a movie or the pool or a friend's house.

"What is a dachshund?" Edie says.

"What is a papaya?"

"Who is Daphne du Maurier?" Allegra says, triumphantly adding, "Beat you," to Libba.

"Only because I couldn't read the answer," Libba says. The television sits on a rolling cart. Libba, who's refused to consider a wheelchair, is not. "It's too far away."

Alice pulls the set closer. A segue has taken place at Creek Cabin, a transition. Libba has told Allegra that the easiest way of making time pass in fiction is simply to pick up a character as if it were a chess piece and place the character forward in time. After a terrible fight between husband and wife on a Tuesday night, say, or a crippling ice storm, it isn't necessary to tell what happened on Wednesday, or how everyone felt. "If it needs to be Sunday so the neighbor can drop by and move the plot forward, simply make it Sunday," Libba told Allegra. "Open the chapter with the neighbor at the door while the church bells chime. Then it's Sunday, and neither the character, nor the author, nor the reader, has had to suffer through three days of telling."

So has art become life for Libba. The sisters aren't certain when Libba began to spend more time in a horizontal position than a vertical one. She'd tried the back porch but its lumpy sofa wasn't bed enough, smelled of mildew, and grew damp from exposure. And the double bed in her downstairs room seemed isolated, and the sisters understood this, the way as sick children they'd wanted to be where the action, the daily living, took place.

So in the same way that not making a decision becomes one, Libba decided on the small daybed fitted beneath the stairs leading to the second floor. Lit by a wall lamp with a forty-watt bulb, it's an intimate hollow, a kind of nest complete with quilt and pillows, with headroom enough beneath the risers only to sit up, back propped to the wall. A space not so different from the triangular speaker space Alice had closeted herself inside to memorize the words to Broadway soundtracks, picking up the needle and putting it down again over and over on "Surrey with a Fringe on Top." Soundtracks that are here as well. "Put on *A Little Night Music*," Libba says when Alex Trebek signs off a five-day champion.

Alice opens a woven tote whose bottom is frayed and worn from years of hauling projects and takes out a novel she must read for her book club. "Can you have the meeting at your house," Margaret had asked, "since you don't work?" The question's sly superiority and presumptions still nag Alice. She unpacks Boy Scout badges to be sewn on a sash, a new address book in which to enter addresses from her old one scruffy with erasures, cents-off coupons to be sorted. Trivial tasks, drone work, the same kind of projects she'd accomplished while her mother lay—Alice pushes the thought away and says, "The photinia are gone."

"'Photinia'?"

"The shrubs I planted along the chain-link fence at Mother's grave to make it look nicer. Someone stole them, dug them up by the roots. I worked so hard to plant them. Who would do something so desperate and awful?"

Allegra and Edie look at Alice, unsure how to respond. There's something almost comical in the picture. "Maybe there's a black market for shrubs," Edie says.

"Grave Alice," Libba says, quoting her poetic namesake.

"And the Final Jeopardy answer is: 'The title to this novella which won the Pulitzer Prize in 1953 has six words, each with three letters.'" The contestants frown, ponder. Like Allegra and Edie, they clearly have no idea.

"*The Old Man and the Sea*," Libba says. "Didn't I tell you to read the Pulitzers?"

They'd woken to chilly dampness, heavy fog that obscured the Vade Mecum valley all day, tucking itself like a shroud into any available space, enveloping trees and cabins in a damp, day-long, motionless gloom. Nuts and branches and skittering squirrels had thumped on the roof throughout the long hours. Whether it had ever actually rained or simply misted had been debated for so long that Alice had put on her mother's old slicker and left them to it.

Until *Jeopardy!* Libba slept most of the day, sedated with morphine and exhaustion. Edie and Allegra read or puttered while Alice wandered. "Where have you been?" Edie asks Alice when she comes in, shaking droplets of condensation from her hair.

"Watching the day campers rock hopping." The sisters had done this as children themselves, dressed in old bathing suits and tennis shoes and leapt from rock to rock in the stream, inevitably slipping into the water. "They don't even notice the weather."

"That used to be a blast," Allegra says. "We'd do it until our fingers got pruny."

Alice gazes at her hands. "After forty your fingers are wrinkled all the time." She goes into the kitchen. "What should we have for supper?"

Guessing, suggesting something Libba will eat, accept, is a daily challenge. Something appealing will come to mind, but by the time it's prepared it swells in her mouth, her stomach is off, she's tired, she hurts. "There's that steak place out on the interstate," Allegra says. "How does a baked potato with sour cream and butter sound?"

Instead of answering, Libba speaks as if talking to herself. "When Allegra had her tonsils out she could only eat ice cream. Vanilla and vanilla and vanilla. Watery, one-flavor hospital ice cream she refused to eat. One night, late, Frances said, 'If you could have anything to eat, Allegra, what would it be?' And Allegra said, 'Coffee ice cream from Howard Johnson's.'" Libba reaches up to turn off the light that hurts her eyes. "You couldn't buy coffee ice cream in grocery stores then. And Frances got in the car and drove out to the highway and went to Howard Johnson's for coffee ice cream, and brought it back to her."

Alice grips the refrigerator handle. She remembers being a child when a neighbor's husband was killed in a car accident, how she'd watched people coming and going with their pies and cakes, platters of fried chicken, bowls of fruit. And how Frances had gone over to the house at dusk with nothing more than a bunch of fresh spinach. She'd cooked it there in the neighbor's kitchen, sauteed it in butter, and the woman had eaten every bite. Simple spinach, limp and warm and easy on the palate, had finally been what the grieving woman managed to eat, though she hadn't known what she wanted herself. How, Alice wonders, had her mother known?

She opens the refrigerator's vegetable bin, takes out a bag of spinach, and answers her own question. "I think a spinach salad sounds good. There's probably a recipe for dressing in one of these old cookbooks." She chooses one and opens it. On nearly every page she finds her mother's handwriting beside a recipe, a single numeral beside most—4, 7, 5—and the occasional *don't do again*. Alice puts the book on the counter, realizing what the numbers signify. Her mother had rated the recipes from one to ten; she'd found a pen and taken the time to grade the meal she'd cooked before returning the book to the shelf. Alice snaps the volume shut.

She looks through lower cabinets for the lettuce spinner. Most of the cooking utensils in Creek Cabin are ancient—graters grimed with rust, old-fashioned swing-handled can openers, dented colanders, pans missing their lids—but she knows there's a lettuce spinner. She knows because she gave it to her mother one year for Christmas, and the ridiculously domestic gift Alice had been so proud of especially selecting had found its way to Creek Cabin. But it isn't in the cabinets, and it won't fit in the drawers.

Alice opens the slender door of the pantry, a door she's opened a thousand times. This time, though, she looks not for cereal or flour. This time she looks toward the deep, high, uppermost shelf large enough for oversized boxes and items, and this time, she sees something else in her mother's handwriting, a neatly numbered list on a curling piece of notepaper tacked to the dead dark center of a knothole between shelves.

1. Unbutton collar
2. Turn over, press collar outside
3. Press one arm sleeve and crease it on top and bottom
4. Press other sleeve
5. Press front of shirt, one side at a time
6. Press in between each button
7. Do other half of the front where the buttonholes are
8. The back

Alice studies this list of steps for ironing a man's shirt, a list that embodies for Alice something that is ludicrous and poignant and heartbreaking and futile about Frances Wilson's life, and her own. She turns away from it, takes two eggs from the carton in the refrigerator, puts them in a small saucepan, runs water into it, and sets it on the stove to boil. With her thumbnail she breaks stems from spinach leaves, rinses them, tears them, and dries them with paper towels. She finds the big wooden salad bowl, measures vinegar and oil and spices from the cabinet into another, and whisks the mixture. She wipes mushrooms free of grit, breaks off the stems, and slices them. There's a plastic container in the freezer filled with a pound of bacon she's already cooked and drained and carefully placed, strip by separate strip, on waxed paper so it won't stick. She does this at home, too, so her family can conveniently reheat bacon for sandwiches and hamburgers and breakfasts.

But as Alice moves toward the counter where the ingredients are assembled, she drops the container. It falls to the floor, the lid snaps off, and twenty strips of bacon, frozen and fragile, shatter into dozens of crumbs. Alice stares at the greasy brown bits littering the floor. From *Oliver!* on the stereo, Nancy extolls what a fine life it is, and something detonates inside Alice. "I'm sick of being competent," she spits.

Allegra looks up from her book. "I'm sick of being the drunk."

"I'm sick of being the youngest," Edie says.

"I'm sick of being sick," Libba says as Alice walks away from the bacon, away from the kitchen, away from the three women, and toward the stairs, the bed, the comforter.

"I've decided something I feel like eating: a baked potato from the steak house on the interstate," Libba announces. "And I want Alice to take me."

March 27, 1975

"Should I be worried? We haven't exchanged a word in an hour."

"Are you mad at me?" Libba replied.

At Frances's baffled expression she went on, "Didn't you hate that, when you were in seventh grade? *'Are you mad at me?'* someone would ask if you hadn't spoken to them in school that day. Only girls do it."

Frances rested her chin in her palm. "Maybe we have nothing to talk about anymore because our lives are so different. Maybe—"

"Know what dialogue tag lines are?" Libba interrupted her. "They identify the speaker, what they're feeling. You and I don't need tag lines. We're *beyond* that, Frances. We don't need to fill the silences."

July 16, 1976

As the porch swing moved slowly to and fro, they dragged their bare feet along the smooth worn floorboards. They'd put the book of photographs aside, pages one or the other had turned without the need to ask *Are you ready?*, knowing instinctively in a private pas de deux when the other was finished. From the bottom of the hill the tiny outdoor chapel's bell rang for the Sunday service.

"I have an enduring fantasy of walking down our church aisle stark naked except for black patent leather heels, spike, with a handbag to match," Frances said.

"Twenty-five years of marriage and that's your fantasy? I hate to be the one to break this to you, but I doubt anyone would even look up. Those old blue hairs, the biddy brigade."

Laughing, Frances leaned her head over the back of the swing. The stretched cords of her throat striped the graceful length of her neck. "Don't ever let me be a blue hair, Libba. Promise me."

August 15, 1979

Libba watched Frances knot a length of royal blue wool. "I'm having a distinct déjà vu of fifteen years ago."

"How so?"

"You with wool in your fingers. Always working on a sweater for one of the girls."

"Fifteen years ago I was knitting. This is needlepointing."

"Same thing."

Frances smiled. "Like romance novels and biographies are the same thing?" She rummaged through a denim bag for scissors. "The girls hated those homemade sweaters, far preferred whatever you sent from Best & Company. Remember the buttons in the shape of anchors I used for—?"

"I know whose sweater you used them for."

"You and Sam bought them some little place in the Village."

"That must have been the last thing we did as a couple."

Frances dropped the scissors back into the bag. "Don't you ever wonder if—"

Libba interrupted her. "Never."

"Careful with the nevers."

Libba sighed noisily. "Alright, wonder what? If he knew, whether we'd have stayed together? If he knew, whether he'd have let me to go through with it? If he knew, whether he'd have wanted it? Now what about this scenario: whether Alice was all there was."

Frances's knuckles whitened on the needle.

Libba rose, took the broom that always stood behind the door and swept away leaves from under the swing. "Lift your feet." Frances obediently did. "Some topics aren't worth speculating about." She swiped at corner cobwebs. "It's alright, Frances. When a person has you and John as the standard, well . . . I made wrong choices with men. Still do. But not with friends." Libba pointed to the cabin's side beyond the swing. "Look."

Frances glanced up. "At a knothole?"

"It's a moth, camouflaged to look like the wood grain. What are they called, lunar moths? Mammoth moths?" She inspected it—huge and hulking yet delicate and fragile, the wings sleek as mink and brown as dirt but for a pair of identical honeydew green oval markings that seem to gaze out like fixated eyes—and reached for it.

"Don't!" Frances said. "Even a single touch brushes off microscopic feathers. Eventually it won't be able to fly even though it looks just the same."

Libba stared at Frances, surprised by the unexpected intensity. "Okay," she said, and examined the faint dusty smudge on her finger. "Poor old moths. Waiting all day long for nighttime just to beat themselves senseless getting to anything bright as day. Never get to be butterflies."

Frances shifted the heavy dun-colored canvas in her lap. "Maybe fewer moths are asphyxiated with alcohol and pinned to Styrofoam than butterflies," she said quietly. "Or captured in jars. Or eaten by birds. Invisibility has its advantages."

Libba replaced the broom and clasped Frances's neck from behind in a quick, fierce hug. "I may be the writer, but you're the one who always knows just what to say."

CHAPTER 16

In the mist-muted glow of a neon steer beaming BLUE OX STEAKS above the car, it looks as though Alice wears lavender gloves. She holds the warmth to her chest for a moment, then hands the tin-foiled oblong across the seat. Libba peels back the silver wrapping and steam rises from the fragrant split potato. "I should have told you just butter."

"Yes," Alice says, "you should have." She pulls out of the pitted parking lot and dark specks spill across Libba's lap.

"More bacon bits," Libba says.

Alice drives in silence, navigating the gradual rise of the looped exit to Stockton whose familiar curves are obscured by the mist, a nearly opaque fog that seems to suck possessively at the car. She switches from high beams to low and back to bright, both no more effective than flashlights. She squints through the windshield at the curving road, gray pavement barely distinguishable from the fog that mocks the headlights, and searches for the white lines on the shoulder that are her sole means of navigation on a road that normally is as familiar as her name. Landmarks are obliterated, and a pair of headlights spark and vanish.

It leaps from the vaporous nowhere toward the car, a ghostly beige blur illuminated for a fraction of a second in Alice's peripheral vision. The deer collides with the car, a sickening rubbery thunk, and Alice cries out, slams foot to brake, throwing Libba toward the dash. Heart in her throat and dread in her gut, Alice flings open the door expecting carnage, a violent and horrific scene: shredded fur, a pulp of blood and gristle.

But there's no slain or wounded animal on the pavement, its moist eyes wide with terror. Nor is there damage to the car; not the slightest dent, nothing red but the taillights blinking in the lazily swirling fog. Alice searches the shoulder, the ditch, listening for bleats.

"But I saw the deer," she says. "I heard it." The awful meaty noise. A flank, a chest, a slender furry snout. She gets in the car, peers toward the dark woods as though the creature might materialize again and runs her hand over the fender. "You'd never know it happened." She gets in the car, stares through the windshield, then drives on. "Not a single trace."

Just beyond the rock arch entrance Libba crumples the potato skin inside the foil. "Surely you have one of those car litter bins. Given your four children. Given your efficiency."

Alice snatches the metal wad, rolls down the window, and pitches it out into the blackness.

"Stop the car. Right here. Stop it," Libba says.

Alice brakes so abruptly that Libba reaches for the dash again. The car sits between the row of trampolines and Lake Sarah. "Once, when Frances and I were on the back porch, a bear ran right beside Creek Cabin towards Shoals Creek. Not ten feet from us."

"I don't want to talk about Mother."

"I think that's exactly who you want to talk about."

"She's dead."

"I noticed."

"So why talk about her? She lived, she married, she had children, she died. She's sitting on a cloud up in heaven and someone is saying 'What did you do when you were alive?' And she's fluffing up that cloud, making things nice, and saying, 'I was just a wife and mother. Send down a replacement, they're millions more like me.'"

Swift as the switch of a light Libba reaches across the seat and strikes Alice with all the strength she has left. "You little shit."

Alice's hand flies to her arm. She reaches for the gear shift.

"Just wait a minute," Libba says.

"Fine."

"Fine."

"I'll wait long as you want. I'm an expert waiter. In fact, it's one of the few things I'm expert *at*. It's on-the-job training with children. You spend five and ten and fifteen years waiting for the next thing—the next meal, or the next place they have to be—school and practices and lessons and friends' houses and sports, and then you wait some more, for school and lessons and sports to be over. And in between you get things for them and cook things for them and wash things for them and your life is a series of waiting for the next thing you do for them. That's fine, it's rote, it's what you chose, isn't it?"

"How heinous. It sucks."

Alice's eyes flash recognition at her children's over used adjectives. She takes a breath. "And then," she exhales noisily, "all the waiting and doing and providing dwindles away because they can do and provide for themselves. And you're so astonished, and delighted, and grateful, and pleased. Until one empty minute when you realize there's nothing to do or provide or wait for any longer and then where are you? *Who* are you? I'll tell you who you are. You're a middle-aged woman who's made no mark to show she ever existed. Except for you, of course. *You* are sui generis."

Alice gazes at headlights of other cars swimming through the fog, and the steam rising from Lake Sarah's placid surface, and laughs a little. "Whenever I leave home I always make sure there's a full kettle of water on the stove. Know why? So Rob can hear the whistle and remember. Because no matter how many times I tell him, he forgets to turn off the eye after he's heated water for his coffee. This is the kind of detail my life consists of: a full kettle on the eye. You carefully fold the shirt sleeves, make the beds so the blanket won't itch, slice the celery so the tuna salad isn't too chunky, peel price tags from the presents and wrap them so the labels don't show through the paper. And whatever you've done—folded or wrapped or chopped—is eaten, wrinkled, opened, slept in without a thought, and then you start over. Nothing is left to show that you've ever done anything, or done it carefully, and well."

"What do you think writing is? You labor over a single word, a portion of a sentence, and someone reads it in a fraction of a second and turns the page. No one exclaims, 'Oh that fabulous setting! Oh, that divine dialogue!' And then what? They read it, shut it, forget it."

"You can touch books. You can hold them and stack them and say this what I did in sixty years. They make you immortal."

"My *deathless* prose? Eight of ten are out of print."

Alice stares stubbornly ahead.

"Can we find a lowest common denominator here?" Libba says. "You're starved for thanks, a case of gratitude deprivation? Or is it resentment against me for having the cottage, for having books with my name on them, for having used your life—though you don't think it's much of a life, evidently—in selfsame books. Is that a complete list?"

Alice seems not to have heard her. "An unremarkable life. Just. Like. Mine."

"So this *is* about Frances. What is it that you—is blame the word? I think it's closer to scorn."

"You forgot angry."

"Angry?"

"That she was conventional. Predictable."

"And ordinary."

"Yes. She settled for being ordinary."

Libba's hands drop in her lap, and she looks out her own window. "Why, you're absolutely right. Frances coulda been a contender. But she was too busy taking the television to school so your class could watch the astronauts land, and writing clues for a scavenger hunt, and returning your books to the library, and reassuring you that your going back to touch the doorknob twice because you didn't do it right the first time was okay, *normal*. She was too busy locating Dracula teeth for your Halloween costume, and calling out your spelling words, and buying graduation presents for your one thousand and one friends. Multiplied by three children."

Alice slaps her palm against the seat. "And that's just it!" She rolls her forehead back and forth on the hard ridged edge of the steering wheel and begins to cry. "So worthless, all of it."

Libba leans against the door. "You think that little of the life Frances led, the one you're leading?"

"Yes," Alice chokes. "No. It's . . . complicated."

Libba lets her cry, intently watching. "Your children have no idea what you do all day, Alice, do they."

"No."

"They don't know that you're folding their clean clothes and cleaning out the dryer lint trap and arranging who will pick them up at the same time you're making sure you have the right change for the piano teacher and frying bacon, do they?"

"No."

"They come in and eat that bacon like potato chips before you've even finished washing the pan, don't they? Put another dirty glass on the counter after they've finished their Coke and go outside, don't they?"

"Yes."

"It's incredible, their oblivion, isn't it."

She sniffs, nods. "Yes."

"Children have no idea what their mother does all day, do they."

"No! I told you, no."

"Self-absorbed little bundles of egocentricity, aren't they?"

"Why are you doing this?" Alice cries. "What is it you want me to say?"

Libba stares at her. "Neither did you, when you were a child. So were you."

Alice's head whips toward Libba's. "It's worse than that, though." Her cheeks glisten. "I'm afraid, too."

"Of what?"

"That I'm just like Mother. And I'm ashamed of what I'm afraid of because it's petty when you're sitting here . . ."

"Nothing significant to show at all. A wasted life."

"Yes," Alice gulps.

"Oh, and that would be terrible now. Grim."

"All my life I've been organizing. Organizing vacations and Christmas and birthdays. Organizing for fundraisers. Organizing meals and dentist appointments and camp physicals. And for *what*? So somebody can put on my tombstone 'She Did Errands.' And don't bother planting bushes around my grave. Someone will steal them."

"You've led a decent life."

"Decent. Swell. Just what I wanted to grow up to be."

"You have Frannie and Catherine and Luke and Thomas."

Alice drags an arm across her damp eyes.

"Do you have the gall to imagine you're some kind of renegade, the first to be disappointed with domestic status quo? You think Frances never thought, what's it all for, that she never suffered just-a-mother syndrome, that yours is some new angst spawned by seventies feminism or recent ravings from generation X? Frances and every other fifties housewife were your foot soldiers. Frances respected herself and what she did every day. Isn't it enough to live a life honorably and steadily and dependably? Isn't that valid and noble and *enough*? If you think there's no honor in the ordinary, then ordinary is *precisely* what you are.

"I can't sing you a hymn to motherhood because I was too frightened to learn the words. I was only lucky enough to be an intimate friend of someone who did. So that I knew *her* specifics, *her* details.

That she always took wax paper to the park for you to go down the sliding board. That she stopped what she was doing to go outside and hook up the sprinkler for you to run through. That she saved shoeboxes so there would always be one available for your homework dioramas.

"I'd arrive for a visit and find cucumbers floating in the sink, the first step of homemade pickles. Pickles you mindlessly ate, pickles you gave your teachers for presents without a thought. While Frances and I talked she'd replace all the buttons on a pea coat because that's the way you wanted it, had to have it. With *brass* buttons, not *tortoiseshell*. What do you call that, Alice, obligation? Nothing better to do? Frances got in the car and went to the store and bought new buttons. She snipped off the old ones and got out the sewing kit, threaded the needle and sat down and sewed on new ones. You think that teaching you three to write thank-you-notes, and all the other quotidian details I created my *immortal* fiction from, has no validity? Don't you denigrate an extraordinary *minute* of your mother's ordinary life."

Alice thinks she might be sick. She opens the car door and leans out into the damp coolness.

"Books get packed up no differently than the belongings you and your sisters sorted through. But people go on living. And even if they don't go on living, they have other people who do: their children."

Alice thinks of Rob. Of Luke, Frannie, Catherine, Thomas. The products of her forty years of living. Thirty feet ahead the row of trampolines lies taut and black, coiled springs gleaming in the car's headlights. The day after day of living, doing, sleeping, being.

"Whoever did it didn't know much about plants." Libba says.

"Did what?"

"Stole your cemetery photinia. Frances's photinia," she corrects herself. "Plants die if you transplant in the summer, need autumn to harden off. Common horticultural fact. Another *useless* detail Frances taught me."

Alice shifts her legs from under the steering wheel, places her feet on the rocky ground, and leaves the idling car, and Libba. She slices through the headlights, fog rising about her as she walks through the thinning mist toward the deserted trampolines. Beneath the black rectangles the earthen hollows are even blacker, opaque and solid as a piano key. Like graves.

Alice lifts a foot across the foot-wide expanse of springs. She hangs there momentarily, then steps onto elastic slick with moisture. The webbing yields beneath her, sags and stretches, and she thinks fleetingly of quicksand. She bounces tentatively, a single bounce, feet never leaving the mesh. Again, and her stomach drops into her pelvis. And again, stiff-legged and straight-spined. And again. And again.

The car and Libba blur like crayon shavings in waxed paper beneath her mother's warm iron to make stained-glass windows. Waxed paper with which her mother separated chocolate-chip cookies, and took to the park sliding board; small gestures that had been her mother's way of making a mark on the world instead of saving it. Making herself immortal in ordinary ways.

With every bounce Alice grins wider, springs higher and higher forgetting how silly and spastic she surely appears. It's an alien sensation, this imbalance, an effortless freedom bound only by the high infinity of the dark heavens, where her mother sits on a star. She surrenders to the springing, the giddy weightlessness, and laughs out loud.

"Are you alright, ma'am?"

Alice tumbles to the tramp, panting. She hadn't realized jumping on a trampoline was such exercise. She focuses breathlessly on the Vade Mecum night watchman making his rounds. *Poor man*, she thinks, *grounded by gravity*. "I'm fine. One hundred percent fine."

"Uh," he begins, confused. But he's grounded in duty as well. "You're not supposed to jump with shoes on."

Alice looks at her sneakered feet. "Right," she says. "I knew that, too."

"Too?"

"But I'm finished jumping, anyway. I'm all through here." She dramatically salutes the watchman and staggers toward the car, stooping once in the headlights' beacon. Still winded, she flings herself into the driver's seat. "I found the trash," she says to Libba, and holds out the crumpled wad. "And I do have a litter bin," she laughs. "It's in the back. Where the children sit."

But Libba doesn't answer. She's slumped against the door, eyes shut, head bowed to her chest.

"Libba?" Alice grasps a shoulder, but there's no response beneath the soft nap of the silver cardigan. She jerks the gear from Park, flicks the heat to high and reverses, sending gravel and grass clumps flying, a tire gashing the wet ground beside the road. Heedlessly she speeds through the dark retreat, jouncing over speed bumps glaring whitely in her headlights, past the stone buildings, bulky behemoths looming beside the occasional overhead streetlight. She ignores the pedestrian crossing at the dam, passes Lake Sarah, steers swiftly up the hill past the silent cottages, past Creek Cabin's lit interior. Panting, panicked, she runs up the steps and beats on the door beneath the yellow porch bulb of Dennis Chandler's cabin.

"Alice?" he says, smoothing his white thatch of hair. "Are you—"

"It's Libba," she pants. "She won't respond, she's—"

"Where?" he says instantly, picking up a battered leather bag behind the door.

No figure is visible through the car windshield. She's crumpled across the wide sofa seat of the front. Dennis crouches inside while Alice stands helplessly outside, unable to decipher the low tones of Dennis's murmuring. She hears the clink of instruments, silence, a groan. Dennis holds Libba beneath her armpits, bodily lifts her to a sitting position. "Yes," he says.

Alice peers over his shoulder. "What?"

"Yes," Dennis says again, but not to Alice.

Libba's head lolls on the back of the seat. Her eyes open, take in the snowy head bent close to hers, Alice's figure in the clearing fog. She lifts a hand, presses her palm to her forehead, curving her lips in a rictus of pain. "No," she gasps, and then with absolute vehemence, "*No hospital!* Now or ever."

At Creek Cabin, Dennis lifts Libba from the car, carries her up the stony path and into the cottage, onto the narrow bed beneath the stairs. Libba is too weak to undress, and as Alice undoes the overall straps, her knuckles knock accidentally against Libba's chin, rousing her. She stirs, looks up, recognizes who's standing above her. "Alice," she says, "they may not remember all the peanut butter sandwiches. But you will."

March 2, 1980

Giggling and cursing, they scrambled through the open window into their shared room and tumbled clumsily to the floor. Oranges spilled from beneath their robes embroidered with the spa's bold logo.

"Shit! I scraped all the skin off my shin. Prowling around groves in the dark, stealing fruit. I can't believe I've stooped so low. This better be worth it."

"We're starving," Frances laughed. "That dinner wasn't dinner, it was animal feed. Whose idea was this, anyway?"

"A week of luxury, relaxation, and renewal at a high-class spa is our fiftieth birthday present to ourselves, remember?"

"This isn't R&R. It's starvation and confinement. *Expensive* starvation and confinement."

"Remember throwing oranges out the window at Em Sem?" Libba said.

"*You* threw them. I was the good girl," Frances said. "Here, have a purloined orange."

They frantically dug fingernails into the tough hide, ripped away the peelings and ravenously pressed the fruit to their mouths. But Libba spluttered, spat pulp to the floor, and Frances grimaced at the tart sourness. "We got lemons!"

"These aren't lemons, they're oranges. I cased the groves during that frigging hike."

"They aren't ripe yet!"

"Curses, foiled again. And still starving."

Frances wiped her mouth. "Damn things chapped my lips." They fell to their backs on the floor, terry robes twisted around their legs, and laughed hysterically at the entire ridiculous scene.

"You know," Libba said between gasps, "I wrote a book last year in which a character had a face lift, and my publisher refused it because she said feminists don't have plastic surgery." She rolled to her side, toward Frances. "Wait, am I a feminist? How did I get to be a feminist at fifty? Someone forgot to tell me. I've written nothing but domestic dramas my entire adult life."

Frances kicked, laughed harder.

"It's the first rejection I got that ever made me laugh," Libba said, weak with hilarity. "Not that I wasn't disappointed all the same," she added, and this sent them off again, shaking.

"Get up," Libba finally managed, glancing at the mess of peelings and pulp around them. "We have to destroy the evidence before the spa police discover it."

Frances picked at a soggy section of uneaten orange. "How?"

Libba gestured to the bathroom. "The time-honored method: down the toilet."

Hands full of shredded oranges, they stood on either side of the commode. "Look at us," Libba said, pointing to the mirror. They saw themselves, two middle-aged women in bulky robes, hunched over a toilet, tearing sour oranges into tiny pieces. "It comes to this: two biddies flushing forbidden food."

"This all feels familiar to me," Frances mused. "I used to get rid of outgrown toys, stuff the girls wouldn't part with, by putting them in the diaper pail. Nobody ever looked there." Libba howled, grabbed a towel rack for balance. "Even a few of John's ties found their way into ye olde diaper pail," Frances laughed, and gave the commode's handle a final push. As they rinsed their sticky hands beneath the sink faucet, she added, "Promise me you won't ever tell Alice and Allegra and Edie about this."

"That you steal oranges?"

"That I went away to get beautiful. They think I'm just away with you somewhere, again."

"Right, one more thing to hold against me: taking you away, leaving them out."

"It's not that," Frances laughed. "I don't want them to think I'm vain. I want them to think I'm *perfect*."

CHAPTER 17

While others in the wide world prepare for school's opening and a seasons's beginning, four women in Creek Cabin prepare for an ending. As Libba has progressed from ability to inability, the sisters have progressed from tending her in the low lean-to bed under the slant of stairs to the bed proper in her downstairs bedroom. Libba has her music and her books, the only things she craves. The sisters have Dennis stopping by daily and the compassionate tones in which he discusses end-stage cancer.

"Fourteen milligrams morphine sulfate."

"Is she making water?"

"It's moved into her stomach and liver and intestines and lungs."

Both accelerated and prolonged, the days blend and merge. One sister is always at her side. And when she's able and coherent, they talk with her. Simply talk. Thus they do with Libba as she did with their dying mother, though they have no idea of this unconscious imitation of the not-too-distant past. They are honoring a commitment: something else they don't know.

"Is my pal Bertie still at large?"

"There's nothing in the paper."

A slow shake of the head where the hair is still thick but brittle against the pillow. "Don't draw out the tension too much when you're writing. A reader forgets there *is* tension if you delay it."

"How will I know if I am?" Allegra asks.

"Instinct. You'll know."

She is so very ill. Often her speech is slurred, or there are long pauses between sentences. But the mind in the collapsing body never falters. "Have you ever noticed how people say someone was 'a great lady'? I want someone to say, 'She was a great dame' about me. Unfortunately no one's still a dame by the time they die."

"Yes, you are." Her hands are scaly, shaky. They coat them, and her lips, and her feet, with Vaseline. "You're still a dame."

"Don't give me that fake smile."

Alice looks into yellowed and watery eyes, the silver filmed. "It's not fake."

"Huh. You used to practice smiling in front of the mirror so your gums wouldn't show."

Alice can't help herself, breaks a promise not to tire her. "Is there *anything* you don't remember of our lives?"

"I remember because Frances isn't here to do it for you. Friendship has obligations."

"No sentimental stuff." A tiny beam beside the daybed clicks on, the diminutive book light Dennis brought. "Know what sentiment is?"

"No."

"Sentiment is 'Leavin' on a Jet Plane,' which you went around the house singing for an entire month when you were fourteen."

Edie, who can still recite every word, blushes.

"'Sentiment is giving something more tenderness than God intended it to have.' I can't remember who said that."

Except that *tenderness* has a new definition. Tenderness is brushing her teeth, putting ice cubes to lips. Tenderness is back rubs, gentle massages with lotion. Tenderness is sponge baths, carrying her to the toilet.

"Still at large," she says, referring to Bertie, and herself. "Let's get all the euphemisms out of our systems." Her own system is failing; bowels blocked, infection likely, legs swollen in an otherwise gaunt body. "Giving up the ghost."

"What?"

"I used to make my students do this as an exercise."

"No."

"Yes. Croak. Check out."

"Kick the bucket," Allegra says, choking on the words. "Meet your maker."

"Excellent. Buy the farm."

"Pass away."

"Dull, but acceptable. Push up daisies. Called up."

"Bite the bullet."

"No, no, no, wrong euphemism."

"No, it's not."

"Yes, it is. Go get the thesaurus at the bottom of the cardboard box." When she returns, Libba takes the opportunity. "You're the one who's going to do it. Dennis will sign the certificate as doctor of record. He's used to that."

Allegra looks down.

"'Ermengarde, stop sniveling, don't cry on the valises.'"

"What is *Hello, Dolly!* And I'm not crying, it's allergies."

Her stomach has bloated, so filled with fluid that any pressure on her abdomen is unbearable. Instead she lies on her back and looks at the ceiling, though some days her vision is blurred and she can only see shadows. "Is it hayfever time? September already?"

"Almost."

"I'm the only person in the world who went into a decline when the jonquils began blooming. Winter's the best time for writing." She reaches, fingers the glossy leaves in the tiny vase. "Bring some fresh water. I want the galax to go on living."

And still she tells stories.

"Frances's New Year's resolution one year was to be annoyingly optimistic."

"This is what Frances would say when she called me: *You're going to love this . . .*"

"Frances didn't really fall in love with John until they went to the beach together and he wouldn't lift his arms because he didn't have any hair in his armpits."

"Frances always brought food when she visited me. Homemade soup, shepherd's pie. She knew I never ate, didn't take care of myself. Imagine. Held casseroles on her lap in the airplane."

"Frances drew a cartoon satire of *The Scarlet Letter* at Em Sem. A wild-eyed witchy Hester with stick hair and A-line dress to fit her initial."

They stare at her, amazed that she can still amaze them with stories of their mother, from the smallest detail to the greatest revelation; piecemeal recollections of more than four decades that they have access to only through Libba Charles. The novels are but a minuscule portion of the stories she knows.

One lifts while the other two swiftly change the sheets. "Is that a hospital corner?" she asks.

Alice looks at the sheet. "I guess it is."

"Frances taught me how to make hospital corners. I never got it right. Like she taught me about necessary sadness."

"'Necessary sadness'?" Allegra echoes.

"Things happen that are sad, and hurt, but eventually you can look at them and be reconciled and better for it. That's what I always wrote about, but Frances named: a current of bittersweet that runs through everything. Sometimes it's a flood, and sometimes it's a trickle, and the reasons behind everyone's current are different. But they all flow in the same direction."

"Like the Continental Divide," Edie says.

Alice picks up needle and thread and a Mile-Swim badge. But she can't thread the needle for shaking hands and brimming eyes. "I'll never have a Premier Friendship of the Century like you did with Mother. What was it between you?" she says desperately.

"I know," Allegra says. "You each had something the other needed. You had freedom and irresponsibility. Mother had family and stability. Nonconforming and convention. The oldest story. That's it, isn't it. Isn't it?" she begs. "Tell us."

"Hush," Edie says. She can't bear it. None of it.

"Look after each other," Libba says.

"What?"

"But . . ." And why not, now? "That's what she told us to do, before we left for dinner the night she died. *'Look after Libba.'*"

"Did she." Libba tries to smile, fails. "We made promises, Frances and I. That's what we had between us." The watery eyes look at Alice and Allegra and Edie in turn, but she only points to one. "I promised her you," she tells Allegra.

● ● ●

December 28, 1955

But for light leaking from the edges of the open door, the hospital room was nearly as dark as the December night outside. A single bed, a single chair. No flowers graced the bedside table, no cards bearing holiday greetings or congratulations, no slick ceramic kitten or teddy bear filled with hard candies. In the bed, one black head bent so near to a tiny dark one that the pair seemed a single figure when Frances quietly—tentatively—opened the door a bit wider, and entered.

"Libba,"she said softly, "it's me."

Blinking as though woken, she looked up at the sound of her name, then down, and they were one again.

Frances felt an intruder suddenly, struck timid, as though she'd trespassed upon a scene too tender and intimate for exposure. But she had to begin somewhere, after all these months of silence and secrets. "I promised to be there for all your important occasions, but how could I be here when I didn't *know*."

Libba didn't look up, only fit her palm to the head, the bottom, said nothing.

"You hid away, like a pregnant nineteenth-century-novel heroine." Frances approached the high bed. "The airport was crazy with Christmas travelers. I got the first flight after Dennis called. And then renting a car and finding the hospital at this time of night. I was so afraid that I might have missed seeing her before — that you might have already given her . . ." Her prattling died. "Libba?"

But she only tucked the flannel blanket possessively round the child in her arms. Tighter. Closer. And asked of no one, "Where do they learn to wrap them so neatly? No dangling edges, no flapping . . . seams. A perfect package."

Frances pressed her fingertips to her lips, unsure how to respond to this peculiar opener.

"Makes her feel secure, they told me. Safe. Must be nice, feeling that safe."

It wasn't the reunion Frances envisioned. Not this different, unfamiliar Libba.

"I knew it would be a girl. I always knew. Even when I—when I almost didn't have a—" She broke off, fingered the bracelet of white beads like teeth circling the plump wrist, whose bold black letters Frances easily read: BABY GIRL CHARLES.

"Do you get to—are you allowed to name her before she, before you—?"

"Daughter. My daughter. 'Time for school, Daughter,' my mother used to say. 'What are you reading these days, Daughter?' she says now.' " She frowned slightly. "I had a name."

Frances laced her fingers to stop herself from reaching. To comfort the friend, to touch the child. But it was Libba's child, and Libba was touching her, rubbing her cheek to the baby's own. "It's warmer than satin, but smoother than velvet. More like a petal in the sun. A broad petal. Magnolia. No, too leathery. Camellia. Peony."

Frances barely breathed, uneasy with this altered person. Passive, distant, reflective.

"Poor little girl," Libba said, not sadly, but wistfully. "Now she's one of us, and one day she'll have to decide, too."

"Why poor?"

"Because we're the ones fitted out to have babies. So we're the ones who have to decide whether to have them. Or whether we want to farm, or sell cars, or run a hotel, or write books. Whether we want to be a mother or be something that's not a mother. Decide whether we can possibly do both. That's the crux of it all. No matter what any kind of scientist or sociologist or any other-*ist* claims, no matter how culture or society changes or progresses, in the end it's a woman's conflict. Our awful, wonderful, terrifying, eternal conflict."

"No, Libba, John wanted—"

"Because when a man walks away, his child is still there, still living. But it's our body, and what our body produces ultimately depends on us. It does. That's just the way of the world. An immutable fact, fair or unfair. Someone is going to have a big problem figuring that out, someday soon. It's coming."

Frances swallowed. She'd rehearsed a repertoire of responses in the twenty-four hours since the shocking phone call had come.

Frances? This is Dennis Chandler.

Dennis? Why are you—

I'm in Vade Mecum. With your friend Libba Charles, and her baby.

Baby?

She wanted me to call and tell you never to underestimate a friend's power of persuasion. She said you'd know what she meant. She came a few weeks early, but both are fine.

'She'?

It's a baby girl. I'm handling all the adoption details. But she wanted you to know.

She hadn't known. Hadn't know that Libba had not had an abortion. Hadn't known that Libba had called, talked to John with no hint of her plans, moved to Creek Cabin alone, arranged for Dennis Chandler to deliver the baby in the Asheville hospital, where she would give her up for adoption. Frances had come prepared to rejoice and console and agree and apologize. Not for this . . . solitary discourse. "How do you feel?" she asked.

Libba gingerly touched her bound breasts, her belly, between her legs. "Full and tight here. Saggy here. Soggy here."

There, Frances thought, *There's my Libba*, and smiled. "Tell me everything."

Finally Libba looked at her, cocked her head. "But you never told me. You should have. It's not the same, reading about having a baby, or holding someone else's baby. Not the same at all."

Frances's smile faded. "I'm sorry. I thought those kind of details might bore you. Contractions and labor and episiotomies and forceps."

"No, no, you're not meant to apologize. I can describe pain and blood and instruments. Anyone can. A man can. I mean the—the *untellable*. There aren't nouns, no adjectives. I've tried, Frances, lain here and searched for the words to convey what it feels like to, to open your legs and have a living thing push its way into, come out—Frances!" Her exclamation was anguished. "'Come out'! See? There's no adequate language! It's untellable. Poor men, too, who never get to experience—suppose I had lived my whole life without knowing that?"

A nurse appeared at the door. "Everything all right in here?"

"We're fine," Frances assured her, and pulling the single chair close to the bed, put her hand on Libba's bare arm, inches from the infant's head. "Are you cold? Do you want anything?"

Libba didn't hear her. "Someday," she said, "someone you love will be allowed in the delivery room. Someday mothers will insist on staying awake to watch everything happen."

Frances nodded. "I hope so."

But Libba moved on. "They told me that I kept repeating 'I'm not good.' Over and over during her delivery. 'I'm not a good person.'"

"People say ridiculous things under twilight anesthesia. They don't mean anything. Remember the way I wailed when I realized they were taking me to surgery? They covered my head with a blanket so everyone in the hospital couldn't hear my keening."

"But you were *losing* a child, not having one." She watched tiny fingers close instinctively around her thumb. "Before I went under they asked who was with me, the father, my family? Wanted to know who they needed to check with in the waiting room."

"I'm your family. John and I."

The reassurance was lost on her. "I'm not . . . safe," she said with a kind of wonder. "I'm interesting, and I'm determined and I'm even passionate, but I'm not safe. My life is no good for a child."

"You could make it good," Frances said, grasping at a glimmer, the sudden possibility that Libba had changed her mind, decided to keep the baby after all.

Libba stroked the wispy hair, smoothed it forward on the skull. "It grows in one direction." And did the same with the fringe at the back, a mother cat grooming a kitten. "Six pounds. A whole person, six pounds. Six pounds is . . . flour, potatoes. A dictionary. Think of it in there, every organ of a human being perfect and whole and . . . unimaginably small. Lungs and brain and liver and kidneys, and heart. All there, working away. I'm holding all that with a single hand."

"Miraculous, isn't it? Going in as one and coming out as two."

"'Miraculous'?"

Relief that Libba heard her, answered, flooded Frances. And evaporated just as swiftly.

"More frightening than miraculous. When you *want* a baby, when you've hoped and planned and tried, you're ready. When the baby is put in your arms she's no less than you expected, precisely what you've waited for. But I wasn't prepared. Not for the terror of her vulnerability, the helplessness."

From her chair Frances glimpsed a second tiny fist appear above the blanket. Nothing more than that: a curve of head, a fist no larger than a walnut. Libba held the child too closely to see anything more.

"It's beyond our scope of imagining, that utter powerlessness. Think of it, think of my power. I'm holding a living thing absolutely at my mercy, at my disposal. I could walk away. I could leave her in a bathroom stall, beside a cage at the zoo. She couldn't cry out, couldn't blame me. She can barely turn her head." Libba's voice was faint and small with realization and horror.

"The only thing she can do for herself is breathe. She's dependent upon me for everything but air. Looking at her, seeing and understanding how entirely, wholly helpless she is has made me tremble for all the ones who aren't wanted, who suffer, whom wicked, unthinkable things are done to, here and alive through no fault of their own, it's . . . not fair. It's not their fault."

Afraid herself, bewildered by this quiet intensity, Frances said nothing.

"Who did I think I was to take on such a thing? What gall I had, what *effrontery*. What have I done? Such responsibility has scared me so that they've had to give me sedatives to sleep at night."

Libba's distress was so naked that Frances stood, hoisted herself and sat on the elevated bed to be nearer. Libba didn't even notice the mattress's tilt. She ran a finger down the infant's nose. "And yet they love you. They have to love you. It's so appealing, to consider that. And appalling. Someone who'd love me blindly. Just because I'm there. She's like a blank page in the typewriter. Pure and untouched. Waiting to be written. Heart-flutter time. Everything's there. You just wait for it to unfold, happen."

A shadow fell across the door as an orderly passed in the hall.

She pressed her lips to the fuzzy scalp. "It does pulse, the soft spot. It jumps. I watch it, count the beats. It's like a mirror of her brain, a window to her heart. They explained 'rooting' to me. 'Rooting,'" she repeated. "'Soft spots.' Having a baby has its own language."

Frances leaned back, aware that Libba wasn't talking to her.

Libba was talking to herself, and Frances let her.

"I wouldn't go back to being a child for anything. All that dependency. All the awful realizations. All the thwarted loves, the things that are taken from you, or slip from your grasp unnoticed until it's too late to get them back. All the useless knowledge of school, the betrayals of recess, the backyard plots and not-chosens. Homesick nausea. Crying in bed. Nightmares. Hating your hair. Being sent to your room. Cabbage and cod and liver. Wanting what someone else has. Falling on concrete, bloody scraped palms. The failures and disappointments."

Frances listened to a flow of words not gushed or tumbling or fervent, but calm and unhurried, a steady stream from a well whose untapped lapping depths she could only guess at.

The crackling PA system paged a Dr. Holland. And again.

"But oh, I'd go back tomorrow, tonight, this minute," Libba said. "Helium balloons, a home run, an A-plus. Catching a fish. Being tired at night. Building a snowman, new shoes, the hiding places in trees and under beds, the diaries and drawings. Finding a bird's nest, holding a puppy. A fat new raft on an ocean wave, the last piece of a puzzle, candy bars in the freezer, blowing out candles. Wanting something so badly you know, you *know* it will happen, appear. So much lies before her. She's only been alive for forty-eight hours of an entire life. I *created* a human being."

A wail rose down the hall and for an instant Frances mistook it for her own. The tranced monologue broke everything in her: her heart, her silence, her good intentions. She cried out, "Libba, how can you give her up? To strangers. To never see her again, what she'll be, and do, and love."

Libba lifted a forearm no longer than her finger. "She already has wrinkles on her wrist. She already has a tiny hangnail, and a scratch thin as a thread. Already," she said softly, then tore her eyes away, and clasped Frances's wrist, lying on the woven blanket. "Be fair, Frances. Fair to her. I am unmarried, unemployed. This is nineteen fifty-five. Do you think for a minute that someone with no husband, living hand to mouth in a walk-up apartment or by-the-month hotel room or temporary housing at a prep school would be welcome in the PTA or the Hospital Auxiliary, asked to teach Sunday School or head up the Library Bazaar? It's not even in the realm of possibility."

"Make something up," Frances said. "Give yourself a history, an explanation."

"Look at me, Frances. Would you put your child in my Brownie troop? I don't even know how to *cook* brownies, much less *lead* them."

"You'll regret it. It will haunt you all your life! You don't know!"

Libba reached for the Venetian blind cord, winced, and lifted the blinds to a starry cold midnight beyond. "I can see the mountains in the daytime." The measured evenness of her voice was sharp contrast to the vehemence of Frances's. "But I do know. I know myself all too well. Even if I managed to do those things—join and participate, eventually I'd feel caged and trapped. I'm afraid."

"You've never been afraid of anything," Frances said.

"This is a different kind of fear. I'm afraid I'd come to resent that prescribed life, and then come to resent her. Or the other side of the coin—become a martyr. I know what a martyred mother does to a child. I was raised by, well, at least one."

"And it will always lie between us, this, this—this irreversible action."

Libba's eyes traveled from the blank black window to Frances's. "You'd hold it against me, then?"

Frances looked at her feet, shamed.

Libba rested her head against the pillows and looked up at the cracked plaster ceiling of the country hospital. "I want her to have a tricycle, and a wagon, and a hula hoop, and a Betsy Wetsy doll and English sandals in the spring and saddle shoes in the winter and penny loafers when she's fifteen. A record player to listen to Broadway soundtracks. A yard, and a sandbox, and a swing set, and lessons—piano and ballet and even baton. Pencils with her name on them. And a straw hat trailing ribbons to chew on during church and an elastic chin band that itches. A middy blouse."

"You can give her those."

"I can't give her an address without a hyphen in it. A permanent one to put on stationery and luggage tags and a library card and bookplates. I want her to have a neighborhood, and a driveway for a two-wheeler and a hopscotch grid and a basketball goal and a lemonade stand. I can't give her those.

"I want someone to teach her how to part her hair. To plait. Someone to remind her to wash her stockings every time she wears them. Someone to sing in the car with her during trips, to help her with long division and fractions and rate-times-time-equals-distance word problems." She lowered her head, looked across the bed. "That's it, isn't it? Rate times time equals distance?"

"Libba—"

"I don't have a sunny windowsill. Not in the kitchen or bathroom, or bedroom, or living room, and those are the only rooms I have."

"Why a sunny windowsill?"

"To stick toothpicks in the end of a carrot over water in a Pyrex dish and watch it sprout white roots and feathery green tops."

"You think growing a carrot is a childhood necessity?"

"I think a direct source of sunlight is."

"How can you even imagine those details?"

"Because imagining is what I do for a living. A book is an accumulation of details. So is a life."

"It's not too late. You have a choice."

"All those choices," Libba said, and Frances saw her drift away again, lost in her ruminations. "Choice of having her, choice of keeping her. If a mother's inner turmoil affects a baby, I don't want to ponder what her temperament will be like."

"Why turmoil?"

Libba took a deep breath, answered with a question. "Don't you want to hold her? I want to watch you hold her. She wouldn't be here but for you."

"I more than anything."

"'More than anything'?" Libba repeated.

"No. Not more than anything." Frances nestled the newborn beneath her chin, cooed into the pink shell of ear. Then her eyes filled at what would come, what must come. "More than anything I want you to keep her. She and Alice could be like sisters."

"How? Six states away today, tomorrow nine, next July when I'm in Florida or Connecticut, how many states away then? No, they couldn't."

"You know what I mean."

"Sisters don't live in different towns. They don't even live in separate houses. Sisters have the same time-for-bed rules and clean-your-room rules and be-in-by-eleven rules. Sisters have the same chores of setting the table or feeding the dog or bringing in the paper so they can have the same arguments about whose turn it is to do them. Sisters have to wear matching dresses and hand-me-downs."

"At least you and I were spared that."

"Spared? Spared having someone to dye eggs with at Easter and write your name with a sparkler on the Fourth of July? Spared, or deprived?"

"We were only children. It wasn't our fault. Besides, it bound us. It's what's between us."

"What's between us is that we know each other's down-deep fears and shames as well as we know each other's triumphs and joys. You know what my lucky pen looks like, and I know you hated the graduation dress your mother picked out."

"Only children have their parents' full attention," Frances tried to defend. "And devotion. And affection."

"Devotion and affection and attention? Or disaffection in my case, suffocation in yours?"

Frances rose, walked to the single window, away from Libba, and the truth.

"You know I like grapefruit with salt on it and I know you won't eat cubed steak. I know how to put on makeup because you taught me. Because we know each other like sisters."

"Don't tell me those things," Frances pleaded. "It's cruel. Alice is an only child."

"Who won't have someone to be glad she was caught for misbehaving, then squirm with sympathy when she's punished. Like you did for me at Em Sem. An only child of only children of only children. Just like this one. Not again, Frances. Not for Alice. Not for . . . my baby."

Long before the question came, Frances had heard it; had heard it in the somber soliloquies, the voice tinged with wonder, worry, hope.

"They don't have to be only children," Libba said. "We can spare them that."

Frances's heart lifted, lodged so thickly in her throat that she could barely ask a question to stalled her rising hope. "Can I feed her?"

"You've forgotten what you want more than anything."

Frances wormed a finger within the blanket folds, into the thick wad of diaper. "I think she might be wet."

"And you won't have another."

She traced the shell of ear, a fingernail no larger than a tiny pearl.

"And what you want more than anything is just—" the voice faltered "— exactly what I want more than anything, too."

Frances's fingers ceased their gentle caressing and the child opened its mouth in a first silent protest at denial of pleasure.

"I had a choice nine months ago and you helped me make it," Libba said. "Now you have one, too, and I can help you."

And Frances had intuited it, of course, realized it in Libba's rambling, the reasonings and reassurings. Realized she'd listened to Libba convincing herself, forgiving herself.

"But no, not as a favor to me; not as pity or charity for you. It's what's best for *her*. You're the reason *this* child is here."

Frances's eyes filled and she brought the bundle to her face to hide them, unsure whether she was crying out of terror or relief or simple, silent joy.

"You're moving, starting over in a new place, a new state. The same state where you have a cottage where you could have hidden, gone to stay and be cared for by me during a difficult, dangerous pregnancy. The same state where this child was born. No one will question it. The only thing everyone knows is that you and John started trying to get pregnant again the minute you recovered from the tubal. Only a few people will need to know the truth."

As Frances already knew the question, she already knew the answer.

"Dennis will see to the official records and the legalities. I'll help with finances. Will you help me? Help me with the hardest scene I'll ever write, the hardest thing I'll ever do. Yet the easiest. Can you see her as a gift? A gift for four of us. To me from you. To you from me. To only-child Alice. A gift, most of all, to her from both of us. Say you will."

Without another thought, another minute. *Yes*. "Yes," she whispered, "More than anything, yes."

A spasm shuddered Libba. She clutched the blanket, squeezed her eyes tightly shut and tilted her head to the ceiling again, away from the child she has borne, and birthed, and yielded, yet loved. "Pr—" She flattened her palm to her chest, the torque of heart-hurt. "Promise me."

"Yes."

"That you will love her like she was yours and John's."

"Yes."

"Promise me, no references, or jokes, no mention of resemblances. Nothing."

"Yes."

"But everything else—the first step, the first word. Her first haircut and heartbreak. Everything about her, everything that happens to her, everything she does. You must tell me. Promise you will."

"Yes."

"Yes," she repeated, and finally gazed at the friend whom she'd asked the world of, and given the world to, and sighed, grinned ruefully. "Perhaps she'll be the best of both of us."

And only then did Frances doubt. "But she'll—*we'll* be so far away from you."

"I'll come so often you'll have to evict me." She drew the sheet to her breasts, and reached for the baby. "You need to make a phone call."

Puzzled, Frances said, "Wh—?"

"To someone who'll tell her not to use his razor and that she doesn't look good in low-waisted dresses and even after a tragic haircut will tell her that she's still beautiful. Because she needs a father who wants her, too."

Frances wordlessly stood, relinquished the bundled baby to her mother's arms, and went to find a phone.

Left alone, Libba rested her child on her lap, propped against her raised knees to savor and memorize. She needed two hands.

She touched the cheeks, the tiny O's of nostrils, the translucent eyelids, the scant strands of eyebrows. She traced each finger of both hands no larger than a locket, unwrapped the snug blanket and touched each stub of toe, the limp limbs, the bandaged stump of navel. She stroked the loose wrinkled skin of the baby's back, the folds of neck, at the wrinkled joints of bent knees and elbows and legs bowed by the diaper, the blue veins of the inner wrist, the tiny lips that pursed beneath her fingertip. The round chin, and ears, and eyelashes that fluttered slightly even as the child slumbered on, unaware. Unknowing. "Hello, baby," she said softly, then kissed her. "Good-bye, Allegra."

Once more Frances entered the room, came to the bed, and clumsily folded her friend to a face flushed with gladness, eyes radiant with disbelief and gratitude, a contrast to the paled beauty of the person in her arms.

"Promise me that you will never tell her what I've done."

"What *we've* done, Libba."

"Never," Libba insisted, "unless it's life or death."

Frances's laugh—raucous and spontaneous—rang out in the otherwise silent room, and the infant startled, stared with liquid, unfocused eyes at her two mothers. "We're twenty-five, Libba! Life or death? That's a simple promise." Frances laughed again, and at that noisy familiar burst Libba smiled, too, sharing her friend's delight in the remoteness of such an inconceivable circumstance; at the utterly preposterous notion that either of them would ever die.

CHAPTER 18

"You're a carbon copy," Libba says to Alice, "your mother's child."

"And you," she says to Edie, "are your father's, so like him."

"And you," she says to Allegra, "are me, through and through. Even when you weren't, you were. Mine. Through and through."

They stare. Yet now that every story has been told, it changes everything, and not a particle.

Dennis has told them what to expect, what will happen. No intake, no voiding, labored respiration, weak pulse, clammy skin, pupils constricted, rigid legs. And though they've heard it, this is all they hear: *Look after Libba.* She has a choice, he'd said, much pain but fairly conscious, or comfortable but sedated. They have a choice too.

No one says, *We were wrong. You didn't take away our mother after all. Au contraire, as you yourself would say: You have given her back to us, you have given us back ourselves. You've given us so much, told us all we need to know.*

"I was always there because that's where you were," she'd said.

"All of you."

They are, at last, each other's closest friends.

Alice the efficient wipes the wet circle left by a glass on the bed-side table, folds the sheet over the blanket the way her mother taught her, and turns to the window, away.

Allegra, the reader, holds books from the nightstand. E. B. White is on top and she recalls its final line. *She was in a class by herself. It is not often that someone comes along who is a true friend and a good writer. Charlotte was both.* And turns away too.

So that it's Edie who finally commits to something; Edie who reaches, covers the mouth and holds the nostrils. They do for Libba, their friend and their mother's friend, what she did for Frances, their mother and her friend. They let her go.

●　●　●

June 20, 1993

"Do we have to do this?" Libba asked.

"Yes."

"Why?"

Frances singsonged a familiar five-note melody: "'Because I said so.'" The tune was an old insurance advertisement jingle—*because you love them*—that she'd appropriated decades earlier as a response to her daughters whenever they questioned a chore or directive: *because I said so.*

Libba opened the jewelry box, searched through the jumble of jewelry—strands of glass beads, a cloisonné bracelet, gold bangles, earrings in the cutwork cursive of Frances's married monogram—and came up with the square onyx class ring of Emerson Seminary on her thumb, and a wry grimace on her face. "I used to have one of these."

"Until you threw it in the ocean that summer we spent in Maine. I seem to recall a speech about how I was throwing away my life and our histories, trading that ring for a wedding ring. Here's your chance to get it back."

Libba slipped the ring from her finger. "I don't think so."

"Edie can have the ring. She wanted to wear it so people would think she'd graduated from college. She can have all the silver, too, my little hippie lovechild."

"Edie was a child during the sixties, too young to be a bona fide hippie."

"And we were too old." She picked up two gold bracelets, one of chained links and the other a circlet of brushed bamboo. "Allegra lost most of her jewelry at college. She should have the gold."

"And since I have nothing to give her."

"Except her existence," Frances said. She unzipped a satin pouch and withdrew a strand of creamy pearls.

"Your twenty-fifth-anniversary present from John," Libba said.

Frances pressed the cool spheres to her cheek. "One night when I was digging through the jewelry box looking for these, John got irritated. He thought I should keep the pearls in a separate pouch, so they wouldn't get scratched. So ridiculous. We had a fight about it."

"I know you did."

"Of course you do." Frances eyed her friend for a long moment. "Who should have the unblemished pearls?"

"Alice," Libba said without hesitation.

Frances smiled. "Like you say, 'If you know your characters well enough, the story's already there,' right?" Libba nodded. Frances leaned back against the pillows. "They've no idea how well you know them. No idea." She waved a bony hand over the glittery tangle, holding tight to Libba's with the other. "Nothing among all my earthly treasures you desire?"

Libba flicked the catch of a charm bracelet. "No one to help me with the catches."

"Aren't you going to—"

Libba pressed her fingers against Frances's lips. "She's a grown woman."

"A bangle, then. You can manage that, or a—"

Libba closed her hand around Frances's frail one, taking care not to crush the metal against the thin skin, veined and punctured. "Your girls should have your things." She closed the lid. "Alice and Allegra and Edie."

July 3, 1993

"Wish I'd made a list."

"Of what?"

"All the things I wanted to do."

"Frances."

"Travel around the world. Spend all my money. Watch the whales, ride in a hot air balloon. Eat sweetbreads."

"No loss there."

She gazed out the window, where full branches grazed the shutters. "Another beautiful spring gone. And now I've missed summer too, cooped up and captive."

"You haven't missed summer. It's barely July."

"Libba," Frances chastised gently, then said, "Open the window."

"It's ninety degrees outside, stifling."

"I'm already stifled. I want to sweat. I want to feel. I want to hear the trees."

She raised the window. "You can't hear trees."

"Hush, listen." From outside came a distinct rustle, the faint shift and rasp of twig and branch and leaf.

"I argued with an Em Sem teacher once whether you could hear a smile," Libba said. "I'd written that a character could hear her friend's smile over the phone while they were talking. The teacher disputed it."

Frances closed her eyes. "But you were right. Because I can hear you smiling now." She smoothed the sheet folded at her waist. "I have a terrible confession. I don't think about not being here for John or my girls. I don't think about not seeing my grandchildren graduate or get married. You know what I think about? That I'll never walk barefoot on grass again. I will never eat raspberries again or pick up the dry-cleaning again or hear it thunder again."

"Stop, Frances."

"But it's true. Nobody does that, nobody says, now, *now* is the last time I will ever look through the mail. Nobody ever notices, realizes that this, *this* is the last time I will make a bed, or fix a cup of tea, or even," she laughed weakly, "put on pantyhose. But we couldn't bear it, could we? If we knew? We only remember the first things, the first kiss, the first day of school, the first time we flew on an airplane or water-skied. But there's not an adult alive who can say, I remember that Thursday afternoon when I was eleven because it was the last time I ever climbed a tree. That Saturday in October was the last time I ever rode a bicycle."

Libba lowered her head to Frances's lap. "What will I do without you?"

August 12, 1993

Frances plucked at the bedclothes. "Libba."

"What."

"I don't want my girls to suffer. Or John."

"They're stronger than you think."

"Look at me, Libba. No heroic intervention. You understand? I have Advanced Directives, dying instructions."

Libba coiled a ribbon from a get-well gift around her finger.

"Is 'Advanced Directives' a euphemism?" Frances asked playfully.

"Don't."

Her voice rose sharply. "Is it?"

"I don't know."

"You should. You have an opinion on everything."

"I know." She plucked a fading Gerbera daisy from an arrangement on the windowsill, moved another gift plant to ineffectually conceal the bedside pharmacopeia.

"Libba."

"What."

"Me either."

"You either what?"

"I don't want to."

"What."

"Suffer."

September 18, 1993

The voice was faint as a kitten's mewling. "Libba."

She stroked the bony forehead, the sunken cheeks. "I'm here."

Her eyes were closed, but the words were clear. "Be a hero."

CHAPTER 19

November 7, 1994

How to start? Allegra thinks.

"If you know your characters well enough, the story is already there," Libba claimed.

Though Allegra doubts the veracity of this writerly adage, she doesn't have one book to her name, much less ten. What she does have is Libba's bulletin board, looking no differently now in November, two months after Libba's death, than it had in June when Allegra and her sisters had arrived at Creek Cabin. It had seemed an intrusion then, an alien presence among their mother's Creek Cabin things. The same corkboard Pamela Simpson had tripped over the day Frances and Libba met at Em Sem, now covered with bits of paper, clippings, photographs, and *New Yorker* cartoons.

Neither Edie nor Alice had shown any interest in the bulletin board. Alice is busy with her new business, called Straighten Up!, just as their mother used to tell them when they were misbehaving. "Write what you know about," Libba had also said, and in a weird parallel Alice did just that. She'll organize whatever you want—

desk, attic, checkbook, possessions, bookshelves, kitchen cabinet contents. She's paid well to plan a dinner party, or clean out and box up and file and mail and list and wrap: books, hand-me-down clothing, receipts, even the dregs of inheritance. You'd be surprised at the number of people who want their grocery lists arranged in the order in which the items appear on the market shelves. It's surprising, too, how many people think rating cookbook recipes is a good idea, because few individuals have memories like Libba.

Edie is busy, too, if it's no more busyness than fending off Teddy's hovering, bringing crackers to bed in the morning, and dropping by at lunch, and taking her to the obstetrician, though she's barely begun to show. When Edie told her sisters she was pregnant, Alice had said, "Are you married, then?" and Edie had smiled at Allegra and said, "One thing at a time, one day at a time. Right?"

"Some things never change," Alice said. She and Allegra are hoping for a girl, and so is Teddy ("We'll call her Teedie," he suggested, "for Peedie and Teddy."). Edie, though, just wants a precious darling, a child she'll upend her life for, as her mother did for her.

Most weekends Allegra comes with her family to Creek Cabin and tries to write. Her sisters and her father, who's finished with both the project and Bree, are coming for Thanksgiving. As they had with their mother, the sisters have begun again a year of first-afters: first Thanksgiving after Libba died.

Libba, Allegra thinks, *Mother*. Two words with identical meanings, but not listed in any thesaurus, are still strange on her tongue. They'd agreed not to tell anyone, she and Alice and Edie. Some promises last forever, even if the people who made them don't.

There'd been no discussion or agreements, as there had been with Divvy Day, about dividing Creek Cabin. Now and forever to be maintained through Libba Charles's royalties, Creek Cabin belongs to them all. Sticky notes still flag items here and there, but by now the colored squares have acquired a coating of dust, and soon, like the autumn leaves falling outside, they'll float silently to the floor, their adhesive exhausted.

Libba had forgotten to include the bulletin board in the blaze, the "bonfire of the vanities," as she termed it. Allegra remembers that night. She and her sisters were in Libba's bathroom, Libba in the bed, of course.

Alice had brought her makeup case downstairs—a flowery, quilted pouch—and was plucking jars and bottles and wands and brushes and tubes from it. The crowded room, the warm light from lampshades dim with age, the scent of perfumed makeup, and the steamy moistness of the summer night was like those nights they'd hovered in their mother's room as children, watching as she dressed for a party or a dinner out, warm and fragrant and intimate with her bath, the feminine mysteries of her preparations.

"Your problem," Alice told Edie, "is that your appearance isn't a way of life for you yet."

"Since when is that a problem?" Libba asked.

"It's a problem for anyone who wasn't born as gorgeous as you." They were accustomed to Libba's looks then, the gradual, daily ravagement, as they'd never grown accustomed to her astonishing beauty when they were children. "Foundation first," Alice said.

"Maybe we should put on *West Side Story*, and 'I Feel Pretty,'" Libba said.

"No," Allegra said, whose healthy beauty was fully restored. And no wonder: it wasn't only her mother's talent and personality she'd inherited. "It's time for *Jeopardy!*" She switched on the television that they'd pulled into the sickroom.

"Try an eye pencil."

"Frances told me that I needed to be careful with my eyes because steely-gray eyes can be intimidating," Libba said.

They laughed at the absurd idea that Libba could ever have been intimidating, having forgotten ,that's exactly what she was.

"What is détente."

"What is a tuberose."

"Who is Bobby Goldsboro."

"Oh no," Libba complained. "Peninsulas, Sports Legends. Ungettable categories."

"I don't want to play Beauty Salon," Edie said. "Teddy doesn't like makeup."

"At least finish your eyes!" Alice said. "You never finish anything."

"I've finished taking the pill," Edie said shyly. Libba only smiled like a sphinx, but Alice and Allegra whooped.

"Good, they've gotten to Famous Trios," Libba said. "I might have a chance with this one. Who are Larry, Curly, and Moe."

"Who are Shadrach, Meshach, and Abednego," Allegra said.

"What are the three blind mice," Edie said.

An answer flashed across the screen, white lettering against the bright blue background: LONGFELLOW'S POETIC DAUGHTERS. Three voices shrieked in unison, "Who are grave Alice and laughing Allegra and Edith with golden hair!"

Allegra poked around in Alice's flowered bag. "Do you still use black soap to wash your face? All that splashing twenty-times?"

"This isn't sibling rivalry, it's sibling persecution," Alice said. "That black soap regime was an expensive twentieth birthday present to myself. Now I'm saving for plastic surgery."

"So vain!" Edie said.

"Frances had a face-lift," Libba said, an old slyness restored to her fading voice. Alice and Allegra and Edie were shocked. They'd never hear enough, learn enough, get enough.

"I can't believe Daddy cared that much about Mother's looks."

Libba rolled her sunken eyes. "You don't do it for *them*. You do it for *yourself*."

"She never told," Alice said

"We had a secret or two," Libba said, then held up her hands. "I had my hands chemically peeled, and Frances had an eye lift, and then we went to a spa to hide and recuperate." She sighed. "'Vanity, vanity, all is vanity.'"

The sisters waited, accustomed by now to these fragments, bits of quotes. "*Brideshead Revisited*," Libba provided. "Where's my designated reader?" Allegra unfolded herself from the floor beside the bathroom cabinet. Throughout the summer it had been she who read to Libba, lines Libba already knew by heart. Alice and Edie didn't begrudge their sister the privilege, the pleasure of bringing Libba pleasure. They'd come too far to hold grudges. Libba was right again: like regret, resentment is a useless emotion.

They crowded beside Libba on the bed as Allegra read, grown women posed as Little Women, except that it wasn't Beth who was dying. The passages were simple to find, the pages dog-eared with folding. "Which one?" Allegra asked.

"Alice Munro. *Lives of Girls and Women*. She understands," Libba said. "Here," and Allegra read.

"*People's lives, in Jubilee as elsewhere, were dull, simple, amazing and unfathomable—deep caves paved with kitchen linoleum. It did not occur to me then that one day I would be so greedy for Jubilee . . . I would want to write things down. I would try to make lists. A list of all the stores and businesses going up and down the main street and who owned them, a list of family names, names on the tombstones in the cemetery and any inscriptions underneath . . . Names of the streets and the pattern they lay in. The hope of accuracy we bring to such tasks is crazy, heartbreaking. And no list could hold what I wanted, for what I wanted was every last thing, every layer of speech and thought, stroke of light on bark or walls, every smell, pothole, pain, crack, delusion, held still and held together—radiant, everlasting.*"

Allegra finished, swallowed. "Is that enough?"

"The beginning of *Brideshead*."

Though Allegra found the page, the underlined words, her voice went dry. She wordlessly handed the volume to Libba.

"*My theme is memory*," Libba read, "'*that winged host that soared about me one grey morning . . .*,'" and could go no further. Alice groped for her sisters' hands beneath the folds of quilt.

"Let's have a fire," Libba said. "A bonfire of my vanities."

"But—"

"When I said there'd be no grand gestures, I lied. This is it. I don't want anything left for posthumous scrutiny. Bring the boxes." She made a move to rise from the bed, failed, and looked up into three pair of eyes. "Carry me."

So they had. Had stacked the books, the records, the files and scribbled notes on napkins within the ring of stones atop the gray ashes of past campfires. Bree's splendid gazing ball was an imperial purple sphere beside the humble cardboard boxes.

They'd struck matches and retreated from the leaping flames, holding Libba between them, their arms and legs and faces warmed and eerily illuminated in the early darkness. "I've never seen vinyl burn, have you?" Libba murmured.

"No, but I put a six-pack of Cokes in a fire once to see if they'd explode," Allegra said. "Does that count?"

"How did you get to be so bad?" Libba laughed.

"Good genes."

As they watched the consuming flickers snapping and crackling, smoke and sparks rising, the mirrored ball simply vanished, collapsed with a *whisk*, a noise as delicate as the object itself. "Ah," Libba had said, "Not with a bang, but a whimper."

If she were to write that vanity of vanities scene, Allegra thinks, it would be insignificant, too. Silly, superficial, or simply too difficult to convey the level of love necessary for this scene—neither climax nor epiphany nor finale—to have even taken place. There was no adequate language to describe or explain what it represented, the distance they'd covered. Untellable.

"Fiction has to have a heart-hurt," Libba said.

Allegra can't imagine where to begin. Yet it's all so clear, those last days and quiet nights; the stories. What she remembers are the conversations, what Libba said, just as her mother had invoked her friend after she'd left Frances to her family again. *"Libba said,"* *"Libba says."* But like Frances, Libba would not be coming back this time.

Still, Allegra wants to tell it. As though inspiration will spring forth from the bulletin board, she flips through its papers, layers upon layers of Libba Charles. There's no Evelyn Waugh there, but she recognizes the final paragraphs from *The Great Gatsby,* the exact handout she'd brought home from a boarding school English class and shown Libba. "Isn't it *wonderful?*" Allegra had said, rapturous.

"Sophomore swoon," Libba had derisively replied. "Everyone goes through an F. Scott amour."

Yet here it was, preserved all these years, and Allegra thinks, Contradictory to the end. Here is a yellowed paperback book page whose lines she knows are Faulkner's Nobel Prize speech. Here is a newspaper article detailing the search methods being used by the FBI to capture Bert Miller. The lawmen have dismantled their command post now, believe the outlaw to be dead of starvation or exposure. But Allegra has taken up Libba's cause and likes to think her elusive fugitive is still at large, hiding, haunting the mountains the way Libba and Frances haunt Creek Cabin.

And here, printed in Libba's hand on lined paper are one-word lists. Allegra knows they're chapter titles of Libba's last novels, and one she'd thought to finish but didn't. Libba never wrote a word until she knew exactly what was going to happen, and perhaps the cancer wasn't responsible for the unfinished book; perhaps Libba didn't yet know how it was going to end.

But of course she did know; she'd planned it.

In small font is a typewritten list, another conference hand-out:

"WHAT DO YOUR CHARACTERS WANT?"

1. Character's name:
2. Character's nickname:
3. Sex:
4. Age:
5. Looks:
6. Education:
7. Vocation/Occupation:
8. Status and money:
9. Marital status:
10. Family; ethnicity:
11. Diction, accent, etc.:
12. Relationships:
13. Places (home office car, etc.):
14. Possessions:
15. Recreation, hobbies:
16. Obsessions:
17. Beliefs:
18. Politics:
19. Sexual history:
20. Ambitions:
21. Religion:
22. Superstitions:
23. Fears:
24. Attitudes:
25. Character flaws:
26. Character strengths:
27: Pets:
28: Taste in books, music, etc.:
29. Journal entries:

30. Correspondence:
31. Food preferences:
32: Handwriting
33: Astrological sign:
34. Talents:

Allegra has no idea what her sisters' astrological signs are. She's amused to find "Character flaws" nearly as far down the list as "Pets."

She frowns; these are traits, not "wants." Then she thinks of Libba's adage again, and knows why they're related. If you know your characters, you know what they want. When she and her sisters had come to Creek Cabin in June they'd all needed something. What they'd wanted wasn't as obvious: they'd wanted what their mother had with Libba. "All I wanted," Libba said, "was to create characters who were were honest, difficult, endearing, troubled, and ordinary. Like you three. And Frances."

Libba, though, was the real character. A piece of work. A living outrage. An old shoe. And a mother.

Deciding she has to start somewhere, Allegra writes *It's no given that daughters know their mother.*

"No dice," she can hear Libba saying. "Mother/daughter novels are claustrophobic."

Allegra dramatically crumples the page, begins afresh. *Once upon a time there were three sisters and their dead mother and their dead mother's friend.*

"Now there's a hook." She can hear Libba laugh.

Allegra drops the pencil and listens for Brent's and Sasha's shrieks as they rock-hop with Dal in Shoals Stream, prettily choked now with autumn leaves. The nostalgic scent of woodsmoke scents the cabin as she gazes at the bulletin board again, puzzling over a fire escape plan taken from the back of a motel room door. There is the exit diagram, there are the formally worded cautions and warnings. And there at the bottom is the reason Libba kept it. DON'T GIVE UP reads the final exhortation.

Allegra tugs the sleeves of her mother's silver-gray sweater, picks up the pencil, and begins again. *What you need to know*, she writes.